# From *The Black Stocking*

He took the key to his father's tomb from its hook and slipped it into his pocket. Better investigate thoroughly, while he was about it. Probably John had just been babbling, but he had to make sure. He disliked the idea of entering the mausoleum, but John's mutterings made it necessary to check on it.

As they made their way across the lawn, Irene began to feel decidedly nervous—rather to her own surprise. She decided that it must be the gray early-morning light, because she was not afraid of Doris Miller, even if she was insane.

Ross went ahead through the straggling little path, and she followed, trying to preserve her stockings from the undergrowth.

The summerhouse was deserted and empty. Ross attempted to turn on the electric bulb and found that it did not work, but it was quite light enough to see that the place was unoccupied.

Irene found herself drawing a breath of relief as she said unnecessarily, "No one here."

"No. Come on, we'll try the other place," Ross said, and started off again. He had never been inside the tomb, but he knew the coffin had not been sealed, and he decided, grimly, that he'd have to open it and see that everything was in order.

The small, neat little building looked gray and blank in the dawn, and Irene stopped, some distance from the door, and protested rather breathlessly: "You—you're not going in there?"

Ross fitted the key into the lock and glanced back at her. "Sorry. I'm afraid it's necessary."

"But she wouldn't be there. How could she?"

The lock turned easily and smoothly, and Ross said, "There's no need for you to come in. I'll bring her out if she's here."

Irene set her teeth and followed him in. She peered fearfully over his shoulder and saw at a glance that the musty little room, with its stained-glass window, was bare, save for the coffin set up in the center. She took a step backward and was horrified to see Ross advance toward the coffin and lay a hand on the lid. He fumbled with it for a moment and then raised it, and stood for so long looking down inside that she crept forward. She clutched at his arm, gave his face a quick, frightened glance, and then looked down into the satin-lined box.

It was empty.

Books by Constance & Gwenyth Little

*The Grey Mist Murders* (1938)
*The Black Headed Pins* (1938)
*The Black Gloves* (1939)
*Black Corridors* (1940)
*The Black Paw* (1941)
*The Black Shrouds* (1941)
*The Black Thumb* (1942)
*The Black Rustle* (1943)
*The Black Honeymoon* (1944)
*Great Black Kanba* (1944)
*The Black Eye* (1945)
*The Black Stocking* (1946)
*The Black Goatee* (1947)
*The Black Coat* (1948)
*The Black Piano* (1948)
*The Black Smith* (1950)
*The Black House* (1950)
*The Blackout* (1951)
*The Black Dream* (1952)
*The Black Curl* (1953)
*The Black Iris* (1953)

# The Black Stocking

By Constance & Gwenyth Little

The Rue Morgue Press
Boulder, Colorado

*The Black Stocking*



ISBN: 0-915230-30-5



The Rue Morgue Press
P.O. Box 4119
Boulder, CO 80306

PRINTED IN THE UNITED STATES OF AMERICA

# The Black Stocking

# About the Littles

Although all but one of their books had "black" in the title, the 21 mysteries of Constance (1899-1980) and Gwenyth (1903-1985) Little were far from somber affairs. The two Australian-born sisters from East Orange, New Jersey, were far more interested in coaxing chuckles than in inducing chills from their readers.

Indeed, after their first book, *The Grey Mist Murders*, appeared in 1938, Constance rebuked an interviewer for suggesting that their murders weren't realistic by saying, "Our murderers strangle. We have no sliced-up corpses in our books." However, as the books mounted, the Littles did go in for all sorts of gruesome murder methods—"horrible," was the way their own mother described them—which included the occasional sliced-up corpse.

But the murders were always off stage and tempered by comic scenes in which bodies and other objects, including swimming pools, were constantly disappearing and reappearing. The action took place in large old mansions, boarding houses, hospitals, hotels, or on trains or ocean liners, anywhere the Littles could gather together a large cast of eccentric characters, many of whom seemed to have escaped from a Kaufman play or a Capra movie. The typical Little heroine—each book was a stand-alone—often fell under suspicion herself and turned detective to keep the police from slapping the cuffs on. Whether she was a working woman or a spoiled little rich brat, she always spoke her mind, kept her sense of humor, and got her man, both murderer and husband. But if marriage was in the offing, it was always on her terms and the vows were taken with more than a touch of cynicism. Love was grand, but it was even grander if the husband could either pitch in with the cooking and cleaning or was wealthy enough to hire household help.

The Littles wrote all their books in bed—"Chairs give one backaches," Gwenyth complained—with Constance providing detailed plot outlines while Gwenyth did the final drafts. Over the years that pattern changed somewhat but Constance always insisted that Gwen "not mess up my clues." Those clues were everywhere and the Littles made sure there were no loose ends. Seemingly irrelevant events were revealed to be of major significance in the final summation.

The Littles published their two final novels, *The Black Curl* and *The Black Iris*, in 1953, and if they missed writing after that, they were at least able to devote more time to their real passion—traveling. The two made at least three trips around the world at a time when that would have been a major expedition. For more information on the Littles and their books, see the introductions by Tom & Enid Schantz to The Rue Morgue Press editions of *The Black Gloves* and *The Black Honeymoon*.

# ONE

HOT sun glared down onto the highway and burned through the cloth top of the car, and Irene Hastings shifted her sticky hands on the steering wheel and thought longingly of the swim she intended to take as soon as she reached Tilton. Even if it were midnight—or later. She sighed a little and glanced at her silent companion. It was unfortunate that Ann Miller should have held her up, when she had only a week of vacation. Not that the state hospital was much out of her way, but it would mean a long wait. Ann's sister had been committed some time ago, and poor Ann always crept out on visitors' day and stayed as long as the rule permitted.

Irene moved uncomfortably on the hot leather seat and frowned at the winding concrete in front of her. She hadn't wanted to refuse timid, mousy little Ann when she had asked for a lift to Tilton and time to visit her sister at the mental hospital on the way—but it was annoying. She'd undoubtedly spend an hour, at the least, weeping over Sister Doris—and then there was a strong possibility that there would be no accommodation for her at the Tilton hotel.

"I simply *can't* share my room with her," Irene thought, in sudden panic, and broke a lengthy silence by asking abruptly, "Have you reserved a room at the hotel at Tilton?"

Ann stirred, and her hands, which had been lying limply in her lap, suddenly tensed and locked together with the knuckles showing white.

"No, I—it's all right. I mean, it will be all right."

"But you should have telephoned. They may not have a thing for you."

"It doesn't matter—I—have a friend there. He'll arrange something."

Irene gave her a quick, curious look and then concentrated on the road again. The look was wasted, because Ann wore a large, rather floppy hat, and only part of one cheek and her chin were visible, but the curiosity remained, since Ann did not go around with men at all—

not even the dry sticks on the outer fringes.

"Anyone I know?" Irene asked casually.

"Oh no—no, I don't think so."

Silence again, and Irene speeded up the car a little and then dropped it down again at sight of a state policeman resplendently mounted on a motorcycle.

Ann cleared her throat, coughed, and fingered her white purse, which had been inadequately cleaned and had left two white smudges on her green-and-yellow print dress. "We're almost there—just a few miles now."

Irene said, "Mmm," and swallowed a yawn which brought tears to her eyes.

Ann cleared her throat again.

"I hope Doris will be in a good mood—I'm *sure* they'll let her out soon—they must see that the whole thing was a mistake. Doris wasn't insane—and anyway, she certainly isn't now."

Irene drew a quick, impatient breath. She'd heard that before—many times—and had merely offered sympathy, but now she said, with a touch of irritation, "Why did they put her in, then?"

Ann, perspiring in the hot little car, suddenly shivered. "They—it was a frame-up—Doris told me. One of the other nurses—"

"Doris was a nurse?"

"Yes—yes, she was—a very good one. But there was this other nurse who hated her, and she started to make out that Doris was doing queer things. Oh, it was dreadful! And Doris didn't realize it in time to defend herself, and she was committed before she could do a thing. She tried to tell them, and I did what I could, but nobody would listen. It was wicked and unfair, and I—I *hate* them!"

Tears seemed to be imminent, and Irene said hastily, "All right—you mustn't get all excited just when you're going to see her—you'll only upset her. If she's all right, they're bound to find it out—and they certainly don't want to keep anyone when it isn't necessary. All the hospitals are pushed for space, these days."

"Yes—but it's been two years now—and she's still there." She sighed and added with sudden tension, "Oh—here we are, I guess."

Irene drove up to a pair of formidable iron gates, stopped the car, and turned off the ignition.

"Don't be any longer than you can help," she said as Ann clutched her bag and straightened the floppy hat. "We still have a long way to go, and we don't want to be too late."

"I'll try to hurry. But I forgot to tell you—my friend—this man—is meeting me just outside of Tilton. It's a big old white house—you can't miss it—a private hospital. He'll be there, standing out in front, and I'll—I'll leave you there."

Irene nodded and watched the girl as she made her way, drooping and badly dressed, toward the gates. You never could tell, she reflected, about these timid, quiet people. Evidently Ann had a boyfriend at Tilton—a complete dark horse—and a rendezvous was in prospect.

Irene lit a cigarette and slumped down behind the wheel. She had known Ann Miller for only a few months—they worked in the same office—and she had learned that Ann's whole life seemed to be devoted to the sister—who emerged, purely by reference, as a far more forceful character. That Ann should be meeting a man in Tilton, and presumably spending the weekend with him, seemed utterly and absurdly out of character.

She shrugged, threw away the butt of her cigarette, and yawned. She had two beaux of her own—a soldier and a sailor—and as a matter of fact, they both wanted to marry her. She liked them equally well, and she reflected comfortably that there was no hurry about deciding between them. When they were demobilized and were at home again—A friend of hers had warned her not to marry either one of them, since she obviously was in love with neither—but the advice did not impress her. She'd been in love all right—twice—and she'd have married both of them if she'd had the remotest chance of doing so. Later, when she'd recovered, she was mildly horrified to think that she had been willing to tie up with either one of such impossible characters.

She'd explained it to her mother, Elise, who knew all there was to know on the subject and who listened with a poised, critical ear.

"There's no use marrying when you're in love," Irene had said dubiously, "because you're blinded and can't see or reason properly. But Bill and George are both nice boys, and I couldn't go wrong by marrying either one of them."

Elise, busy with one of her long crimson nails, had raised a pair of shapely eyebrows and observed, "I don't know what you mean when you say you're not in love with them. You must be, because you're completely blind to the fact that neither of them has any money."

Irene, remembering it, smiled and reached for another cigarette. Elise had been married three times and had done well, financially, each time—and if she were not so extravagant, she wouldn't be under the present necessity of looking around again. She'd find someone, too—with money—and Irene hoped idly that he'd be nice as well. Nicer than the last one, anyway.

She was startled out of her thoughts when the car door was suddenly wrenched open and Ann almost fell in. She did not say anything, but settled back against the seat with her head turned away and the floppy hat hiding her face.

Irene supposed that she was crying, as she usually did after one of these visits, and asked merely, "All set?"

Ann nodded without replying, and Irene started the car and slid out onto the highway. She was vaguely uneasy, for no definite reason, and after a glance or two at the silent figure she said apologetically, "I didn't want you to cut your visit quite that short—it's just that I'd like to get to Tilton in time for a swim."

Ann hunched her shoulders but seemed incapable of further response, and Irene left her alone and presently forgot her.

She was deep in her own thoughts when she ran into the outskirts of Tilton and was suddenly reminded again of Ann and her mysterious rendezvous.

"Where is this place?" she asked abruptly. "Where do you want to be dropped, I mean?"

"Just a little way down the road, here, I'll tell you."

Irene, instantly conscious of something wrong or different in the voice, jerked her head around to stare—and at that moment a gust of wind blew the brim of the floppy hat out and up.

It was not Ann who sat beside her, but someone dressed in Ann's clothes.

## TWO

IRENE'S foot went automatically to the brake, but the car had scarcely slowed before she pulled it away again. There was no use stopping there alone on the highway, she thought wildly—she needed someone to help her. It was Doris who sat beside her, and Doris had been certified as insane. Evidently the two girls had managed to change clothes without being seen—and the man who was meeting Doris must be in on the plot too.

Slick, the way they used me, Irene thought angrily, and continued to drive with her eyes straight ahead. And it had all gone smoothly, too. Ann had explained about the man who would be waiting in front of the white house, so that Doris need not talk and give herself away. But what was her next move? What ought she to do? No use trying to take Doris beyond the point of her rendezvous and into the town—it would be inviting attack and injury—and equally hopeless to try and reason with her in any way. Drop her, and allow her to escape—and then make for the nearest policeman or telephone.

"Right here," Doris said suddenly.

Irene braked and turned off the highway in front of a large white house with a circular driveway. She started to turn into the driveway, when a firm hand came down upon her arm.

"No. Just stop here."

Irene twisted the wheel and came to a stop just beyond the driveway. There was no one in sight, and the summer afternoon lay hot and still over the white house and the deserted highway. She could feel goose-pimples pricking her skin when at last she broke the silence to say nervously, "It doesn't look like a hospital—more like a private house."

Doris moved restlessly and muttered, "Where is he? He should have been looking out for us. I can't afford to be hanging around on an open road, like this."

"No," Irene murmured unthinkingly, "I expect the alarm is out by this time."

She felt her heart begin to pound furiously as Doris turned abruptly and glared at her.

"You keep your mouth shut! I knew you'd wise up— Ann and I aren't much alike."

And yet they were. There was a noticeable resemblance in their features, and the hair seemed identical—an ordinary medium brown. This girl, though, had more force and personality in a single gesture than Ann could have found in her entire makeup, and although they were both pretty, this Doris was far more attractive.

"Well—what are you staring at?"

"I was just thinking," Irene said meekly, "that you *are* rather like Ann—except when you speak, of course."

"Oh, sure—we speak different. That's why I didn't say anything to you back there. Only I can see now you're a good sport, bringing me straight here without any trouble. It was a cinch getting out. They usually had someone watching when Ann visited, but they haven't bothered so much lately—and then, going out, I made like I was crying all the way, and nobody could see my face much. It was easy." She stretched her arms above her head and added, "It's swell to be on the outside. They'll never get me back in that dump—never."

She dropped her arms and then turned her head quickly. "Here he comes now." She slipped out of the car with one lithe, almost stealthy movement, and Irene edged over to the vacated seat and called, "Is it all right if I go on now?"

"No, wait a minute," Doris said under her breath. "He has someone with him."

"Probably a friend. You'll be all right now—I think I'd better go."

She started to slide back under the wheel, when Doris's hand came down upon her arm again—catlike in its swift strength.

"No! I might want to make a getaway—I don't know who's with him. I'm not going back to that place—"

Two men emerged from the driveway, both young, the obviously younger in the lead and with an anxious look on his face. He gave the two girls a quick, comprehensive glance and then circled around Doris and caught Irene's head between his hands.

"Darling," he said clearly, looking down into her eyes, "it's wonderful to see you again."

As Irene jerked her head back, Doris made an exclamation of some sort, and he turned to her quickly.

"You must be Irene Hastings. It was awfully good of you to bring Doris out here—we're both grateful. I know you're in a hurry, and we won't try to detain you. By the way, if you're hungry, you can get a good meal at the Indian Head just down the road a short distance, on your right—very good food."

"Wait a minute," Irene said shrilly, "you've made a mistake. I—"

"Hush, darling—it's all right. Come on." He reached into the car and lifted her out as though she had been a small child.

Doris slid in behind the wheel at once, and the car shot away, spitting gravel from the rear wheels until it swung onto the concrete of the highway.

Irene, trying to struggle away from the strong arms that held her, attempted to protest and explain in a terrified jumble of words that were drowned out by the man's deeper voice.

"Darling, please—it's no use. Ross found out about our plans, and he's making things awkward. He's a doctor, of course, and he says he can't connive at a thing like this. We'll have to go in and try to talk it over with him."

The other man spoke for the first time. "Clark, go and get your car—you'll have to take her back. I'll telephone to say you're coming."

Irene, fighting angry tears, tried to protest, and was again talked down by Clark.

"I can't—I've a flat tire and engine trouble of some sort. We'll have to keep her here until they can send for her—hush, darling—and you can look her over. I'm convinced that you'll agree with me about her sanity, and perhaps we can get her released. Come on, Ross, be reasonable, can't you?"

Ross jammed his hands into his pockets and muttered, "You're a damn fool."

Irene had suddenly stopped struggling and protesting and was quietly watching the two of them. This man Ross apparently had found out about the plans for Doris's escape, but Clark, thinking quickly at the last moment, had saved the situation anyway and as soon as he could get away would meet Doris at the Indian Head place.

"Mr. Ross " she began, and was promptly interrupted by Clark, who laughed loudly and falsely.

"It's Munster, darling—my nephew, Dr. Ross Munster."

The designated nephew was certainly several years older than his uncle, and Irene began to have a confused feeling that she had been caught in a web of general insanity.

Nephew Ross, dark-browed and forbidding, said abruptly, "We'd better take her inside—although where the devil you think we're going to be able to put her is beyond me."

"You're not going to put me anywhere. I have a reservation at the hotel, and that's where I'm going to stay. You can phone the hospital and get a description of Doris Miller—and you'll find out then that you've made a mistake."

Ross gave her a strictly clinical look and turned away, and Clark laughed deprecatingly.

"It's no use, Dorrie—I'm afraid we'll just have to face it."

Ross had already started up the driveway, and Irene, urged along in the firm grip of her captor, had perforce to follow. She glanced up into his anxious face and grinned for the first time.

"You mean *you'll* have to face it—as soon as he gets the description of Doris."

"Oh, shut up!" Clark muttered furiously. "The damn nosy busybody! Always butting into my affairs."

Irene suddenly twisted herself free from him. "You can let me go now—my car's gone, and I've nowhere to run to. But as soon as he clears the thing up, you'll have to see that I get transportation to the hotel."

Ross waited at the foot of the veranda steps until they caught up with him and, after another rather searching look at Irene, said flatly, "Bring her into my office while I phone the hospital."

Clark nodded. "You'd better be careful what you say, I mean, explain that it was the sister who helped her to escape and that Irene Hastings wasn't in on the thing at all. You can take my word for that."

Ross was still frowning. "They'll have to send for her tonight. We haven't room for her here."

"Oh, for God's sake—why can't you be human? I want you to look her over—give her a chance—"

They herded Irene into the office—a rather pleasant room with a low ceiling, windows reaching to the floor, and polished brass andirons in the fireplace under an Adam mantel.

Irene sat down and kept her eyes on Ross, who went to a mahogany desk and began to riffle through the telephone book.

"You're going to feel pretty silly as soon as you get that description," she observed almost airily.

Ross tossed aside the book, picked up the telephone, and said briefly, "Fair enough."

"You're fighting a losing battle, Dorrie," Clark said rather desperately. "I assure you, Ross, that a description won't be necessary."

Ross ignored him and barked a number into the instrument, and presently he began a low-voiced explanation, while the other two waited in dead silence. He asked for a description of the escaped patient and then raised his eyes and looked full at Irene.

"Light brown hair, yes—blue eyes, yes—medium height, slim figure, right. What's that? Oh, attractive—yes, very. She's Doris Miller, all right."

## THREE

IRENE heard Clark release a breath that had been held overlong, and in sudden fury at his evident relief, she stood up abruptly.

"Dr. Ross—"

"Munster," Clark murmured amiably.

"I don't care how that description tallies—I am not Doris Miller. If you'll come with me to that Indian Head restaurant, I can prove—"

Dr. Munster, still hanging onto the telephone, paid no slightest heed to her. His eyes were angry, and he presently barked into the mouthpiece, "I tell you I haven't room here—the place is filled to the doors. My own uncle is forced to sleep in a tent on the grounds, as it is— What? . . . Certainly I have my own room; it is necessary for me to be near the patients at all times. This is a private hospital, and I have only one other doctor here. What's that? My room? I'll be damned if I will!"

Irene gathered that they hung up on him at that point, because he banged the phone down in a fury and brooded for a while. When he looked up at last he discovered that Clark had quietly departed. He got to his feet and yelled, "Clark!" and Irene gave a chilly laugh.

"Don't delay him, he's in a hurry—he has to get to that Indian Head place and pick up Doris—and the two of them will go off in my car.

You'd better come, too, and see for yourself, because you're going to look silly if you can't produce Doris when they come for her."

He wasn't listening, and she turned away with a sudden desperate desire to get out of the place, even if she had to let her car go for the time being and was forced to trudge along the highway, hitchhiking her way into Tilton. She went quickly to the door and out into the hall, but she had taken only a few steps before she was jerked to a stop, her arms pinioned firmly from behind.

Ross Munster stood there with her for a while, inwardly cursing everybody and everything, then with a magnificent effort he controlled his temper. He marched Irene to the elevator—a handsome structure installed by his late father at great expense, and well worth it to the orderly—pushed her in, and held her with one powerfully muscled arm while he banged the door with the other.

"You're making a priceless fool out of yourself," Irene cried furiously. "You could tell that I'm not insane if you'd take two minutes to look at me."

"I haven't two minutes to spare," he said shortly and without relaxing his grip on her. "I know that damn fool Clark has gone after that girl—he chases any pretty face that comes in sight. You're caught, and he can't get you—so he might as well have a try at the other one. The best thing you can do is to forget him."

Irene felt her tense body relax a little, and unexpectedly the whole thing began to seem funny to her. She glanced up at the good-looking angry face and asked mildly, "Is that a nice way to speak to a poor loony?"

But he was not amused. The elevator came to a stop, and they got out and pounded up another flight of stairs. Irene, panting, observed that they were now in the attic—a rather gloomy hall boxed in by closed doors. But the room which they entered immediately was almost startling in its sunny charm. It was carpeted in an odd, soft shade of blue and furnished in mellow old mahogany, with a cheerful and yet quiet chintz at the windows. A pair of french doors opened onto a small, white-painted balcony.

Ross, silent now and grim, put Irene into a chair and proceeded to close the french doors and lock them. He dropped the key into his pocket and walked over to another door which opened into a gleaming little bathroom. He collected his old-fashioned razor and the extra blades, and after a quick glance around the room he went out, closed the door behind him, and locked it.

He went slowly down the stairs, frowning and still fuming inwardly. It was quite by accident that he had discovered Clark's plan of going off with this girl, and he had felt that he had to put a stop to it—and now there was all this mess and trouble. The people at the asylum had been relieved and happy to hear that their patient was being held at a hospital, under the eye of a doctor, and had been cheerfully vague about when they'd be able to pick her up. Ross ground his teeth together and vowed to himself that the next time Clark got into trouble he'd do it entirely by himself—and that included the getting out too.

In the lower hall he ran into his assistant, Dr. John Girsted. Dr. John was small, middle-aged, and gray-haired, with mild blue eyes peering through his glasses.

He said unhappily, "Is there any trouble, Ross? I hear you took a girl up to your room. I mean it seems to be all over the hospital. Nurses and patients, you know "

Ross ran a hand wildly through his hair and exploded furiously, "What the devil are you talking about! I only just took her up—how could they possibly be jabbering about it already!"

Dr. John lowered his eyes and pulled uncomfortably at his ear. Ross was always doing things of which he disapproved, but it seemed to him that this was pretty close to the limit—dragging a girl up to his room in broad daylight.

Ross let out an exasperated breath and said more calmly, "You'd better go around and explain the thing. The girl escaped from the state hospital sometime today, and I'm holding her until they can come for her. They can't—or won't—make it until tomorrow, and if you can think of any other place to keep her—your room—for example—I'll be only too happy."

"What do you mean?" Dr. John asked agitatedly. "Are you telling me that the girl is insane? How did she come here?"

"She's insane, and how she came here is a long story—and we're both busy, so let's get on with it."

"Wait a minute! Good heavens, Ross! We can't let that story get around. If there were the slightest suspicion that we are harboring a lunatic, we would not have a patient left by nightfall. And no one could blame them! It's monstrous!"

Ross muttered, "Oh God! I suppose you're right. We'll have to think of something else."

Dr. John nodded, and the mild blue eyes were suddenly fired with quiet anger. Ross is just like his father, he thought. If they hadn't had me here with them all these years, they'd have ruined the place in no time. He gave a quick sigh and wondered again, as he had wondered a thousand times, why Ross's father, Dr. Horace Munster, had failed to keep his word. He had promised to leave the hospital to Dr. John—had bound him to the place all those years by that promise—and now he was dead and had died intestate.

"Look here," Ross said suddenly, "we'll say she was eloping and her father got me to stop the thing and hold her until he could come for her."

Dr. John frowned. "She'd have to be under eighteen for that," he objected. "How old does she look?"

"Oh, I don't know—what does it matter? The young ones look old, and the old ones look young, these days, anyhow. We can say she's seventeen."

"If you say so, of course. But I think you'd be better advised to take her back yourself—tonight."

"I can't," Ross declared peevishly. "I'm busy, and I need my sleep—I'm operating in the morning. They'll pick her up tomorrow—and in the meantime the patients will enjoy the story of a broken elopement—be a bit of spice in their gray lives."

He went off, and Dr. John followed more slowly, shaking his head a little. These young doctors, he thought, lacked the wisdom of experience. Ross would find out, as the years went by, that a gray life was the best kind for a patient.

Upstairs, in Ross's attic bedroom, Irene had settled into a philosophic attitude. No use getting into a stew—the thing was bound to be straightened out in due time. It was odd how the description of Doris had fitted herself, and yet they were not at all alike really. Descriptions of that sort were obviously pretty useless. She wondered vaguely what they would do with poor, foolish Ann.

She took a restless turn around the room and discovered that there were two telephones on the bedside table. The one with the blank surface was a house phone, she supposed, but the other bore a plaque with its number inscribed on it and was evidently an outside telephone. She looked at it for a thoughtful moment and then reached out her hand, lifted it, and dialed for an operator. She gave her mother's number and exchange and waited with a little smile pulling at her mouth.

Elise, after listening with unusual patience to the whole story, was definitely intrigued.

"My dear, I know you're slightly cracked about some things—I've always said so—but you are not certifiable. I shall come down there immediately and get you out."

"Don't be silly," Irene protested. "It would only be a long trip for nothing. They wouldn't just take your word for it—and anyway, it will all be settled tomorrow."

But Elise had hung up, and Irene knew that she was coming anyway. She always liked to have a finger in every pie and hated missing anything. Anyway, she would probably annoy the Ross man to the point of frenzy—and that was all to the good.

She wandered over to the french doors and, after a brief inspection of the lock, picked it with comparative ease and the help of a nail file and went out onto the balcony. It had a gay little awning overhead and two comfortably cushioned garden chairs and was altogether a pleasant spot. It overlooked the side lawn and part of the back, and Irene noticed a tent standing against a background of hollyhocks. Uncle Clark's residence, she thought, and made a face at it—and then wondered if she wasn't acting a little like a loony at that.

Considerably farther back the lawn ended abruptly in a thick woods, and right at the edge there was a little white stone building, its straight lines sharply etched against the dark trees directly behind it. In the midst of the woods, and partly concealed by them, there seemed to be an old summerhouse.

A movement from the tent drew her eyes back to it, and she saw Clark Munster emerge with a suitcase in his hand.

## FOUR

IRENE watched Clark hurrying across the lawn with his suitcase, and fury quickened her breath again. He was going away with Doris, of course, and the two of them would go flying off in her car without giving a thought to the tires, which were none too good.

The thing was not funny—it was annoying and exasperating. She flung back into the room and went over and tried to pick the lock of the door into the hall, but it resisted all her efforts and the accompanying bad language, and she had to give up. Oh well, she thought resignedly, no use fussing. She glanced at her watch and saw that it was almost six. They should be sending her up some food pretty soon, but perhaps they'd just forget her. She lay down on the bed and hoped that her shoes would soil the creamy chenille spread, and although she had no thought of going to sleep, her long trip and the early hour at which she had crawled out of bed were too much for her. She closed her eyes and went off at once.

Ross sat down to his dinner at half-past eight. He was tired and still annoyed at Clark's stupid behavior. Further, he could think of no possible place where he might comfortably lay his head during the coming night. Unless he put Clark out of the tent, of course. The thought cheered him up a little.

Dr. John was just finishing his coffee and, after a glance or two at his morose companion, asked hesitantly, "What is it? Are you worrying about that girl?"

Ross raised his head and made a rather obvious effort to be patient and even courteous.

"Oh no, I'm more or less resigned to it. I was simply wondering where I'm going to sleep."

"Ah yes—of course. It is rather a problem. That couch in the waiting room—"

"Out of the question," Ross said shortly. "Old Dave Cattledge is going out on us—any minute, I should think—and his relatives are apt to be draped around the waiting room all night."

"Yes, yes, I see. It's awkward. You never told me how the girl got here."

"It's Clark's doing—he ought to be certified along with the girl. You'd better ask him about it. I think I'll take his bed in the tent, and he can spend the night in his favorite bar."

"No, no, Ross," Dr. John protested agitatedly. "You know Clark should never be encouraged to drink. It isn't the boy's fault—your father was always too easy on him, and that's why he's irresponsible now."

"He was easy on me too," Ross said, "and I'm not irresponsible—in fact, I work like a blasted beaver, and have for years. By this time I wouldn't know what to do with a bit of leisure if someone handed it to me."

"But what about your army service? Surely that was not so bad?"

"Not as bad as this," Ross admitted, "but I didn't exactly sit around and contemplate my navel. When I got my discharge I thought it would be a pleasant change to spend a bit of time with my private patients, but of course Father died and I had to step in here at once. We should be able to get some extra help pretty soon, though, don't you think, John?"

They were interrupted by the entrance of a big, handsome blonde woman, neatly garbed in nurse's uniform. She came from the kitchen and was carrying a plate of steaming food, which she placed on the table. John hurried to hold her chair, while she greeted them both cheerfully.

Ross grinned at her, and the smile lingered as he watched Dr. John's courteous ministrations. They had been what Beatrice, the night switchboard girl, described as "going steady" for the last twenty years, and people were still wondering when and if they were going to be married. Lucky thing for the hospital that the romance had stalled, Ross reflected. Myrtle was a combination of head nurse, housekeeper, and general boss, and she was very nearly indispensable.

She attacked her meal with enthusiasm and, with her mouth still full, said to Ross, "I heard you handing out that sob story to John a minute ago. Can you name one single reason why you want to spend more time with your private patients?"

"Certainly," Ross replied with dignity. "I have time only to listen to an installment of their life histories—after which it is always too late to get around to boring them with mine."

Myrtle opened her wide mouth and laughed heartily, and Dr. John shifted uncomfortably in his chair and wished that she would take time to swallow before giving way to such wholehearted mirth. He quietly changed the subject.

"Where's Clark?"

"I don't know where that loafer is," Myrtle declared, still cheerful. "And I don't think I'd tell you, if I did. You might want to lend him another dollar to go and look for a job."

"I don't think that's funny, Myrtle," Dr. John said, looking offended. "You know that I'm fond of the boy and I want to help him if I can."

Myrtle patted her bosom, belched in a ladylike fashion, and then nodded agreeably. "All right, John, I know how you feel. But there's no need to worry about him—he'll straighten out in time. Anyway, even if he doesn't, there's always room here at the hospital for him, and he can help around some, the way he's been doing since they chucked him out of the army."

She gave a small sigh and was silent for a while, although she continued to eat. She thought wryly, Why couldn't John have been fond of Ross, who was full of solid worth ? But he didn't care for Ross at all—it was quite obvious. His affection and concern were centered on Clark, who was a wastrel and probably never would be anything else. Clark had come very late in his mother's life—her first son, Horace, already married with a son of his own. The elder Mrs. Munster had died at the birth, and Horace had cared for his little brother and brought him up with his own son, Ross. Myrtle sighed again and speared a large piece of potato with her fork.

"If you are determined to put Clark out of his tent, I don't see where he can sleep tonight," Dr. John said fretfully to Ross.

"He can have the waiting-room couch. The Cattledge gang won't mind him—they'll think he's an expectant father."

Myrtle looked from one to the other of them and asked, "What in the name of Pete are you talking about?"

Dr. John patiently gave her the whole story. She grasped it perfectly at the first telling and made no exclamations or protests, which was an indication of one of the reasons why she was so nearly indispensable to them.

"Isn't there room for two cots in the tent?" she asked after a moment's thought.

Dr. John shook his head. "No. Unfortunately."

"Hmm. Well, there must be some place you can put a bed—some corner— Let me think."

She half closed her eyes and stopped eating while she presumably thought, although what actually came into her head was that her new coat did not exactly please her and she was inclined to take it back.

"Even if you can think of a corner," Ross said after a moment, "there's nothing to put in it. There are no extra cots or beds left."

"There are two beds in your room," Myrtle pointed out, "and one is a double, at that."

"One's a built-in day bed," Ross told her, "so it won't come out, and it would be altogether too much of a sweat to take down that great mahogany thing and lug it out."

"But then where is Clark to sleep?" Dr. John asked.

Myrtle put her new coat firmly out of her mind, concentrated for about thirty seconds, and then said, "Well, look. Why should you bother taking the bed out, anyway? The girl's a patient, isn't she? Just give her something to make her sleep, and as soon as she goes off, go to bed yourself. Once she's safely out, you can sleep in peace. I mean you won't have to worry about her getting up and tying your toes together—or whatever her particular brand of insanity prompts her to do."

Dr. John was scandalized. "Myrtle, whatever possesses you to think of these mad things? Ross sleeping in the same room with a girl—a patient! Good God! Supposing a thing like that ever got out?"

"What in hell would we do without you, Myrtle?" Ross said admiringly. "Just as simple as that. Only, be sure that it doesn't get around. You too, John—keep it under your hat."

"But, Ross, you can't do a thing like that—I tell you it's insane. If it ever got out, not one single soul would ever believe that you were innocent."

Ross got up and yawned. "So maybe they'd be right."

Myrtle giggled, and Dr. John blushed all the way down to his collar.

He'll ruin the place, he thought wildly, after all the work I've put into it—years and years—sticking it out because of Horace's promise, and now there's nothing—no will.

Dr. John had looked everywhere for that will, quietly but persistently. He wanted so desperately to find it and take it to Ross and show it to him. Ross strutting around as the owner, because he was next of kin. Horace had said, "You'll have to find the will, John—for once in your life you'll have to show a little ingenuity."

Ross left the room, and Myrtle presently went out to the kitchen for something, but Dr. John sat on, obsessed by the thought of that will. He had come slowly and painfully to the conclusion that Horace had actually made a will leaving the place to him, and then had hidden it where it would never be found. Thus he kept his word to John and at the same time secured the place for Ross. It was natural that he had wanted the boy to have it, since he had done so well in medical school and in the army. But Horace should have been honest about it, should have admitted that he intended to break his promise.

Dr. John wiped his forehead with his handkerchief and realized vaguely that it was hot. He got up slowly and walked over to the french doors and out onto the stone terrace. After standing there for a while, slapping at mosquitoes, he stepped onto the lawn and made his way over to Clark's tent. But it was in darkness, and Clark was not there. He went on, worrying a little and hoping that Clark was not out drinking again. What had Ross meant by blaming the arrival of that insane patient on Clark? He blamed Clark for everything. Ross was too young and inexperienced to be running a hospital of this size, anyway—it needed a man like himself.

He supposed that he should have got out years ago and built up his own practice, and then he could have married Myrtle. She had wanted it—she had minded very much their not getting married—although somehow she didn't seem to mind any more. He hadn't been fair to her—he'd been afraid to marry her. And she'd been faithful to him all these years, and kind to him as well. But perhaps she was better off. She had a good position, and sometimes it wasn't easy to make ends meet when you were married to a country doctor.

He raised his head and found that he was approaching the small white stone building at the end of the garden. He stood staring at it, while anger welled up in him. Horace lying in there in his handsome black coffin that was lined in white satin, and all dressed up in a white tie and tails. Why should he have thought that his carcass was worthy of being surrounded by white stone, a stained-glass window, and a bronze door? The Tilton cemetery was a hallowed and decent resting place.

His anger, as always, died away in futility, and he sighed. If you were going to be absolutely fair, you had to admit that this appalling little mausoleum was quite unlike Horace—he had always liked simple things. And yet he had had this place built shortly before his death and had been explicit about wanting to be interred here

Suddenly, in that hot, humid darkness, Dr. John went quite cold and could feel his hair pricking along his scalp.

The will was there—inside there, with Horace.

## FIVE

IRENE awoke to a dark room and a sharp hunger. She stretched an exploring arm and, after some fumbling, found a lamp on the bedside table and switched it on. The clock said half-past eight, and she blinked at it for a moment and then frowned. No one had brought her any food—unless they had left a tray somewhere. She pulled herself off the bed, yawning and pushing her hair away from her forehead.

There was no tray in the room. She prowled around for a while, irritated and increasingly hungry, until her eye fell on the house phone, and she went straight over and picked it up.

"Yes?" a voice said wearily.

"Will you kindly send up my dinner."

"Huh?" said the voice, becoming perplexed.

"Dinner. You know—things to eat. I'm starving, and I've evidently been forgotten."

"Oh. Er—you in the doctor's room?"

"Yes," said Irene, "I am in the doctor's room. I wish to be fed, and the sooner somebody attends to it, the pleasanter it will be all around."

"The trays went up at five forty-five, same as usual," the voice informed her. "I—er—I guess they missed you out. What name shall I say?"

Irene thought it over. "Well," she said after a moment, "suppose we keep personalities out of it. You can inform the kitchen that a tray is wanted for the doctor's girlfriend."

She heard the sound of a sharply indrawn breath before she replaced the phone, and she muttered defiantly, "Maybe that'll hold them for a while."

She heard the sound of a key in the lock and turned toward the door as Ross walked in, holding a glass of milk.

Irene looked at the glass and then at him and shook her head.

"That won't do. The trouble is supposedly in my head, you know—not my stomach. I want something more on the order of a medium-rare steak."

Ross said, "Oh damn! Of course, you've had nothing to eat. Sorry—I forgot to tell them. Drink this milk, anyway, and I'll have something brought up for you."

He offered the doctored milk, hopefully, but she merely shook her head.

"I hate milk. I never touch the stuff."

Ross banged the glass down onto the bedside table and started for the door. "All right—I'll go down and see what I can do."

"You'd better check with the switchboard girl first. I've already phoned in an order."

He stopped dead and turned around. "You've—what?"

Irene closed her eyes and bawled out in complete exasperation, "I phoned down for *food.*"

Ross came back, sat down, and took out a cigarette. He lit it, inhaled deeply, and, as the smoke drifted out again, said almost casually, "Well, that's interesting—that ought to fix everything. Who did you say you were?"

Irene turned away and walked over to the window, and he said grimly, "Oh. So you did give a name to yourself. What, for instance?"

"I am still anonymous. I merely ordered dinner."

"Beatrice must have asked for your name. What did you say?"

Irene abandoned the window and came back to glare at him.

"I'll tell you what I *didn't* say. I did not describe myself as an escaped loony, because it isn't the truth. But since the girl seemed to know that I was in your room, I confirmed what she was thinking anyway and told her I was your girlfriend."

The cigarette fell from Ross's fingers, and Irene picked it up and handed it back to him because she had taken a fancy to the carpet and hated to see it marred by a burn. Ross accepted it mechanically and gave her a dazed stare. He seemed incapable of speech for a few moments, and then at last he said almost feebly, "Haven't you any shame?"

"There was no use in my telling her I was your aunt Julia," Irene pointed out reasonably. "If she's smart enough to run a switchboard, she knows better than that."

"I'd like to have five minutes alone with Clark right now," Ross said wistfully. "Just five minutes—that's all I'd ask."

He thought of John spreading that story of the eloping young woman being held until her father could come for her and shuddered.

He looked full at Irene and really saw her as she was for the first time. She was older than seventeen—in her twenties somewhere. Smartly dressed and good-looking. Pity about her, and odd that she showed no sign of it.

Irene had been watching him, and she asked curiously, "Can't you tell that I'm perfectly normal? I should think that you could—you're supposed to be a doctor."

He was silent for a moment, turning the cigarette in his fingers. "Did you ever hear them give a name to your trouble? Or don't you know?"

She shook her head. "I don't know what Doris's trouble is—specifically, I mean. Her sister thinks it's all a big mistake, but I don't suppose she knows much about it really. Anyway, the doctors won't release Doris, and they ought to know what they're doing."

There was a knock on the door, and Ross got up wearily, unlocked it, and admitted Myrtle, who was bearing a full tray. She gave Irene an interested look and set the tray down on a table.

"Here you are, dear—a nice hot meal for you."

Irene hastily established herself in front of the tray and began to eat hungrily, and Myrtle turned to Ross.

"You've got yourself into a nice fix this time. You should have cut the telephone wires."

"There's no use telling me what I should have done," Ross said gloomily. "What's going on now? Did John circulate that story about the elopement?"

Myrtle sat down, sighing as though she were tired, and took one of Ross's cigarettes. Irene, absorbed in her meal, noticed nevertheless that they talked about her as though she were a small child who was incapable of understanding them.

Myrtle took a pull on her cigarette and shook her head. "John thought up something that he figured was better. He told them that you were merely showing the young lady over the hospital and that the young lady had already left. And then the young lady phones down to that popeyed Beatrice—from your *bedroom*—and says she's the doctor's girlfriend. How do you like that?"

But Ross had already heard the worst, so he merely shrugged.

Myrtle was a bit annoyed that her bombshell had fallen so flat, and she asked tartly, "Do you realize what this means? You know our patients are very refined people—mostly elderly and somewhat Victorian. They're certainly not going to patronize a hospital if they think the head is indulging in—in illicit—er—debauchery."

Irene choked over a piece of bread and, when she got her breath, laughed aloud for some time. The other two glanced at her idly but took no further notice, and she presently realized that they regarded her rude mirth as being merely an aspect of her infirmity. She turned back to her dinner and finished it up with dispatch.

"You'll have to think of something," Ross was saying to Myrtle. "You're good at that sort of thing, anyway. Only don't let John have a hand in it this time. He's apt to muck it."

Irene moved back from the depleted tray and observed, "You people have no imagination. It's really quite simple. The doctor can grab me and run me out the front door, in full view of the popeyed Beatrice. He throws me down the front steps and then goes back in, dusting his hands and saying loud enough for Beatrice to hear, 'Awful the way some women throw themselves at a man's head.' "

Myrtle threw back her head and laughed loudly, while Ross scowled.

"It's not such a bad idea, at that," she said presently. "I'll be waiting outside to get her as she comes tumbling down the steps, and then I'll smuggle her in again, through the kitchen. Anyway, I'm too tired to think of anything else."

"You're too tired to talk sense," Ross said coldly.

He glanced at Irene and the tray and raised his eyebrows at Myrtle, who nodded back. She said obscurely, "She'll go off at any time, now, and sleep like a fool."

"Who—me?" Irene asked, startled. She looked at her empty cup and then at both their faces. They ignored her, and for a minute she was frightened, until she realized that they could hardly have any intention of harming her. Evidently they'd given her something that would put her to sleep so that she'd be no further trouble to them until the morning.

Ross said to her with fatherly kindness, "You just get into bed, now, and have a good night's rest."

Myrtle picked up the tray. "Good night, honey—pleasant dreams."

The two of them went out and locked the door firmly behind them.

Irene shrugged and, after thinking it over for a while, began slowly to undress. If she were going to sleep, whether she wanted to or not, she might as well make herself comfortable first. Clark had had the unexpected decency to remove her suitcase from the car, and Ross had brought it up to her later, so that she had everything she needed.

She got into bed, but instead of being sleepy, she felt restless and excited, and after turning over several times she got out again and went onto the balcony. But the night was very dark, and there was nothing to see, so that she presently went in—and stubbed her toe sharply on some piece of furniture while she was feeling her way to the bed. She cursed freely, climbed into bed once more, and had barely got her head onto the pillow when she heard the lock turn and the door open. Her heart seemed to stop beating as she heard someone creep quietly into the room and relock the door. She could see a dark figure silhouetted for a moment against the french doors, and then it moved on into the bathroom and shut the door.

After the first shock she realized that it was probably Ross, come back to use his own bathroom, and she began to breathe again, although her whole body was tense and her hands clenched.

The bathroom door presently opened cautiously, and he came out. Irene, sweating with nervousness, thought confusedly that he must have changed his clothes—he seemed, now, to be wearing a white suit. It was not until he had made his way silently to the day bed, stretched out on it, and pulled a sheet over him that she realized he was wearing pajamas.

## SIX

THIS was entirely *too* much, Irene decided—in fact, it was outrageous. She spoke out clearly into the darkness.

"Even if I were what you think I am, it would be hardly fair of you to kick my reputation around like this."

There was a hollow groan from the day bed, and Ross sat up. "Oh God! Are you still awake?"

"Certainly I'm awake. I feel a bit fuzzy around the edges, but I know what I'm doing. That stuff that your nurse Myrtle put into my food must have been pure birdseed."

Ross got up, switched on a light, and draped himself in a bathrobe while he wondered irritably what was the matter with Myrtle, anyway.

Irene yawned. "My mother won't like it, you know. It's bad enough when you hold me against my will and lock me up in a room, but when she hears that you came and slept in with me, she'll be definitely annoyed. My guess is that she'll sue you."

Ross lit a cigarette and said morosely, "You were quick enough to tell the switchboard girl that you are my girlfriend—but when I merely try to sleep in my own room, quite innocently, you talk about suing me. What's the matter with you?"

He began to pace the room, wondering why he bothered to try and talk to the girl. But he had to do something—he needed sleep badly. He glanced out onto the balcony and thought suddenly, That's it—I can fix up some sort of a bed out there. Be cool, if nothing else.

He turned to Irene in time to get the end of what had been rather a long sentence.

"—should think that she'll be here at any minute."

"Who?"

"I've just finished telling you. My mother."

"But—how does she know where you are?"

"I phoned her. She said she'd come right on out, and—this is just a friendly warning—I think you'd better be out of this room by the time she gets here."

Ross agreed with her. No mother, he thought glumly, would take kindly to Myrtle's silly idea of putting the patient to sleep so that the doctor could bed down in the same room.

He looked at the girl with a faintly puzzled frown. She was half sitting against the pillows, with the sheet pulled up around her, but there was a glimpse here and there of a delicate shell-pink nightgown. Her hair was pushed childishly back from her face in damp, disordered curls, and the blue eyes looked dark and sleepy. He thought, with sudden pity, that the poor kid had expected to go on a honeymoon—and Clark hadn't put up much of a fight for her. He wondered why not; if it had been himself, he'd have fought for her, all right.

He saw that her eyes were closing up, although she was fighting to stay awake, and he said quickly, "All right, "I'll go, and you can sleep in peace. I'm sorry about it—we're short of beds—and besides, I wanted to be sure you'd be all right."

Irene muttered, "Please shut up," and slid lower into the pillows.

Ross tramped across the room, noisily let himself out, and locked the door. He seated himself on the top step of the stairs and prepared to wait.

He wondered a little about the mother. The girl might actually have phoned her, at that—and perhaps she really was on her way down here. It was only eleven o'clock—she might turn up tonight. He ought to phone down to Beatrice, only what was he going to say to her ? He sighed and rumpled his hair and wished for Clark's neck between his two hands.

He presently went quietly back to his room and opened the door with infinite care. The light was still on, and the girl was out this time—not a doubt of it. He was going to sleep on the day bed and be damned to it; he'd be dressed and out before the girl woke up in the morning, anyway, and only Myrtle and John would ever know, and they were quite safe.

Only there was that infernal woman, the mother. He ought to prepare Beatrice for her, in case she showed up— but how? He absentmindedly picked up the glass of milk he had brought for Irene and drank it down. He went over to the day bed and sat down and tried to think, and then he stretched full length on the bed, in order to think some more. He went out as though someone had hit him over the head.

* * *

Elise drove her coral-colored sedan up to the hospital at shortly before one in the morning. She parked in the driveway and then stretched her cramped muscles and yawned. She was tired, but she was glad she'd come. Anything for a change. She got out and hauled her small suitcase down from the seat. They'd have to put her up at the hospital for the night—it was too late to go anywhere else, away out in the country here.

Beatrice was busy doing her nails when Elise walked in. She saw a slim, middle-aged lady, dressed in smart but restrained navy blue and quietly embellished with diamonds and sapphires as worn in the best of taste. Beatrice stared.

Elise walked straight up to the desk and said, "Young lady, I want to see the manager of this establishment at once." Irene, she knew, had given her several names, including that of the doctor in charge—but she had forgotten all of them, which was quite usual with her.

Beatrice, busy eying the diamonds and sapphires, asked, "Who is it you wanna see, madam?"

"Whoever it is that mismanages this hospital, and at once."

Beatrice said, "But, madam—" and discovered at once that she was outclassed.

Elise slapped a shapely hand on the desk and snapped, "Come, now—hurry up. I've had a long journey, and I am in no mood for inanities. Furthermore, I object to being addressed as 'Madam,' since I do not run an establishment for the purpose of—"

"Yes ma'am, right away," Beatrice said hastily, and plugged in to Myrtle's room.

Myrtle, roused from a sound sleep, was far from amiable. "Find out which patient the woman wants to see. If it's old Pop Cattledge, it's all right—he's going out. Or if it's a complaint, tell her to write it down. Try and handle the thing yourself, for once—I'm in bed."

Beatrice disconnected, slipped her gum under her tongue, and tried once more—if feebly—for mastery of the situation.

"If you'll tell me which patient you wish to see, I'll—"

Elise slapped the desk again, and her rings clicked on the polished surface. "I do not wish to see any of your miserable patients. Do I look morbid? You get that person—whoever it is—on the phone again and say I'm here about Irene—or Doris—and if he isn't down here within five minutes, I shall go up and look for him."

Beatrice plugged in again in a hurry. So there was something going on, she thought excitedly—and Myrt and the two doctors were trying to keep it quiet. There was a girl up in Dr. Ross's room, and her name was Irene alias Doris.

She broke in on Myrtle's peeved exclamations and gave her a low-voiced hurried outline of the situation. Myrtle groaned and, breaking in before the end, said curtly, "All right—tell her I'll be right down."

She dressed rapidly, to an accompaniment of nagging worry. It must have to do with that girl upstairs, and she had not yet thought of any explanation to give Beatrice. She supposed she'd have to use some variation of the girl's own story. She came down, to be confronted by Elise in all her elegance, and she found herself wishing that she'd taken a bit more care over her dressing.

"You wished to see me?" she asked coldly.

"Some afternoon at tea, perhaps," said Elise, looking her over, "but not at one in the morning—if you don't mind? I came to see the owner of this place, and my patience is wearing thin. It's an important matter, and he'd hardly care to have it spread around."

Myrtle quickly urged her toward the waiting room and said, "You might as well have a seat while I'm getting him up."

She closed the door behind them and then asked rather desperately, "Will you please tell me who you are?"

Elise took a long breath. "My dear woman, I am Mrs. De Petro, and I have come for my daughter, who is being detained here against her will. I should certainly have brought a policeman or a lawyer along with me but for the fact that my daughter tells me it was an honest mistake on the part of your doctor. Apparently the man is a fool, and since I am sorry for fools, I'll do nothing more than sue you for the inconvenience my daughter and I have suffered."

Myrtle swallowed, twice. "Please don't be upset, Mrs. De Petro. If there has been a mistake, it will certainly be set right in the morning. Your daughter is perfectly all right—she's sleeping soundly at the moment—and it would be foolish to wake her, since we can't let you take her away until we check on it. You know how that is—red tape."

Elise was getting a bit tired of it, and she decided that it would be more fun to continue it in the morning, after she'd had her coffee and orange juice.

She said abruptly, "Very well. Show me to a bedroom, and we shall conclude this absurd business tomorrow."

A bedroom. Myrtle felt a cold, flat sensation somewhere in the region of her stomach.

Elise was tapping a small foot, exquisitely shod in navy blue. "Now don't try to tell me that you haven't a bedroom, because I wouldn't believe you."

"No," said Myrtle, "oh no—I wouldn't believe it myself. We have a very comfortable bedroom with bath attached. And a picture of my rich aunt on the dressing table."

"Excellent," said Elise. "Suppose we go up. You can take the picture of your aunt out—I don't believe I'd care for it."

Myrtle had to remake her bed with fresh sheets and then collect her uniform and a few other essentials, while Elise looked on in stony silence. In the end, they wished each other a sarcastic good night.

Myrtle, on her way up to Ross's room, stopped at the linen closet to pick up a blanket. Ross would have to get out of there without delay, she thought feverishly.

The door was locked, and it proved unexpectedly hard to wake him. She dared not make too much noise, and she was afraid, too, of waking the girl. She gave a fairly hefty bang, at last, and heard him mutter and stumble out. He unlocked the door, and she pushed in, crowding him back. She flung the blanket at him and hissed, "Get out on the balcony—quickly—and don't make any noise. The girl's mother is downstairs in my room."

Ross muttered vaguely, "To hell with her," but made his way out onto the balcony obediently. He wrapped himself up in the blanket, stretched out on the floor, and then lay blinking confusedly down at the lawn. There seemed to be a faint light at the end of the garden, somewhere in the direction of his father's tomb.

## SEVEN

ROSS blinked away his confusion and stood up to get a better view, and it was then he realized that the light was not at the mausoleum but to the right a little, and back in the woods. The light went out as he stood there, and he could not decide whether it had been a lantern or a flashlight—more like an ordinary electric bulb, perhaps. And that's what it was, he thought suddenly—Horace had had the old summerhouse wired, used to go out there and read on hot nights. Horace, being impervious to mosquitoes, was the only one who had ever used it, since it was merely a floor and roof supported by uprights with morning glory and honeysuckle vine climbing over and around it. And the light had undoubtedly been over in that direction. It was odd, Ross mused, because, as far as he knew, no one had been near the summerhouse since the old man's death.

He gave it up with a shrug and lay down again. Some tramp, perhaps—he'd better go out and look at the place tomorrow. He rolled up in the blanket and went straight off to sleep, still without realizing that he had taken a glassful of drugged milk.

In the room behind him, Myrtle had discovered that Irene was sitting up in bed, looking at her.

She sighed deeply and said, “Go to sleep, my dear.”

“Why should I?” Irene asked, and added childishly, “I’m afraid to. Every time I go to sleep you people are up to something. Anyway, since my mother is here, I’d like to see her.”

“You can’t wake her in the small hours of the morning,” Myrtle explained patiently. “She was very tired and went straight to bed. You’ll see her tomorrow.”

Irene raised her sleepy eyes, still heavy with the drug, and asked simply, “Why do you call me ‘my dear’ and act so pleasant when you’d really like to bat me over the head ?”

“Because I’ve learned that it pays to keep your temper,” Myrtle snapped, losing it. “I work hard all day, and you and your confounded mother have lost me plenty of sleep tonight.”

But Irene had dropped down into the pillows again and murmured, “Ah, shuddup!” with her eyes already closed. To Myrtle’s practiced eye she looked thoroughly uncomfortable, but Myrtle stopped herself almost in the act of straightening her out. Better leave her alone, she thought—the way she resisted drugs was out of this world, and she didn’t want to wake her again.

She undressed quickly and fell onto the day bed with a groan of fatigue. She hoped that the girl was sufficiently dosed so that she wouldn’t come over, through the night, and cut her throat. Maybe I’d better feel my throat when I wake up, she thought, or shake my head to see if falls off. She was dreaming by this time, and went on to dream that she took her new coat back and exchanged it for a mink.

John was dreaming too—a recurring dream that had haunted him for some time. He thought Horace was there in the room with him, sneering at him, and yet he knew that Horace was dead.

He woke up in a cold sweat of fear and lay there for a moment until he was sufficiently oriented to stretch an arm and switch on the bedside light. He blinked his eyes into focus and then reached for a cigarette. It always took a considerable time before he could get back to sleep after one of those nightmares. He couldn’t seem to get Horace out of his mind any more, day or night—it was becoming an obsession. But he knew it would be all right, everything would be all right, once he found that will.

It was not like Horace to build himself a fancy tomb, but it was exactly like him to figure out some way of giving the place to Ross and at the same time keep his promise to John. And that suit of clothes in which he had been buried—he’d bought it some time before he died, and told everyone it was to be his shroud. The will was probably sewed into the lining, because it might have been discovered in one of the pockets, and Horace hadn't wanted it discovered. He had known perfectly well, too, that John, for all his medical experience, was squeamish about the dead—and he had banked on that.

The key of the mausoleum hung in the dining room with all the house keys. John knew which one it was, and he intended to get it, take a pair of scissors, and then go out to the tomb and rip up the lining of Horace's suit. He'd go tomorrow night and make sure that no one saw him. Probably they wouldn't even be angry, if they knew what he was going to do—they'd laugh, and that was a thousand times worse. And then, if he didn't find the will, he'd never hear the end of it—they'd laugh at him till he died.

Of course he could go tonight—now. He was wide awake, and everybody was in bed, sleeping. But tomorrow night would be better—he was tired—he'd had a hard day, and there was plenty of work waiting for him in the morning.

He put out the cigarette, turned off the light, and lay down again. But he could not sleep, and he knew that he was due for a long stretch of wakefulness. He'd never be able to sleep properly until he got that will. He ought to go now and get it over with. He shuddered and turned his face into the pillow. He'd never be able to go into that silent mausoleum and search through Horace's shroud—violate the dead—it was hideous. He'd have to get help— Myrtle. No, not Myrtle; she'd laugh at him and tell him not to be silly. He ought to go straight to Ross and explain the whole thing to him.

He got slowly out of bed. There was no use—he'd been over it in his mind so many times—he couldn't tell anybody, because nobody would believe him. He'd have to produce the will, and now he knew where it was.

He pulled on his trousers over his pajamas and put on a sweater, and then went to his neatly arranged sewing box and got a pair of scissors. He crept out of the room and then found that he'd forgotten slippers and had to go back. He found an old felt pair that would make no noise and started out again, hoping and praying that there would be no call for him while he was gone.

He went quietly past Ross's room, wondering if he and that poor girl were both sleeping in there. It was just such things that showed how unfitted Ross was to be running a hospital. No proper sense of dignity.

As he started down the stairs he was conscious of sweating hands and a pounding heart. He'd have to watch out for that Edith Dooley—she was always flitting about the place at night, instead of attending to her patients. He'd spoken to Ross about it, but Ross maintained that she had a sixth sense that told her when anyone needed attention.

As he neared the lower hallway he heard voices—low-pitched, but animated—and came to a stop. They belonged to Edith Dooley, on night duty on the second floor, and Catherine Edson, who was night nurse on the ground floor.

"Well, I'm telling you," Edith was saying, "there wasn't a nurse who'd stay with him more than twenty-four hours, and I know for a fact that Ethel had hysterics right there in his bedroom, before she quit."

"I heard he threw the bedpan at her because she hadn't warmed it," Catherine supplied interestedly.

"Sure he did. So then I took him on—and oh, brother, did I let him have it. I told him just where to head in, and I said if he didn't behave himself, so far from warming his bedpans, I'd put them in the ice chest for five minutes before I brought them. So what happened? He shut up and got better. And two years later, when he gets sick again, who does he yell and scream for to come and nurse him? Me."

"Well, sure," Catherine said doubtfully, "but Ethel says—"

"Hey, listen," Edith interrupted. "I gotta go and see if old Pop Cattledge is still breathing. Go and put some coffee on, if you get a chance."

John was furious. These girls were not paid to stand around chatting to each other! And talking in that loose way about former patients. He had told Myrtle a hundred times that she was not strict enough with them, and she had always flouted the traditional subservience of nurse to doctor and told him to mind his own business.

But he must get down past the second floor before Edith came out of Mr. Cattledge's room. He was glad old Dave was Ross's patient; looked as though Ross were due for a call any time—it was a wonder, really, that the old fellow had lived this long. Edith Dooley had no business leaving him to go and gossip.

He got safely through the hall and went on down the back stairs to the lower rear hall and from there into the dining room. It was very dark, and he had no flashlight—he'd have to get one. He groped his way to where the keys were hanging and easily picked out the one that opened the mausoleum. He'd looked at it, and even fingered it, often enough.

There was a flashlight in the drawer of the buffet, he remembered, and he found it after a little quiet fumbling.

Out on the lawn, he was suddenly engulfed in a wave of stark terror. He hurried along, stumbling occasionally, but not daring to stop, because he knew that if he did, he would be lost. He tried to tell himself that he had seen so many dead bodies, but the horror stayed with him.

By the time he reached the little white building he was hoping that the lock would be rusted and would refuse to work, and he sweated afresh when the door swung back easily. He crept in and swung the light of the flash onto the coffin that stood on a raised platform in the middle of the marble floor.

The lid was loose, and when he raised it, there was only the pale glow of the white satin lining. The box was empty.

## EIGHT

IRENE opened her eyes to bright, hot sunshine and closed them again quickly, with a frown. She felt dull and heavy and decidedly cross. She lay there, drowsing uncomfortably, until Ross's voice suddenly brought her sharply awake again.

"Myrtle," he said in a hoarse whisper, "for God's sake come out of there."

She turned her head and saw that he was standing in front of the closed bathroom door, decently belted into a dressing gown.

"She'll take forever," Irene observed. "I know she wears a girdle. That takes a while to pull on, especially in this weather, and then—"

"Spare me the details," Ross said coldly. "It's just like you to wake up at this point."

"If you expect anyone to sleep through the continuous all-night traffic in this room, you ought to hit them over the head with a hammer instead of feeding them little white pills. How many people have been bedding down in here with me, anyway?"

"Just Miss Warner, our head nurse," he said formally. "She was taking care of you."

Irene gave a croaking laugh. "I am batty, after all, then. I counted more than that."

"You were dreaming. The—er—the little white pills, you know. I merely came back to use my bathroom, because my things are in there."

Irene yawned, stretched, and laughed again. She was beginning to feel distinctly more human.

"I remember now. You were sleeping over there on the day bed, and then our Myrtle threw you out onto the balcony and took the day bed herself—because my mother had thrown her out of her bed. Where is my mother, by the way? Have you got her locked up too?"

Ross said, "Myrtle, what in *hell* are you doing in there?"

The bathroom door opened suddenly, and Myrtle appeared fresh and neat in a crisp white uniform and with a little white cap perched on her blonde hair.

"Good morning, Ross," she said cheerfully. "Did you sleep well?"

"Don't be an ass," said Ross, "and I hope you know you're fired—keeping the head doctor waiting in line for his own bathroom."

"O.K.," Myrtle called after him, "but how do you propose to keep my mouth shut?"

Ross went in and slammed the door after him, and Myrtle began to tidy up the room while she sang excerpts from *Madame Butterfly.*

"Don't make the bed until I get out of it," Irene suggested.

Myrtle took a high note before answering—she had a suspicion that her high notes were good. When it had died away, she said, "So you're with us again."

"I can see why you never made the Metropolitan," Irene said coldly.

Myrtle, mindful of the delicate position Ross was in and of that peculiar woman downstairs, forced a bright smile and inquired, "How did you sleep, my dear?"

"Even if I thought you really wanted to know, I wouldn't bother answering that one. Do you suppose your clever young doctor has drowned under that shower? I want to get dressed."

Myrtle sat down on the edge of the bed and said wistfully, "I *would* like to box your ears."

"Don't you be silly. Elise—my mother, you know—has enough on you right now. Uncle Clark certainly put a fast one over on your boyfriend."

Myrtle smiled and settled the cap more firmly on her golden tresses.

"Why, Ross is not my boyfriend, honey—I'm a couple of years older than he is. But I'm certainly flattered to have you think so, because he's a swell person."

"Bit dumb, isn't he?"

"No, my dear, he isn't. I know he's in a spot of trouble with your mother—unless you make it right with her—and actually it was all my fault, anyway. I told him to give you something to make you sleep and then for him to use the day bed. I couldn't see that it mattered—the poor boy works so hard, and he was so tired—and there just literally was no other spot for him to lay his head. We have a full census just now. Clark even had to take to a tent."

"My heart bleeds for Clark, of course, and in fact the whole story is very affecting. Listen, get me some breakfast, will you? I might be in a better mood after I've had some coffee—although I don't promise it."

Myrtle went eagerly for pencil and paper and said, "Anything you want, hon—just order."

Irene ordered, and Myrtle wrote it down carefully. "And you might send my mother up with that," Irene added as an afterthought.

Myrtle hesitated. "Well, look—will you promise not to tell her anything until after you've finished eating?"

"Fair enough," Irene agreed. "It's a promise."

Myrtle rustled out and made her way down the stairs. Perhaps the girl would be reasonable, after all—be a sport about it. But how could you expect her to be reasonable when she was mental? Queer that she showed no sign of it. Perhaps she was all right.

Myrtle shrugged it away and went on to another worry. She hadn't given that popeyed Beatrice any explanation yet, and God knows what sort of lurid stories she was spreading around. Jean would be on now, of course—she'd better give Jean some sort of a story and let her pass it on to Beatrice and the rest.

She approached the switchboard with a sunny smile and said, "Good morning, Jeanie," and draped herself against the desk in a confidential attitude. "Some girls really are the limit, aren't they?"

Jean raised an inquiring eyebrow over a frankly eager eye.

Myrtle, with no previous inspiration, gave a little laugh and made it up as she went along. "Money. Honestly, what some girls won't do! Don't want to go out and work decently like you and I—just spend their time trying to grab a fella with money so they can sit back with their feet up and chew candy all day."

Jean murmured, "Yeah—sure," looking virtuous, and waited.

Myrtle lowered her voice about two tones and yet made it louder.

"Did you see that girl who came in yesterday to look over the hospital? Well, she insisted on seeing Dr. Ross's quarters as well—we thought it was queer at the time—and then she left, and, my dear, somehow she got in again and went up to his room and *stayed* there. Later on she phoned down to Beatrice and asked for dinner and said she was the doctor's girlfriend. Tried to get herself compromised, you see, and thought he'd have to marry her to save her reputation. All because the poor man owns this place and she thinks he must have money."

While Myrtle paused to take breath, Jean quickly gave the switchboard some necessary attention and then turned back with an eager glint in her eye. "So what happened?"

"Well, I took a tray up, and there was the girl, and poor Dr. Ross standing around wondering what to do. It made me mad, and I went straight and phoned the girl's mother. She came right out, but it was so late when she got here, and she was so upset, poor thing, that I had to put her to bed in my room. I went up to Dr. Ross's room and kept an eye on the girl, and he tried to get some sleep out on that little balcony. He wanted to be near so that he could protect me in case the girl got nasty."

Someone said, "Good morning, Nurse," and Myrtle swung around to look straight into Elise's eyes.

She said, "Oh—good morning, Mrs. De Petro," rather breathlessly, and added, "I've been waiting for you. Will you come in to breakfast?"

Elise said she would and, when they had left Jean behind, observed mildly, "I heard every word of that absurd story. You won't be wounded if I tell you that I regard it as a very poor effort on your part?"

Myrtle stammered, "Don't misunderstand—"

"But I do misunderstand—in fact, this place has me thoroughly puzzled. You tell my daughter that she is an escaped lunatic and lock her up—and then you tell the girl at the switchboard a quite different, and highly libelous, story. Now, explain yourself promptly, please—I'll give you that chance before I get the police in."

They had reached the dining room, and as they entered, John arose from his chair and waited to be introduced. Myrtle muttered feebly, "Oh, John—er—"

"I am Mrs. De Petro," Elise told him. "Who are you?"

John explained himself with all due dignity, and he had just finished when Ross walked in, so he introduced him as well.

Elise eyed the new arrival without favor and said simply, "So you're the conceited young ass whom this woman says my daughter is trying to ensnare."

Ross gave her a black look and, without trying to untangle it, seated himself at the table and reached for his orange juice.

John courteously seated Elise, Myrtle shifted for herself, and when they had all settled themselves a neatly aproned young woman came in from the kitchen with a tray of food.

Myrtle waited until she had retired and then said wearily, "Ross, I think I'll go on vacation as of today. I give up."

Elise clicked her tongue. "Never give up and run away from things, my good woman—it doesn't solve anything. Now—"

She was interrupted by the jangle of a telephone in the corner of the room, and Ross got up abruptly and went to answer it. He barked into it briefly for a minute or two and then hung up and returned to the table.

"Fat's in the fire now," he said to no one in particular. "That girl upstairs is not the escaped patient."

## NINE

MYRTLE and Ross resumed their breakfast with a false air of unconcern, but John dropped his fork onto his plate and cried agitatedly, "Good God! What a terrible thing! What are we to do? The hospital will be ruined—ruined. After all the work your father and I put into it."

"Oh, John, don't get so excited," Myrtle said. "It isn't as bad as that." She mopped daintily at her mouth with her napkin and stole a look at Elise, who had rather an air of a sleek cat regarding a saucer of cream.

"I'd like to catch up with Clark," Ross said longingly. "Just long enough to make him see the error of his ways."

"Was that Clark on the phone?" John asked.

"Telegram from him. Said he and the Miller girl were well away, and I'd better release the other one if I wanted to stay out of trouble."

"Only you are in trouble," Elise pointed out. She took a thoughtful sip of coffee and went on. "It is possible, of course, that we can come to some arrangement, satisfactory to all of us, whereby the thing may be kept quiet."

"Elise," Irene said from the doorway. They all turned around, and she walked in, with a glance for Ross. "Lunatic at large. You forgot to lock the door when you went out."

Elise held out a jeweled hand and cried, "My poor baby! What a dreadful thing to have happened to you."

Irene said, "Stow it," and Elise returned serenely to her breakfast, while John hastened to pull out another chair.

Myrtle and Ross, busy with the bacon and eggs, had thrown in the towel altogether and were ignoring everybody, including each other. John was left to cope with the situation, and he rose to it gamely. He saw, first, that Irene was supplied with breakfast, and then he started earnestly. "My dear Miss—er—Hastings? Yes. We are all very sorry to discover that there has been a grievous mistake."

Irene laughed. "Grievous? I suppose you could call it that. Although I can think of another adjective or two."

"We owe you an apology, of course," John went on hastily, "and we do most sincerely hope that you will do nothing to harm the reputation of the hospital."

"Your concern for the hospital's reputation is of very little interest to me," Elise said, "since I suspect that my daughter's has been spotted, to say the least."

Ross sent a meaning stare at Myrtle, who dropped the cutlery she had been plying so busily and made the gesture of throwing up her hands. She gave a quick look around the table and then told all. "It was the only story I could think of," she finished, "since you wanted it kept quiet that she was insane."

John had suffered to the limit of his endurance, and he got up and, with a muttered excuse, left the room.

Elise, to whom battle was the joy and spice of life, looked after him in some surprise. "What's the matter with *him?*"

"He's running," said Myrtle. "He knows the jig's up."

Ross turned to Irene. "I'm sorry, of course. Apologies, and all that. Whatever I can do—"

"I believe we can settle out of court," Elise broke in happily. "You don't want any publicity, naturally—so I think a reasonable—er—"

"Elise," said Irene, "you're speaking out of character. You're wearing the refined-mother outfit."

Elise glanced down at herself. "I know I am—the occasion seemed to call for it. What's the difference, anyway?"

"It doesn't go with blackmail at all."

"Blackmail! Irene, you're exactly like your father—what's his name?—Hastings. Just exactly like him—no head for business. Now, you hold your tongue and allow me to handle this."

"I'll handle it myself," said Irene. "It's my show."

"Then I'll have no more to say," Elise declared, and went on to talk steadily for the next fifteen minutes.

Myrtle and Ross had finished eating and were smoking cigarettes. They sat in complete silence until Elise, stopping to light a cigarette for herself, asked irritably, "Why do you two sit there like a couple of dummies? Can't you join in an intelligent conversation?"

"Just waiting to be sentenced," Myrtle said equably.

Irene looked up. "I was on my way to the hotel at Tilton for a week's vacation. It's pretty crowded, and I've no doubt that my reservation is gone, since I did not turn up to claim it. However, I find that room upstairs very comfortable, and I should like to stay there for the week. That's all."

Ross gave a hollow groan.

"And don't start up all over again about having nowhere to sleep. There's always the tent, since Uncle Clark apparently won't be using it this week."

Myrtle laughed, and Ross stared despairingly at the tip of his cigarette.

"That's fair, isn't it?" Irene prodded him. "All I ask is that no more of my vacation will be lost. If it imposes a hardship on you, remember that it was your mistake."

Ross nodded grimly, but he didn't answer.

Elise, busily hunting through her huge navy-blue purse for something, said abstractedly, "My dear, I think you're perfectly mad—but then you always have been. That man Hastings was an error on my part. However, if you're bound to stay in this odd place, I think I'll stay too."

"No," said Irene hastily, "you go on home—you won't like it here."

Elise closed her purse with a snap. "I shall stay."

"Don't be so silly," Irene said reasonably. "There's nothing for you to do here—you go on home."

"She's quite right, Mrs. De Petro," Myrtle joined in earnestly. "You'd only be bored."

Elise got up. "I'm staying—that's flat." She made her way out of the room and called over her shoulder, just before she disappeared, "I find Dr. John a most interesting person."

"My God!" Myrtle exclaimed. "She already has my room, and now she's out gunning after my man."

"She won't do any man hunting while she's in that outfit," Irene explained. "But you'd better look out if she brought some of her other clothes with her—and some of her other hair."

"You mean that refined-suburban-motherhood look is merely a pose?"

Irene took out a cigarette and shook her head. "Not exactly. It's just that Elise gets bored with being one person—so she changes when it happens to suit her—clothes, hair, personality, and everything."

Ross said, "Look—will you two stop jabbering? I've work to do this morning, and we'll have to get this thing settled."

Myrtle, looking off into space, murmured, "Isn't that cute? Changing yourself into another person whenever you feel like it?"

"I'd know her anywhere," Irene said, "but almost everyone else can be completely fooled."

Ross raised his voice until it thundered through the room. "Will you women kindly shut up and listen to me?"

They turned with one accord and gazed at him out of innocent, limpid eyes.

Ross cleared his throat. "Is your name Miss Hastings? Yes. Well, look—is there anything I can do for you, other than put you up here for a week? We're very short of space, and we work hard and need our sleep."

"No," said Irene flatly. "I like it here—I like my room, and I like the company. Hospitals have always been interesting to me, but I'm so healthy that I've never had a chance to go and live in one. This is a God-given opportunity, and I don't intend to throw it away. I'll pay for my board—and you can pack up and move over to the tent this afternoon."

Ross pushed his chair back and stood up. "All right, then, stay if you want to—but I'll be eternally damned if I'll move out to the tent. We'll just share the room—it's big enough."

He took himself off, and Irene turned back to Myrtle. "Bluff, isn't it? He knows he can't do that."

"Well—I wouldn't be too sure. But it will be perfectly all right, because you'll have me in there too—unless you can get your mother to go home."

Irene shrugged. "You can work on Elise if you want to—I'm on vacation." She stood up and stretched her arms above her head. "It's wonderful to have nothing to do. May I go on your rounds with you?"

"What rounds?"

"Well—you're head nurse, aren't you? Don't you go around and see that the other nurses are doing their duty—and say good morning to the patients?"

Myrtle stood up and hitched her girdle down firmly on each side. "Listen, girl—like all hospitals, we're short-handed. I haven't any time to go around snooping. I have good solid work to do, and if you come with me, you'll probably find yourself working too."

"All right," Irene agreed. "I don't mind."

"You mean that?"

"Certainly."

"In that case," said Myrtle, "you may come with me provided you promise not to lock the door of that room upstairs when you go to bed—because if we fail to boot your mother out, I have to sleep somewhere."

Irene nodded. "That's all right. It will look better, anyway, since the doctor is sleeping in there too."

"O.K.—come on. Only, who am I going to introduce you as?"

"Surely you haven't forgotten? Irene Hastings, who is madly in love with the doctor and his money."

"Good enough," said Myrtle, and walked out of the room, settling her cap.

Out in the hall she nearly tripped over Ross, who was lying full length on the floor.

## TEN

MYRTLE righted herself, looked down, and exclaimed, "Merciful heavens!"

"What is it?" Irene asked, peering around her.

Myrtle knelt down on the floor and said, "Go and get Dr. John—quick. Out in the front hall—ask the girl at the switchboard."

Irene hurried away, and Myrtle heaved a little sigh of relief as Ross began to stir. There was an abrasion on the side of his head, but it appeared to be unimportant.

"But what could have happened to him?" she murmured, and glanced around the small square hall. There were three doors—one to the dining room, one leading to the front hall, and one opening onto a landing with another door beyond, that led outside—an old carriage entrance.

Her eyes traveled upward, and presently she nodded her head, with a tightening of her lips. There was a wrought-iron hook jutting out from the wall near the dining-room door. There had been a pot of ivy hanging on it, which had been removed—and if Myrtle had said once she had said a thousand times that the hook should be removed, too, because it was dangerous.

She looked down at Ross and saw that he was regarding her with the light of reason once more in his eye.

"What are you doing there?" he asked.

"Just waiting to say, 'I told you so,' " Myrtle replied truthfully.

He struggled up to a sitting position and frowned at her. "What the devil is going on here?"

"Don't you know what hit you?"

"Hit me? No. What are you talking about?"

"You've banged the side of your head, there, and you were out cold for a few minutes. No kidding."

"Are you trying to say that someone struck me?" he asked fiercely. "Here, help me up."

Myrtle helped him to his feet and indicated the iron hook. "Not somebody—something. Have I or have I not said, at least a thousand times, that that thing should be taken out? Now, perhaps, you'll agree with me."

Irene came back, looking concerned, and Myrtle said briskly, "Here, take his other arm—we'll help him into Dr. John's office."

Irene took the arm gingerly, and they walked slowly through to the front hall.

"Let's go into my office," Ross suggested. "It's closer, and I'm getting tired of holding you two up."

Myrtle said, "Nonsense," and at the same time Jean called from the switchboard, "Oh, Dr. Munster, I hope you're not badly hurt—Dr. Girsted is with Mr. Cattledge. He's very low, and Dr. Girsted said to tell you he'd attend to him until you are able to."

Ross nodded to the girl and then muttered, "The patient is always first with John. I might have been struggling with my last breath, for all he knew."

"Yes," said Myrtle, "and if it were your last breath, you'd use it to complain with. Don't be ridiculous—John knew we'd get another doctor for you if we had to—or something. Anyway, we can't let old Dave die without a doctor to stand helplessly by."

The three of them tried to get in the door of Ross's office at the same time, and he was obliged to back up and push the other two in ahead of him. He sat down at his desk at last, a little heavily, and said with some bitterness, "You could have got that doctor on Mapes Avenue—the veterinary."

Myrtle, busily putting a neat little patch on the abrasion, laughed and said easily, "It's quite interesting to me to see how jealous you and John are of that man. I guess he's pretty good, at that. I believe there are several families around here who always call him for the kids—as well as for the cows and horses."

"Say, Myrtle," Irene said suddenly, "are you sure that's blood on him, and not tomato sauce? Maybe it's a stall, so that I'll take pity on him and give him his room back."

Myrtle hooted with laughter and pulled back the edge of the bandage. "Come and see for yourself."

"Myrtle!" Ross roared. "Put that damned thing back on my head—do you think I'm a sideshow at a circus?" He turned to Irene. "What's the matter with you? Why should I be afraid to sleep in the same room with you? Do you take me for a complete stupe?"

"Calm yourself," said Myrtle. "I'll be in there with you, by the way."

"Oh no, you won't," Ross said nastily. "You'll find some other place to sleep. That room is reserved for the girl and myself. Matter of fact, I'm looking forward to it—be company for me."

"You are not scaring me in the slightest," Irene said, avoiding his eye.

The telephone rang, and Ross began to bark into it as usual, until he discovered that it was the rich relative of one of his rich patients, when his tone changed automatically.

Irene and Myrtle left him—Myrtle to plunge into the morning's work, and Irene to follow her around, marveling at how much there was to do. She found that she was working, too, after a while—obeying brief orders hurled at her by Myrtle and trying not to trip over her feet as she obeyed. One old lady complained that someone had put salt in her orange juice, again, and Myrtle glanced at Irene and snapped out a request for a fresh glass of orange juice. Irene took the glass and wandered out but was unable to find orange juice or even oranges. She went back for further enlightenment, but before she could open her mouth, Myrtle said quickly, "There you are, Mrs. Forbes—a nice fresh glassful, with no salt."

Mrs. Forbes drank it down and declared it was the first decent orange juice she'd had for a week, while Irene stood looking at her with open mouth.

Out in the hall again, Myrtle took a long breath and murmured, "I think I'll just take a look at old Dave."

"All right, lead the way."

"You'll have to wait outside—you can't go in there."

"Whatever you say," Irene agreed.

They turned a corner and came to old Dave's door, and Myrtle stopped abruptly. Dr. John was standing there, talking to a woman who stood out like a flame in the drab hallway. Her amber-colored hair lay against her head in smooth and fashionable perfection—her skin had a delicate tan, and her scarlet mouth was wide and attractive. She wore a flawless beige suit, with a large jeweled pin on the lapel. It was an intricate arrangement of diamonds and rubies, and the thing flashed expensively at every movement of the shoulder beneath it.

Myrtle caught her breath, and Irene dug her sharply in the ribs. "It's my mother," she said out of the corner of her mouth.

Elise seemed to be doing all the talking. "So I thought, of course, that if you would allow me to come around with you, I could get the atmosphere of the place—the local color, you see—and then when I write my book, I shall know what I'm talking about."

John, looking completely helpless, swallowed convulsively and then caught sight of Myrtle. Relief flooded into his face, and he said, "Ah, there you are, Miss Warner. Mrs. De Petro would like to be taken around the place—I'm sure you'd be only too glad—I—er—like to do it myself, only—so busy—short-handed—"

"Sure," Myrtle said cheerfully, "I'll take her around. We nurses have nothing to do but clean up a few slops. How's Dave?"

"He seems to have rallied slightly—there'll be nothing for a while. What about Ross?"

Myrtle nodded. "Oh, Ross is all right—false alarm. Come on,

ladies—our first stop is the kitchen."

Elise held back and said, "Just a moment," but Myrtle took her firmly by the arm and walked her off.

John mopped his forehead and then, glancing at his handkerchief, decided he needed a fresh one and climbed the stairs to his room. It was so peaceful up there that he closed the door behind him and wandered over to the window. He could see the little mausoleum, gleaming whitely in the sunlight, and he gazed at it somberly.

Ross had removed that body, he thought—Ross must know about the will, and of course he was desperately anxious to keep it from being found.

He turned away from the window abruptly and began to pace up and down.

Only, why would Ross remove the body? He'd have to hide it or bury it. He needed only to find the will and destroy it—the thing didn't make sense. And if Ross had not taken the body away, then what in God's name was the explanation?

He suddenly sank onto the edge of the bed, his hands twisted together and drops of moisture starting out on his forehead. He knew now—it all fitted in. Horace having a tomb built for himself and directing that his coffin was not to be nailed down.

Horace was still alive.

## ELEVEN

JOHN felt himself seized by a sudden vertigo and clutched at his head until the spasm had passed. He sipped some water from the glass on his bedside table, mopped shakily at his lips, and then went unsteadily to the window and stared out at the tomb.

He had been away when Horace had died—suddenly, of a heart attack, they had said. Ross and Clark were still in the army at the time, and the death had been certified by Horace's old friend Rod Smith—the only other doctor in the vicinity. Outside of that preposterous horse doctor, of course—and what had Myrtle meant by saying that the local inhabitants were receiving treatment from the man?

But about Horace—and Rod Smith. Rod must have been a party to the thing—but Rod had died two weeks ago and taken his life's secrets with him—and Horace had been gone for almost two months. The tomb had been finished about two weeks before Horace's supposed demise, and Horace had told Myrtle that the lid of his coffin was not to be sealed—said that he couldn't trust any doctor but himself, and if some fool had him put away before he was actually gone, he wanted to be able to come back from the tomb without too much trouble.

John's lip curled and he drew a quick, angry breath. That was so like Horace. He had never allowed John to make any important decisions or take any important or interesting cases. No. There was only one god—Allah—and there was only one doctor—Horace. John had always believed in a fitting reverence for the dead, but he felt the old hate burgeoning in him now that he was convinced that Horace was still alive.

It was just one of his usual rotten tricks—pretending to be dead and then living out in that tomb and spying on them all—just the sort of thing he delighted in doing. Probably he would come in, some night, and play ghost, and he'd expect John to scream.

John clenched his fists and was conscious of moisture on his forehead. Well, he wouldn't scream—he'd just look through the old devil and pretend he wasn't there.

The telephone cut sharply into his thoughts, and he started and reached for it. It was a summons—and John could somehow feel the raised eyebrows at the other end of the wire—to one of his patients. He agreed, with nervous haste, to come at once, and felt a spasm of annoyance at himself. He should never have allowed Horace to keep him from his duty—it was inexcusable. And Ross was ailing in some way—he should have seen to him.

Halfway down the stairs, John stopped suddenly, aghast. Ross was operating! But he shouldn't be, if he were not up to par—he should have handed over to John. He went flying off to the operating room and met Ross coming out of the door.

"Ross! You surely did not operate? In your condition!"

"What do you mean, 'my condition'?" Ross asked, cheerful at having got away from the recent muddle into a simple appendectomy that left him with a feeling of admiration for his own smooth work.

"You should have left it to me. You were ill—Myrtle said so. It is not fair to the patient—"

Ross shrugged. "I cooked my head, but I can assure you that I didn't damage the contents—such as they are." He hastily tried a change of subject. "John, who goes out to that old summerhouse? I saw a light there last night."

All concern for the recent appendectomy—now supine on a stretcher and being jockeyed into the elevator by a nurse and the orderly—drained out of John's face and left it white and strained.

Ross had been trying to ease himself away, but he stopped and looked at John in some surprise.

"It wasn't you, surely?" he asked curiously, and added, trying not to smile, "Perhaps you and Myrtle were out there."

John's white face was suddenly flooded with color, and he said stiffly, "Certainly not."

Ross killed the smile—with difficulty—and wondered whether John really supposed that the fact that he and Myrtle had been living together for years was a secret.

John turned away abruptly, his mind already back with Horace. He must be getting bold, he thought, to sit out in the summerhouse with the light on. He swallowed twice and made a resolution to go out and confront him that night.

Myrtle and her two aides had finished their work in the diet kitchen and had gone down to the main kitchen on the first floor. The cook resigned immediately when informed that there would still be two extra for lunch, but Myrtle handled it as she had been handling such situations for years.

"Do as you like, Rowena, of course, but if you're leaving, don't dawdle over it, because this lady is writing a movie around our hospital, and the young lady is to take the leading part—and naturally they want to get the characters settled. It's quite a thrill to have a movie star staying with us, isn't it?"

Elise and Irene raised four eyebrows, and Rowena gave Myrtle a look of dark suspicion, because she was familiar with her tricks. But Irene was arrayed in one of her new vacation outfits, and Elise exactly fitted Rowena's conception of a woman of letters, so that after a certain hesitation she agreed to stay on as a favor to the ladies.

The ladies and Myrtle departed rather hastily, and when they had left Rowena far enough behind, Irene mildly inquired of Myrtle if she were completely cracked.

"Look at all the stories you've told about me. You're going to trip over your feet and come a crasher, if you don't stop it."

"It's all right," Myrtle said composedly. "It seems a pretty good angle to me. Those other stories were all so weak that the idea of your being a movie star, and not wanting it known, will explain them very nicely. I can keep all the help for another week—or as long as you're here—and even if Ross sleeps in with you, they'll consider it only natural. They're just simple,country folk."

They had reached the dining room, and as Elise thundered, "What do you mean, 'if Ross sleeps in with her'?" Myrtle crossed the room and disappeared out onto the terrace without answering.

"Keep your shirt on," Irene said absently. "She's only joking.

Listen, is your car outside? I'll bet Clark left mine parked at the station. I don't know where that telegram was handed in, but I imagine they'd go by train to wherever they were going—the car could be identified and picked up much too easily."

Elise was looking out through the french doors to where Myrtle stood on the terrace smoking a cigarette.

"That woman is really the most facile liar I have ever met. It's beyond all decency."

Irene caught her by the arm and hustled her out into the hall. "Come on and drive me to the station—I want to see if my car is there."

Jean, at the switchboard, stared at them steadily as they went through the front hall, and on the steps of the veranda they ran into three of Dave Cattledge's relatives, who bowed distantly. Elise looked them over with lively interest and suggested that it was a nice day, but they merely gave her a look of staid and somber rebuke. Dave had money to leave them, but after all, he wasn't dead yet.

"Listen," Elise said to Irene crossly, "it's hot, and it's almost lunch time. Can't this excursion wait?"

"Come on," Irene said grimly. "It's the only car I have. It's probably sitting around somewhere with the key in it, waiting to be stolen."

They went first to the railroad station and saw the car at once, neatly parked against the curb. Irene found the keys in the glove case, with a penciled note wrapped around them.

DEAR IRENE,

*Thanks for toeing such a sport. Doris and I will try to make it up to you someday.*

*Gratefully,*

CLARK

*P.S. Tell Ross I distinctly saw the headless nurse last night.*

## TWELVE

ROSS went into his office, closed the door behind him, and sat down at his desk, mopping at his forehead. He was late again—somehow he never could seem to catch up—and he hadn't phoned the damned hospital yet, to tell them not to send the wagon. Well, no use getting in a stew—he might as well put Clark out of his mind. That telegram had come from Chicago—and how had Clark got himself to Chicago? He had no money. The girl must have supplied the funds. Clark was an unmitigated ass, he thought savagely. The girl would probably cut his throat and get all their names in the paper. Even if she refrained—and you couldn't blame even a sane person for playing with the idea—they were bound to be caught in the end.

He picked up the phone and called the state hospital. They were politely annoyed, but he kept his temper and offered the suggestion that they throw out the dragnet in Chicago, because of the telegram. He tried to hang up at that point, but they had more to say, and said it. He was to hold onto the girl until they could get over and have a look at her. He might be making another mistake—and there was an implied suggestion, here, that he had showed himself fully capable of making mistakes—and they would send someone out during the afternoon or evening to check up.

Ross banged the instrument into its cradle and glared at it, and at the same time Myrtle burst into the room. She stopped short and stared at him. He had carefully kept his temper throughout the phone call, so that it was almost a pleasure to lose it freely now.

He stood up and shouted furiously, "Myrtle, I will not have you clumping in here without knocking—I've told you time and time again—and I mean it. This is my private office, and you *are to knock before you enter!*"

"Well! What brought this on?" Myrtle asked, round-eyed. "Anybody would think I'd caught you plucking your eyebrows or something."

"You'd better put that infernal girl on a leash," he said morosely. "They want to have a look at her."

Myrtle brushed it aside impatiently. "Listen, what I came down for—you'd better come and have a look at old Dave. I think he's good for a few more hours, but his relatives are in the hall outside his door waiting around for the end, and they're in the way."

He followed her without enthusiasm and went upstairs. He took a cursory look at Dave Cattledge—who opened one bloodshot eye and appeared to glare at him with it— and then went out and informed the three waiting relatives that there was no change and no immediate danger. The relatives nodded gravely, gave three unconscious sighs at Dave's stubborn persistence, and departed.

Myrtle settled her cap and observed that though lunch was no doubt cold by this time, it might be a good idea to go down and eat it anyway.

Elise and Irene were at the table, about halfway through lunch, but John had already gone, leaving a neatly folded napkin and no crumbs.

Elise greeted them with enthusiasm. "I'm so glad you've come—

Irene has something to show you. Really dreadful! I can't think what he means by it, and I'm simply petrified! Darling, give the doctor the note."

Irene explained about her car and handed over Clark's communication.

Elise shuddered delicately. "Perhaps we should go, after all. A hospital is such a busy place, and we are only in the way."

"Not me," Irene said firmly. "If there's a headless nurse around, I want to see her."

Myrtle stopped her fork midway between her plate and her mouth and swallowed air. Ross glanced over the notes handed it across to her without comment, and started in on his meal.

Myrtle read the note twice and then whispered hollowly, "My God!"

Ross squeezed lemon into a glass of iced tea and said, "Don't be so impressionable. You know Clark drinks like a fish."

"Well—yes—but if it's D.T.s, why a headless nurse? Why not pink elephants or purple rats?"

"Use your head. It's been my experience that people with D.T.s can think up much more lurid things to see than elephants and rats of any color—and since the story of a headless nurse around here was all ready and waiting, it would be the first thing that Clark would see."

Myrtle shook her head. "Clark can sponge it up—but I don't think he's ready for D.T.s yet."

"He must be, if he's seeing headless nurses."

But Myrtle shook her head again and appeared to be unconvinced, and Irene asked curiously, "*Is* there a story of a headless nurse?"

"It was a delirious patient," Ross explained. "Yelled his head off, before he died, about a headless nurse in his room and kept howling for someone to come and get her out."

"Oh!" Elise exclaimed with a gasp. "Mong dew!"

"Some of the other patients heard him," Ross went on, "and it caused a bit of trouble, but Father and John worked hard on the thing until it was forgotten."

"Mong dew!" said Elise.

"Now, if anyone is raving, he raves with the door closed and felt stuffed in the cracks."

Myrtle sighed. "I really didn't think Clark was that bad. We ought to do something about him."

"I wish he were that bad," Ross said bitterly. "I'd like to have him tied into bed where I could keep an eye on him. He probably saw one of the night nurses outside for a breath of air. He'd see the white uniform, and if her head were in shadow and Clark full of whiskey, that's all he'd need. He probably flew back into his tent and pulled the covers over his head."

Elise did another delicate shudder. "I would have done the same," she declared. "Mong dew!"

Myrtle turned on her with slitted eyes and asked belligerently, "Are you swearing?"

"Elise has been to Paris several times," Irene explained. "If a French expression creeps in now and then, it's no more than natural. If she insults you, I'll let you know."

"She doesn't have to speak French to do that," Myrtle said coldly. "I happen to know she can do it in English."

Elise turned to Ross. "I suppose you make a good thing out of this place?"

Ross gave her a blank look, and Irene frowned and said quickly, "Don't be silly. Hospitals are always in debt up to their ears."

"Not this one," Ross countered sharply. "We've done well for a good many years. We don't overcharge the patients, either. It's a matter of hard work, and no graft or waste."

Elise beamed. "Well, I think that's just lovely. We must remember to come here, dear, the next time we get sick. Perhaps you'd better get the doctor to look at your appendix—I have an idea it needs some attention."

Myrtle giggled. "Take a look at the girl's appendix, Ross."

"It will cost anybody a quarter to look at my appendix," Irene said to no one in particular.

Dr. John walked into the room and made his way through and out onto the terrace without appearing to notice any of them. His eyes had an inward look, and his lips moved soundlessly.

Ross sent a worried frown after him and then got up and followed him out.

"What is it, John?" he asked directly. "Something on your mind?"

John passed a vague hand across his forehead and muttered, "Oh, Ross. I think they want you up on the second floor."

"I'm going in a minute. But you look seedy—why don't you lie down and rest for a while?"

"Don't be absurd," John said in sudden anger. "I am perfectly well. Why on earth should you think I need rest?"

Ross shrugged. You never could foresee the old buster's reactions, he thought resignedly, and changed the subject.

"Clark left a note for that girl and told her to tell me he'd seen the headless nurse."

John half turned and staggered, and then his eyes rolled upward and he went down onto the flagstones of the terrace.

## THIRTEEN

JOHN had been put to bed with a quieting dose and strict orders from Ross that he was to stay there. In a way it was a relief to have been declared really ill—to have had all responsibility removed from him—but he could not rest. His mind fought implacably with the drug that Ross had given him, and a savage headache pounded at his temples.

Horace must be trying to ruin the hospital, he thought feverishly—skulking around at night pretending to be the headless nurse. And why? The hospital had been his whole life—he had been so proud of it. And he had been so proud of his son, too—why should he want to ruin Ross? John turned his head restlessly on the pillow. There was one explanation, of course—Horace was insane. He must be insane, boldly putting that light on in the summerhouse for anyone to see. The chilling horror that accompanied this thought was a bit blurred, and he knew that the drug was beginning to work on him. He tried to make his mind a blank, and after a while he slid into an uneasy darkness in which his chattering teeth and the pain in his head swelled into a monstrous nightmare orchestra.

Myrtle was busier even than usual, because she had some of John's work to get through. Ross had told her what she could safely do, and she had sailed in with the utmost confidence—although she knew that poor John would have been horrified if he could have seen her. As a matter of fact, she was quicker and more efficient than John had ever been, and she went down to dinner, at the end of the afternoon, wondering, as she had wondered a thousand times, why she had not trained to be a doctor. And as for poor John—he was far better fitted to be a nurse than a doctor. It was all wrong, Myrtle thought wryly, and tried to take some of her dissatisfaction out on Ross.

"The poor, dithering nurse," she told him warmly, "stands around and takes orders and does all the work, and if the patient recovers, the doctor gets all the credit."

"If you're trying to tell me I don't work as hard as you do," Ross said, outraged, "you ought to have your head examined. I'm dead on my feet—I'm exhausted—I should have had a vacation weeks ago."

"And a nurse is supposed to stand up when a doctor brings his lordly body in, mind you," Myrtle went on, gathering momentum. "Stand up, I'll thank you—with her feet throbbing like an engine because she's been on them for forty-eight hours or so."

"Well, don't bother me about it—I didn't make the blasted rules. Send a letter to the A.M.A."

"Imagine a woman of my—er—a woman like me, springing to my aching feet because a pompous jackass of a doctor walks into the room. And then I have to listen without argument while he tells how to give the patient the wrong treatment—and when the patient dies as a matter of course, like as not I get a bawling out from the doctor—still standing on my raw and bleeding feet—because *I* killed the patient with bad nursing."

"Myrtle!" Ross yelled. "Will you kindly shut up and talk about something else? Where are these two confounded women?"

Myrtle took a long breath, settled her cap, and said that she did not know and was not at all sure that she cared. "But I'll tell you this much, Ross Munster. If you're thinking of making eyes at the young one, you'd better be careful. She looks innocent enough, I'll admit—but I could smell that De Petro woman a mile off."

"Expensive perfume, but too much of it," Ross agreed.

"All right—you can joke about it—but you'll notice she asked you to your face if you're making any money. The woman's an adventuress. I suppose she'll try to get you to marry the girl—probably she wants to get the girl off her hands."

Ross yawned and rubbed a fist across his forehead. "What's the matter with you tonight? You're blowing off like a steam valve. The girl seems to have her own car and her own job—and I don't believe she even lives with her mother, so how can she be on her hands?"

"Very well—you'll see. I know the matchmaker type when I see it, and mark my words, she'll have you in a cutaway coat with a white flower in your buttonhole before you know it."

"Are we late?" Elise asked gaily, from the door.

She was arrayed in a white chiffon dress with long, full skirts that swept the floor around her and long, full sleeves caught in tightly at the wrists. The high neck was caught at one side by a large, curiously wrought pin of diamonds and opals, and matching bracelets banded the wrists. Irene followed, wearing a black dinner dress, unadorned, and a sulky expression because she had been bullied into the dress and the matching slippers, which pinched.

Myrtle and Ross, assailed by an elusive and haunting perfume, felt like a pair of day laborers. Ross seated them all and, urged on by an antagonism he did not analyze, remarked that Elise and Irene were a bit late and it must not happen again, since the Service was difficult and must not be irritated.

Irene said, "I think you're wrong about that. We're supposed to be celebrities, and we're trying to act the part by coming late and overdressed for dinner. All for Myrtle's sake."

A member of the Service entered, just then, and offered food to the guests with restrained enthusiasm, while Ross looked on with a puzzled frown. Myrtle tried to talk of other things, but since the weather was all she could think of, Ross brushed it aside and insisted upon an explanation until he got it.

He was shocked to the point of laying down his knife and fork and giving Myrtle his full and baleful attention.

"You've got to stop telling these silly lies all over the place—do you hear? You'll get yourself and everybody else into trouble."

Myrtle sniffed. "I've been juggling lies for twenty years and never yet had the whole thing crash down on my head. And anyway, this wasn't for myself—it was for you and this sweatshop of a hospital."

Elise, who had been adjusting the opal and diamond pin, gave it a final loving pat and cleared her throat.

"My dears, don't quarrel about it. As far as that goes, I have decided to be a writer, so that part is all right—and I'm quite sure Irene could be a movie star if she really put her mind to it. Of course she might get married—" Elise threw an arch glance around the table, discovered that no one was listening to her, and so shrugged and tackled her own meal—after carefully pushing the potato to one side.

Ross had fallen to wondering, again, where he was going to sleep. He was tired, and the wound on his head was painful—and there was no use considering Clark's tent, because he'd have to be on call all night for John's patients as well as his own. He supposed he'd have to camp out on the balcony again, which was a fairly gloomy prospect.

He glanced at Irene and found her eyes on his face. She allowed them to stay there for a moment, and he found himself wishing that he could simply sleep in his own double bed—with her—and boot Myrtle out entirely. All very nice, no doubt, except that Myrtle and the girl would both object. Myrtle's objection would be valid, since she had nowhere else to lay her head—but as for the rest of it, he was inclined to think that civilization had people tied up in a lot of silly red tape and they'd be better off without it.

"—but then I don't suppose locked doors would be of any help whatever," Myrtle was saying, and Ross realized at once that there was design and purpose behind her apparently idle words. "I don't mind admitting that I'm scared stiff. I mean, imagine waking up in the blackness of the night to find the thing beside your bed, staring down at you.

"Whatever do you mean?" Elise asked, her bracelets sparkling as her hands fluttered nervously. "How could a—a nurse without a head stare at anyone?"

"Well, no—not actually," Myrtle admitted. "But if it were just standing there, you know, with its uniform gleaming in the moonlight—"

Elise gave a little scream. "Irene—*darling*—are you sleeping in a double bed?"

"Why don't you go home, if you're scared?" Irene suggested warily.

"No, no—I wouldn't miss it for anything. But I *cannot* sleep alone—I should never close an eye all night."

"She has a lovely, wide, soft double bed," Myrtle said softly. "You could move right in with her tonight. I'll be glad to help you with your things."

Elise gave her a thoughtful stare but said at last, "Thank you. Then I'll do that."

Irene moaned quietly into her coffee, and Ross grinned at the ceiling. In that case, he thought, I'll sleep on the day bed. I'll put a screen around it. They can yell their heads off, but that's where I'll sleep.

His head hurt, and he raised a tentative hand to Myrtle's bandage—and then he dropped it again, his brows drawing down together.

Myrtle was wrong about that hook in the hall having knocked him out. The wound was on the wrong side.

## FOURTEEN

MYRTLE looked up and said, "That bandage is all right—stop fussing with it."

Ross muttered, "Yes," abstractedly, and went out into the small hall behind the dining room, while the three women looked after him in some astonishment. Myrtle got up and followed him after a moment, asking, "What's the matter with you, anyway?"

He said, "Look—I didn't bang my head this morning—somebody was hiding behind the door and conked me."

"Oh, my stars! What next!" Myrtle groaned. "Don't be so silly—trying to make something out of nothing. I told you how it happened, didn't I?"

She went back into the dining room, and he followed her.

"If you'd just listen a minute," he said impatiently. "It wasn't that hook—it couldn't have been, because it's on the wrong side. Think it over."

Myrtle thought it over for ten seconds and remained unimpressed. "You must have decided to come back into the dining room, and you turned suddenly, that's all. Probably you were in a temper—and that sounds just like you, too."

"I did not decide to come back into the dining room," Ross said coldly. "Nor was I in a temper."

"You wouldn't remember, naturally, after a bang on the head like that."

"I do remember—perfectly. I did not turn around to come back. I suppose it was Butch Cohen who hit me, as a matter of fact. He threatened to get me when I kicked him out last week. He must have come in the side door, and I've told you before that we ought to keep it locked."

"Oh," Myrtle said aggressively, banging her coffee cup down onto its saucer, which split neatly in half. "So now it's my fault because you walk into a hook in a fit of temper. You can leave Butch out of this because he's back on the job."

Ross, obviously in a fury, opened his mouth to bellow, but Myrtle leaped in ahead of him.

"Now wait a minute, Ross Munster—I'm going to have my say first. The nurses are not going to do the orderly's work—I won't have it. You can do it if you don't mind being seen by your stuffed-shirt patients trotting up and down the halls with urinals—empty and full. You know perfectly well that I can't get another orderly in the length and breadth of the country."

"Don't be vulgar," said Ross, "and don't forget to put that saucer on the expense account. I wouldn't want you to pay for it yourself."

Irene and Elise had finished their meals and were smoking. Elise, who always enjoyed a good fight, said, "My dear, I always supposed that it was the nurses who were overworked and downtrodden, but now I see it's the poor doctors who have to bear the brunt."

Ross grinned and found himself in a better humor immediately, while Myrtle, in her hurry to say something stinging, choked over a piece of potato and had to retire temporarily from the fray.

Irene flicked ash from her cigarette and said idly, "Here we are all dressed up for polite conversation, and they sit and snarl at each other over purely hospital matters."

"Hush, dear—not right out in front of them," Elise murmured. "We can discuss it later."

"It isn't my fault," Ross said, still cheerful. "I've been wanting to tell you both how charming you look—but Myrtle's been blowing off, and I haven't had a chance."

"Horseradish," said Myrtle.

A nurse appeared at the door, gave the two guests a thorough going over with her eyes, and then announced someone to see the doctor.

Ross went off, gloomily giving up hope of getting any of the strawberry shortcake, but he was back almost immediately with a man at his side. He indicated Irene and said, "That's the young lady."

The man, an amiable-looking individual, smiled at Irene and shook his head. "Oh no—no, no, no."

"No, what?" Irene asked.

"Dr. Babcock from the state hospital," Ross explained. "Checking up. Won't you sit down, Doctor?"

Dr. Babcock would. He was easily persuaded to have some strawberry shortcake and coffee, and Myrtle went wearily out to the kitchen.

Rowena showed fight as a matter of course, but in the end she agreed to serve an extra wedge of cake.

"There's plenty of cake," Myrtle pointed out, "and gallons of coffee."

"Sure," said Rowena belligerently, "and do you think I can bring the cake in in me hand and put it in his hand—and give his coffee to him through a hose pipe? It's all them extra dishes—and I'm fair sick of it. I'm telling you now—any more guests show up tonight, and they'll get a dog biscuit on a paper plate."

Myrtle carefully waited until she was out of earshot and then observed bitterly, "That would be a lot tastier than some of your biscuits, I'm sure."

Back in the dining room things had become quite gay, and Myrtle felt cheered in spite of herself. It was John who had been getting her down, she thought—something was eating him, she knew—and it worried her. She wished that he could just relax and not torment himself so about things. She sat down at the table, prepared to put John out of her mind and enjoy herself.

Rowena sent in two thirds of a cup of coffee and a thin wedge of cake with half a strawberry on it for the guest, but he was having such a good time that he never noticed it. Elise wanted them all to go out to a night club and had to be reminded that Ross could not leave while John was sick in bed. She gave in cheerfully enough and said that they'd have a party in the dining room instead, and somebody could go out and buy some liquor.

Myrtle stood up with a sigh and a shake of her head. "It would be fun, but I'm afraid there's not a chance. They're waiting to clear the table right now—and the nurses' midnight supper is always laid out here. In fact, we'd better get out before there's trouble."

They got out, and Elise, Irene, and Dr. Babcock drifted out to the warm darkness of the front veranda.

Ross and Myrtle had to leave them because there was work to be done, and Myrtle remarked that the whole thing was nothing less than slavery. "I can't remember when I had a day off—and I don't see any prospect of getting one."

"I know—I feel chained to the place," Ross agreed. "But one of these days we'll be able to get hold of some nurses and another doctor or two—and then we'll celebrate."

"Swell!" Myrtle said glumly. "We'll go to a movie and then get a soda at the drugstore. I'm going to have a look at John."

"He should be sleeping, still," Ross called after her, and she nodded and went on up the stairs. She went into John's room and looked at him, but he appeared to be sleeping quietly, and she presently went out again and closed the door gently behind her.

John opened his eyes cautiously and relaxed with a little sigh. It was not right to fool Myrtle like that—but he didn't want her fussing over him, bringing him food against which his stomach revolted. He had made up his mind that he would go out tonight and find Horace. He was terrified—but determined.

Irene tired of the conversation on the veranda after a while and slipped away, leaving Dr. Babcock in her mother's capable hands. Elise enjoyed the doctor while he lasted and, when he had to go, waved him away with a little sigh because it was such a wonderful night and there didn't seem to be anything left to do with it. So many stars, and no one with whom she could share them. It was a great pity, she thought as she carried her floating draperies inside, that Dr. John was ill in bed.

Beatrice, at the switchboard, stared avidly and called out "Good evening," but Elise swished by with a bare acknowledgment. She made for the dining room, in the hope that someone interesting would be there—Dr. Ross, perhaps—or even Dr. John, recovered and come down for something to eat.

But the dining room was deserted, except for a nurse who disappeared through the swinging door into the pantry as she approached. Elise caught only a glimpse of a white-uniformed back and a cluster of platinum-blonde curls under a neat cap.

She paused, her hand on the back of one of the dining-room chairs and her mind's eye on the platinum curls. Really, they had looked very smart and attractive, and she wondered idly whether she could possibly get away with a similar coiffure. Very nice indeed.

She left the dining room, walking slowly and deciding that she was too mature for platinum curls. It was a pity, but there was nothing you could do about it—the years would go by and leave their mark on you.

In the front hall she ran into Myrtle, who announced that all her things had been moved into Irene's room.

"But, my dear, how nice of you—very kind, I'm sure."

Myrtle, who had been afraid that she might change her mind, drew a breath of relief and said it was nothing.

Elise was still thinking regretfully of the cluster of curls, and she asked, "Who is the nurse with the pretty blonde hair?"

"Blonde?" Myrtle repeated, wrinkling her forehead.

"Platinum blonde."

"Oh no," Myrtle said definitely. "I can't even think of any blondes—but I know there isn't a platinum blonde around here."

## FIFTEEN

"YOU MAY not have had a blonde nurse around here before," Elise said briskly, "but you certainly have one now. I tell you I saw her go into the kitchen. Probably one of your girls blonded her hair today. I wish you'd find out which one it is and let me know—I'd like to ask her where she had it done. I think it would be cute on Irene."

Myrtle started toward the kitchen with a puzzled frown on her face. "I think you've been seeing things—I can't imagine either Catherine or Edith with platinum-blonde hair. They'd look like the devil."

There was no one in the kitchen, and Myrtle shook her head. "You've been dreaming, Mrs. De Petro!"

"I have not been dreaming," Elise said positively. "Let's go and look at those two girls you mentioned."

But Catherine and Edith looked much as usual, and certainly neither of them had blonde hair. Myrtle even took a look at Beatrice, who suspended her gum and stared back warily.

"Oh well," Elise said, shrugging, "it really doesn't matter. Whoever she was, she'll turn up eventually. Look, it's only ten o'clock—what can we do?"

"You'll have to play by yourself now," Myrtle said cheerfully. "I'm going to bed."

"Not really?"

"Yup." Myrtle yawned and began to climb the stairs, and after a moment's hesitation Elise followed her.

They chatted more or less volubly, while Myrtle prepared for bed, and even after she had climbed in and propped two pillows at her back. There was only one hint of unpleasantness, and that was when Elise told Myrtle how to reduce her hips—but when she saw that it was not well received, she dropped it.

Irene had gone up to her room earlier, with the intention of reading and eating some candy in bed. She undressed and put a light robe over her nightgown and then slipped out onto the little balcony to smoke a cigarette. The night was warm and brilliant with stars, and she gave a little sigh of pure pleasure and then laughed quietly to herself. Ross had been in quite a pickle about his bedroom, but of course she did not believe for an instant that he was serious about pushing in and sharing it with her. That had been bluff, to try and scare her out—only she wouldn't scare. She'd have to put up with Elise, of course, but it didn't matter—Elise could use that day bed. In any case, they'd leave in the morning—it wasn't really fair to stay on when these people were so pressed for space and so busy. She'd never actually intended to stay, as a matter of fact—she'd simply been teasing Ross. But she'd go in the morning, and take Elise with her—and leave Dr. John for Myrtle. Elise didn't really want him—she couldn't, because it seemed pretty obvious that he had no money.

Irene had finished her cigarette, and she dropped it onto the floor and stepped on it and then turned back into the room.

Although the bathroom door was closed, it became immediately apparent that someone was having a shower in there—and during her absence on the balcony two large screens had been placed around the day bed.

Irene, standing uncertainly in the middle of the room, caught her lower lip between her teeth and frowned. So he *wasn't* bluffing—he actually intended to use the room. She went over and peered behind the screens, but there was no one there, and after some further frowning indecision she lit another cigarette and seated herself in a chair that faced the bathroom door.

Ross presently emerged, looking clean and fairly cheerful and belting a silk brocade robe securely around his waist.

Irene tapped her slippered foot and flicked ashes from the cigarette.

"I suppose you think you're going to sleep in here?"

"A doctor can never be sure that he's going to sleep anywhere," Ross said, still cheerful. "But I'll have a shot at it— if the patients will only save their bellyaches for the morning."

"Never mind the patients. You'd better start thinking of another place to sleep—because you can't stay here."

He crossed the room to an old mahogany cabinet and, swinging open the door, took out a bottle and two gracefully stemmed sherry glasses.

"This is a particularly good sherry," he said, bringing them to a small table by the chair. "You'll have a glass?"

Irene frowned and said, "No."

He poured the wine, handed her a glass, and sat down opposite her.

"I could have taken a bite out of your ear when you first announced that you were going to stay," he observed, holding his drink up to the light and squinting at it, "but now I'm quite resigned to it. In fact, to be perfectly honest, I like it."

Irene sipped the sherry and said rather helplessly, "But you must realize that you can't stay here."

"Nothing of the sort. I'm sleeping on that day bed, and nothing short of a patient or a fire is going to stop me. What are you worrying about, anyway? You'll have your mother with you—right in the same bed."

Irene gave a loud moan and wailed, "She can't—I won't sleep with Elise—it's impossible! You don't know her!"

Ross smiled happily. "Bad as that? Then perhaps I can fix a bed on the floor for you. It isn't too bad, really—after the first two or three nights, that is."

Irene gave him an oblique look and drained her glass. "I expect it's all right," she agreed politely, "after you're used to it. So why don't you sleep on the floor? Because you're used to it, and I'm not—and that would make everything all right."

Ross picked up the sherry bottle and refilled their glasses.

"No—I'm sorry—I'm out of the army now. Besides, if the head doctor of the hospital were to sleep on the floor, it might get out and make talk."

"I suppose it wouldn't make talk if it got out that you had a couple of women sleeping in your room with you."

"I'm trying to keep that a secret," he said darkly.

Irene laughed heartily and advised him not to waste his energy.

"No—you're right, of course. It will get out, and I'll lose prestige and some patients—but what can I do about it?"

"Well, you've been wanting a rest anyway," she said callously. "And don't try the pathetic angle on me, because I'm not impressed. You could easily avoid any scandal by packing up and going out to the tent."

Ross set his jaw. "I am damned if I'm going to sleep in a tent, ever again."

"Very pitiful."

He ran a hand over his hair and suddenly grinned at her. "Well, I tried threats, coldness, and stern-faced business, but you're still here—so I thought I'd better give the pathetic angle a whirl."

"You should have tried it first. Comfort of the returned soldier—we civilians are helpless before it. But it's a bit late for me to pack, dress, and go, now."

"No, no," Ross said hastily. "I—er—find I enjoy the company, as a matter of fact."

Elise opened the door and walked in, at that point, and was thoroughly shocked to find them sitting there in their robes, drinking. She had always married, herself, and she had no patience with women who didn't.

"Irene!" she roared. "What do you think you're doing?"

Irene said, "Nothing," but Elise had already turned on Ross.

"Young man, you will leave this room instantly."

Ross stood up, said, "Certainly, madam," bowed, and retired behind his screens.

Elise stood for a moment with her mouth hanging open, and then pulled herself together and followed him with fire in her eye.

"I asked you to leave the room," she said shrilly.

"How many rooms do you want me to leave?" he asked reasonably. "I left yours, and now you follow me into mine and want me to leave again."

"Your room?"

He took off his robe and got into bed. "You may have noticed that your room is number 301—this is 301A. Good night, madam—and don't forget that laughter and loud talking is prohibited after 11 P.M."

Elise stood looking at him rather helplessly for a moment and then turned and went back to Irene.

"My dear, what on earth are we going to do? This is *outrageous.*"

Irene flung her robe over a chair and climbed into the double bed.

"If you want to protect my honor, you'd better get in beside me," she said, yawning. "I'm too tired to go anywhere else now."

Elise spent the next ten minutes in walking up and down the room and storming, until Ross rapped on the screen and said sharply, "Will you people in the next room please be quiet—I'm trying to sleep."

Irene giggled, and Elise stood rooted to the spot, wondering whether to tear the screen down and oust him bodily. In the end she came to the conclusion that she probably would not be able to do it, so she called out, "Very well, young man—but you'll pay for this. You and Irene will have to get married at once—you can't play fast and loose with my daughter's reputation."

She had a lot more to say on the same subject, but she had gone into the bathroom, and neither Irene nor Ross could hear her.

John could not hear her either, although he had been listening outside the door. He was thoroughly shocked at Ross for openly breaking the social rules like that—if you had to do such things, they should be done secretly, and then they offended no one. He had done things, himself, that he would not want known—everybody had, surely—but as far as the world knew, he was above reproach. And that was the way it should be.

He went quietly down the stairs and was able to get out without being seen. He wore slacks and a smoking jacket and bedroom slippers that were soon saturated by the wet grass. He should have put something else on his feet, he thought fretfully—it was stupid to ruin a good pair of slippers. But he had not expected such a heavy dew.

He urged himself to go faster, and thought feverishly that if Horace were in the summerhouse tonight, he'd confront him. But perhaps Horace wouldn't be there, he thought hopefully—and tried to tell himself that it would be much better to get it over with.

He picked his way carefully through the narrow path that led to the summerhouse and realized that the encroaching underbrush had almost effaced it. No one used it now, of course.

As he approached the dark little structure, he felt his heart thudding fiercely, and he was afraid that he might faint. The heavy darkness all around seemed to close in and smother him, and the chorus of summer insects beat against his ears and emphasized the utter stillness of all human things. He forced himself to the entrance and peered in.

He could just barely see him—and he would not have been sure had it not been for the glimmer of white shirt front from Horace's funeral suit.

## SIXTEEN

JOHN stood perfectly still, shaking a little, his eyes straining into the darkness of the vine-covered summerhouse. He thought that Horace would speak to him, but there was no sound and no movement. He could not see any face—only the white shirt front and a part of one leg. He seemed to be lying on the battered old wicker chaise tongue—always a favorite spot with him.

Something rustled the leaves of the vine, and John started convulsively and backed up. The false courage he had labored to build up for himself began to crumble, and he glanced wildly about him in the darkness. He tried to tell himself that Horace was sleeping in there and that he should go in—now—at once—and confront him. And then something ran across his foot and demoralized him completely. He turned and fled—stumbling through the overgrown path and panting across the lawn to the side door. He stopped there for a moment, leaning against the jamb, his head dropped, and his breath coming short, and then he went in quietly and crept up the stairs.

He was caught on the second floor. Catherine saw him and came hurrying along the hall, her feet silent in white rubber-soled shoes and her uniform giving out starchy little whispers of sound. John backed up against the wall and stared at her helplessly, but she merely shook her head at him and said, "Doctor, you shouldn't have got up. I know you're anxious about Mrs. Forbes, but I've been taking extra-special care of her for you."

John straightened up and put a hand to his head in a nervous effort to smooth his hair. "I—yes, thank you. I think I'll just take a look at her and go back to bed."

They moved down the hall together, and John wished savagely that the nurses wouldn't change floors like this—Edith had been on this floor, and now Catherine was on it—it made for confusion—but Ross insisted on letting them switch whenever they wanted.

Mrs. Forbes was awake when he and Catherine entered her room, and she smiled at him valiantly.

"I must be a thoroughly fascinating old woman, Doctor—you just can't seem to stay away."

John smiled and laid a finger on her pulse, and after a moment she said querulously, "You'll have to speak to some of the nosy nurses around here—they're always poking through my things."

"We'll put a stop to that," John murmured, and glanced at Catherine, who compressed her lips and gave her head a negative shake.

Mrs. Forbes thought up another complaint and voiced it.

"People coming in and out all the time—it keeps me awake."

Catherine made another face of denial, but John was not looking at her. He promised Mrs. Forbes that things would be changed around to suit her, said good night, and left the room. Catherine followed close behind him, anxious for a few words regarding the fanciful notions of certain patients, but he left her abruptly and went off up to the third floor. His slippers were wet, and he wondered if Catherine had noticed it—and then asked himself why he was so anxious to keep this thing secret. Actually he should walk straight in and tell Ross all about it, and they could confront Horace together. He couldn't do it by himself—he had just proved that.

He heard the sound of music and moved over to Ross's door. There was a radio going—blaring forth dance music —and this was a hospital! Ross should put a stop to it—it was disgraceful. Having a rowdy party of some sort with those two women in his room.

He turned away and headed for his own room and a sleeping pill.

Ross was not involved in any party—he was sleeping peacefully through the din made by the radio, and had been for some time. Elise, propped by pillows and wearing a bed jacket that was a froth of palest green chiffon, had turned on the radio in a last effort to drive Ross from the room. She was reading a book that had been banned in Boston and smoking a cigarette in a delicately carved jade holder.

Irene, lying on her back and staring at the ceiling, was smoking without a holder.

"Elise," she said for the fourth time, "will you kindly shut that blasted thing off and let us all go to sleep? You're not going to get him out that way."

But Elise had reached a point in her book where a spade was being called a spade, and she replied abstractedly, "Just a little while more, my dear, and then I'll give up."

Irene presently crushed out her cigarette, turned over, and went off to sleep with the radio still blaring in her ears.

Elise, lost to everything, continued to read until she had finished the book. She put it aside then, yawned, glanced at her watch, and discovered that it was two o'clock. She said, "Mong dew," got up and turned off the radio, and then hesitated, frowning. She was hungry—so hungry that she was sure she would not be able to sleep unless she got something to eat. She investigated Irene's candy, found only chocolate creams, which she disliked, and then went through some of Ross's drawers but found nothing edible.

She could go down to the kitchen, of course—but it would mean leaving her daughter alone in the bedroom, with that crude man. It was not the right thing to do, certainly—but on the other hand, she must have food. She considered waking Irene and taking her along, but discarded the idea almost immediately. Irene would be vexed, to put it mildly, and would probably refuse to go.

"Oh well," Elise thought resignedly, "I'll just run down quickly and get something, and be back immediately. They're both asleep, anyway."

She crossed quietly to the screens and peered around. Ross was asleep—no doubt about that. His hair was disordered and his mouth slightly open, and Elise tightened her lips. He was really quite good-looking when he was awake and up—but then men were so apt to look crummy when they were asleep. She glanced at Irene and thought with satisfaction that she, at least, looked very young and sweet and pretty. She was wondering, as she started down the stairs, what she herself looked like when she was asleep.

She knew that there were back stairs leading straight to the kitchen from the second floor, and she hoped to get to them without being seen because she liked to be thought of as a person with a delicate and capricious appetite. But as she stepped into the hall she saw Catherine approaching, and she backed hastily into a half-open door to her right.

Catherine came straight to the stairs, sat down cautiously on the top step, and pulled out a cigarette and a small metal box which she used as a combination ashtray and quick snuffer. Elise, peering through the crack of the door, saw these preparations with a certain amount of consternation. The woman was going to sit and smoke a cigarette—and Elise would have to wait in the patient's room, or be seen coming out of it, when she had no earthly business there. The room was dimly lighted, and she glanced around nervously and over at the bed. An old man lay there, his face waxen, and with the bones sharp under the skin. He seemed to be staring at her from under half-closed lids.

Elise gasped and murmured, "Oh—I—beg your pardon."

He made no movement, and after a minute she went over and looked at him more closely. She saw then that he was not looking at her or at anything—the half-opened eyes were blank and expressionless—and he looked as though he were dead. Elise shuddered, even while she realized that he was not dead—she could hear the breath whispering through his throat.

She turned away in a panic, feeling that she must get out of that room, no matter who saw her. As it happened, she was lucky, for Catherine was just disappearing into one of the other rooms as she emerged, and she darted down the back stairs with a little sigh of thankfulness.

She found some chicken in the refrigerator and got some bread and a glass of milk. She took them into the dining room, which was dimly lighted, because she had made it a rule never to eat in the kitchen. She hoped that no one would come in and catch her—and that the chicken would not be missed in the morning.

The food was satisfying, at first, and then she began to grow uneasy. The dining room was big and shadowy about her, and she kept thinking of the old man's bleak, bony face. As she was finishing the milk she remembered the story of the headless nurse and choked badly, and at the same time she distinctly heard a sound from the kitchen. She sprang up, still coughing over the milk, and then paused and firmly pulled herself together. She was not nervous like this, as a rule, but she decided not to come down here in the night for food again. It was too fattening.

She picked up her plate and glass and went straight out to the kitchen, telling herself not to be a weak sissy.

An instant later both plate and glass lay shattered to pieces on the floor—but Elise never noticed them or the noise they made.

The moribund old man was sitting in one of the kitchen chairs, still staring at her.

## SEVENTEEN

MYRTLE came up slowly from a deep, heavy sleep to the shrill insistence of the telephone. She lay perfectly still for a moment, until her head cleared, and then stretched an arm and muttered, "Yes?"

"Miss Warner, you'd better come down," Beatrice said, her voice shaking with excitement. "Somebody is screaming something terrible."

"Well, go and see what it is, you idiot," Myrtle said peevishly. "Do you have to run to me with every little thing? "

Beatrice reminded her, with a touch of reproof, "I can't leave my switchboard, Miss Warner," and added frankly, "Anyway, I'm scared stiff."

Myrtle groaned. "Where's Edith? What's the matter with Edith—or Catherine—" But she knew it was no use and that she'd have to get up anyway. She said curtly, "All right, I'll be down," and hung up.

She pushed her feet into her slippers and was still struggling into her robe as she emerged into the hall. Catherine was leaning over the banisters, looking down, and she called to her, "What is it? What's happened?"

Catherine was pale, and her eyes looked enormous. "I don't know—I think Edith is trying to find out. But the screams were dreadful."

Myrtle went on down to the front hall, where Beatrice, chewing excitedly, pointed toward the dining room. "Edith went that way, Miss Warner. I think maybe it's in the kitchen. It sounded like somebody was being killed."

Myrtle set her teeth and proceeded to the kitchen. She found Edith and Elise—silent, now, and looking white and scared—and she asked sharply, "Well—what is it?"

Still silent, they indicated the old man, and as Myrtle turned and saw him she felt the shock right out to the ends of her toes and fingers. He was propped in Rowena's roomy wooden rocking chair, his thin old legs hanging like sticks and clad only in his little hospital nightshirt.

Myrtle, alarmed and angry, turned on the other two and demanded, "Who did it? Who brought him here?"

"He followed me," Elise cried shrilly. "He saw me and he followed me down here. I've had a dreadful shock—and I think I'm going to faint."

Myrtle, bending over the old man, with her fingers on his wrist, glanced up and said savagely, "If you do, I'll slap you silly."

The pulse was not encouraging, and she said to Edith, "Come on, give me a hand and we'll get him back to bed."

"I'll get Butch," Edith suggested, but Myrtle frowned and shook her head.

"We can't wait—I think he's going. Come on—he weighs practically nothing."

They raised him gently between them and carried him up the back stairs, while Elise trailed along after them, wringing her hands.

Catherine was waiting for them on the landing, and when she saw them she gave a little scream and then clapped her hand to her mouth.

Myrtle said, "Shut up!" and she and Edith labored on to the old man's room, where they carefully settled him in his bed.

Catherine had followed, and Myrtle turned and glared at her. "How do you explain someone coming onto your floor and carrying one of your patients off under your nose?"

"Nobody can say I neglect my patients," Catherine declared wildly. "You know I run my feet off checking up on them—but I can't be two places at once—I don't have eyes in the back of my head. And who could have done a thing like that? Who'd want to?"

"He followed me," Elise said from the doorway, in a sepulchral voice.

Myrtle whispered a word, which somewhat relieved her feelings, and then said out loud, "He is quite incapable of getting out of bed, much less of following you downstairs, Mrs. De Petro!"

"But who could have *done* it?" Edith muttered.

Myrtle straightened up from the bed and fretfully pushed the hair off her forehead. "His legs are scratched and bruised—I think he was dragged down."

Catherine took a deep breath. "Nobody can say I don't take care of my patients. I've never slept on duty or—"

Myrtle said, "Oh God! All right—don't start up again. You two go and keep a watch in your own corridors. I'll have to get Dr. Munster, and I'll want Butch too. Someone is deliberately trying to make trouble."

The two nurses departed, and Myrtle went along to the second-floor phone, with Elise chattering volubly just behind her.

"My dear, such a terrible experience—definitely. I shouldn't be surprised if it has turned my hair gray—although, of course, there's no way of telling about that. I mean, I'd have to let it grow out a bit and watch the part—and why bother? But as I was saying, I'd gone downstairs for some nourishment—I eat so little at a time that I try to force myself to eat frequently—and when I carried my dishes back to the kitchen, there he was. I became a little hysterical, which was only to be expected, and—"

Myrtle lifted the phone, said, "Hush!" and added after a moment, "Beatrice, ring Dr. Munster, and hurry."

In another instant Irene's sleepy voice sounded against her ear, and Myrtle was somewhat surprised to find herself blushing. "I—er—want the doctor, if you don't mind."

"I don't mind at all," Irene said, "but you have the wrong room. This is 301, and he's in 301A."

Myrtle swallowed and then unexpectedly turned on Elise in a fierce aside.

"Why did you leave them up there alone? You ought to have better sense."

Elise fell back a step with one hand on the shell-pink satin bosom of her negligee, but for one of the few times in her life nothing occurred to her that seemed worth saying.

Irene, still half asleep, was hanging onto the phone at the other end, when it was taken abruptly out of her hand, and Ross said, "Three-oh-one A has phoning privileges in 301. It's an easement due to the recent shortage of instruments."

He spoke briefly to Myrtle, dropped the phone, caught up his robe, and disappeared out of the door, leaving it alar behind him.

As soon as she had finished with Ross, Myrtle told Beatrice to ring Butch—and ran into more trouble. Beatrice voiced her state of mind with a very noticeable quaver.

"I'll get him for you, Miss Warner—but you'll have to tell me what's going on, first. I'm all alone out here in this creepy hall—and I'm scared—but good. It don't seem right that I have to stay here with people yelling their heads off. There's plenty jobs—"

Myrtle drew a sigh up from the soles of her feet and headed straight into the wind.

"Beatrice, don't be so silly—and don't try to tell me that you've never heard a drunk sounding off before, because I've known your father for some years. One of our guests—you know, the elder one—overdid it a bit and thought she saw some red alligators or something. I want Butch and the doctor to help me get her back to bed."

Beatrice, satisfied and disappointed at the same time, plugged into Butch's room—which was a compartment that he had constructed himself in a corner of the basement—and Myrtle had barely drawn a breath of relief when she felt a hand on her arm and turned to find Elise's furious face a few inches from her own.

She had forgotten that Elise was still there, and she flushed a hearty red.

"I have never," said Elise in a low, throbbing voice, "been so damnably insulted in my life before. I do not get drunk—I never have been drunk—I never shall be drunk. I drink lightly and daintily—when at all. You'll march yourself down to that girl—with me—and tell her that you have told a deliberate lie."

"All right," Myrtle moaned, "don't get excited—I had to tell her something, or she'd have run out on us. I'll fix it—honestly I will—you just leave it to me."

"I do not like the way you fix things when they're left to you," Elise said frigidly.

Myrtle, wildly rumpling her hair, was already talking to Butch, who was very much put out.

"I ain't no doctor," he whined. "I'm tryin' to get my sleep out, so I can do an honest day's work. If one a those guys you got up there croaked, he'll keep till morning, won't he? He don't have to go on ice right away, for Pete's sake. When do you think I'm gonna get my sleep?"

"When you're on duty in the daytime, as usual," Myrtle snapped. "You get some clothes on and come up here. This is an emergency."

She hung up to forestall further argument, pushed her hair around again, and took three deep breaths in a row.

Irene had pulled on her robe, followed Ross to the door, and watched him as he hurried down the stairs. She wondered vaguely where Elise had gone to—but Elise was quite unpredictable, and there was no telling what idea might come into her head at any hour of the day or night. She never worried about her.

She turned back into the room and got a cigarette, and then thought she heard a noise of some sort on the stairs. She supposed it was Elise and went over to the door to meet her.

But it was not Elise. It was a nurse with platinum-blonde hair—and she was just disappearing into John's room across the hall.

## EIGHTEEN

WHEN Ross arrived on the second floor he found Catherine standing, tight-lipped and grim, in the middle of the hall. He asked her what she thought she was doing, and she replied stiffly that she was on guard.

"Well, go on about your business," he said irritably. "I'll be on guard now."

Catherine swished off to the room of a convalescent patient, who, she knew, would be awake, interested, and sympathetic.

Myrtle and Elise appeared, and when they saw him both started to tell him all about it at once. They stopped, glared at each other, and started again. Ross begged them both to shut up and said all he wanted was the name of the patient who needed attention. He was wondering vaguely, at the same time, where Elise had come from, since he had not noticed, when he left the bedroom, that she was not in bed.

Myrtle managed, finally, to give him the highlights of the story and added, "It's poor old Mr. Herms, and I'm afraid—"

Ross turned on his heel and made for the old man's bedroom. But Robert Herms was dead.

"Why didn't you stay with him?" Ross demanded in a furious undertone. "Or leave Catherine here?"

Myrtle said wildly, "My God! You can have this madhouse. I'll go and get a job at the state asylum, where the nuts are all locked in. I think he was gone by the time we got him back to bed—and I had a bunch of hysterical women on my hands and I thought there must be a maniac running loose in the place and I had to get hold of you and Butch."

"All right, all right," Ross muttered. He considered for a moment, frowning, and then said, "We'd better get the police in. I can't make a proper search of the place by myself. John is too ill to help, and Butch might flush a mouse and faint dead away from shock."

Myrtle nodded. "You go and phone them, and"—she indicated the still figure on the bed— "I'll tie him up. Catherine's in a dither, anyway. He was doing all right, too, wasn't he? It's a shame. Whoever did it, it really amounts to murder."

Ross said, "Shh," and Elise, who had been hovering unnoticed at the door, exclaimed dramatically, "Murder!"

Myrtle spun around, and Ross raised his head sharply.

"Mrs.—er—Elise, will you kindly go upstairs to bed?" he said peremptorily. "We're busy."

Elise looked him squarely in the eye. "Certainly not. In the first place, I have no bed. I am not accustomed to sleeping haphazardly with strange men snoring all around me in the same room. And in any case, when the police come, they will certainly want to question me since I was the one who found him."

Ross gave it up and left the room, and Myrtle followed him out on her way to the linen room. Elise, finding herself alone with the dead, gave a little shriek and departed hastily.

Ross was busy at the telephone, and she could hear Myrtle tearing off strips of cloth in the linen room, so that she found herself at a loose end. All the excitement had made her hungry again, and the temptation to go and make some strong, hot coffee and a chicken sandwich began to tease her. She had already gone off her diet to the extent of having one midnight snack, and if she went wild and had another, the scales would undoubtedly leer at her the next time she weighed herself. Still—she ought to have something to keep her strength up. It wasn't every day that she was an important witness in a—well, in what might turn out to be a murder case.

Food and coffee, she decided, were what she needed, and she made her way down to the dining room. It was deserted and still dimly lighted, and she was surprised to discover that she was shaking with fear. It took all her courage and determination to force herself on into the kitchen, but when she got there she breathed a relaxing sigh of relief.

The kitchen was cheerful with light, and Edith stood at the table, busy with a cup of coffee and some cookies.

"Oh, my dear," Elise said happily, "do give me some coffee, or I shall perish."

"Help yourself," Edith said, and indicated a percolator standing on the stove.

Elise helped herself and decided that cookies would do, instead of a chicken sandwich. She was considerably cheered to find coffee and food already prepared, since she had always hated any type of housework.

"I thought you were supposed to be on guard," she suggested, eying Edith.

"Nope. Butch turned up, and he's doing the guarding. And is he ever fit to be tied!"

"Butch?"

"The orderly." Edith thought for a moment and then added with a certain amount of bitterness, "The day orderly. And should you ask who the night orderly is, I would have to tell you that there is no night orderly. We night nurses simply have to get along the best way we can."

Elise considered, for the first time, the life of a night nurse, and was honestly shocked. It was not the work they had to do—although she felt vaguely that it must be very trying, not to say downright unspeakable, at times—but it appeared to be such a completely manless existence. She decided that patients did not count, because when a man was sick he was simply nothing more nor less than a pest.

She said, with considerable feeling, "It's a shame!"

Edith gave her a more tolerant eye and warmed up.

"Furthermore, do you know how many nurses there are on day

duty here? Four. Four of them looking after the same amount of patients that Catherine and I are supposed to handle at night. And Miss Warner around to help them when they get tired fixing their hair and looking at their fingernails, too."

Elise poured herself some more coffee. "Well, yes—but of course there's more work to be done during the day. I mean, at night everybody goes to sleep, and you girls just have to stand around in case the patients have nightmare or something."

Edith choked badly over her coffee, and Elise was kindly patting her on the back, when Catherine and Ross walked into the room.

Ross said, "Coffee. Good," and Catherine fluttered over to the stove, murmuring, "Can I get you a cup, Doctor?"

Ross asked abstractedly, "How's Mrs. Forbes?"

Catherine handed him a cup of coffee and said, "Why, she's just fine—sleeping like a baby. Dr. Girsted was in to see her tonight, and she loves to have him fuss over her."

Edith had recovered her breath, but she was feeling thoroughly frustrated. With the doctor there, she could not explain to Elise just how much work a nurse had to do during the course of a night.

Ross took two swallows of coffee and then turned suddenly to Catherine. "What did you say—about Dr. Girsted?"

"He was in to see Mrs. Forbes tonight," she explained. "I know he's ill, Dr. Munster, but he worries so about her. I guess he just had to take a look at her."

Edith glanced at the clock and departed reluctantly, with a last glance at Elise, who didn't notice it.

Ross muttered, "But he was under a narcotic. I don't see— Was it late?"

Catherine nodded. "Yes, quite late. But he must have gone outside first for a little air, because his slippers were all wet."

"His feet were wet? You're sure?"

"Oh yes, Doctor, quite sure," Catherine said, hoping it meant something important. She'd had a hunch lately that Dr. Girsted was going a bit queer.

Ross, his face impassive, was undergoing a certain amount of mental turmoil. There could no longer be any doubt that there was something wrong with John. He'd felt it for some time, of course, but he'd supposed that John was simply stewing over one of his interminable little problems. But this sounded serious. And suppose it was John who had dragged poor old Bob Herms downstairs— He'd have to do something about John immediately.

Catherine glanced at the clock and, hoping to be detained from her duties, asked, "Is there anything I can do for you, Doctor?"

Ross said, "No, thanks," and she departed with a faint sigh.

Elise lighted a cigarette, shook an errant flake of ash from the cobwebby lace at her wrist, and settled down for a chat.

"Those nurses, now—they are callous, naturally, but—"

Ross gave her an absent glance and said, "I think you should go back to bed, Mrs.—er—"

"Are you not waiting for the police?" Elise asked with exaggerated patience. "And have I not already told you that I am the key witness? Really—"

"Oh yes. Sorry." But he was not thinking of Elise. His mind was still fretting over John. If John had done this thing, he must be loopy enough to be certified. Better go up and see him, anyway. And at once. He turned abruptly and left the kitchen without hearing Elise's sharp inquiry as to where he was going.

He found John lying limply in bed but was quite unable to rouse him.

## NINETEEN

Ross summoned Myrtle, and they had to work hard over John, who proved to be a stubborn case. "I gave him plenty this afternoon," Ross said worriedly. "Enough to keep him on ice for a while, I thought—but apparently he's been up and out. And now he's taken another dose on his own. He'll kill himself one of these days."

But something had poor old John by the throat, Ross thought, and unless they could find out what it was and set him right, he was heading for a smashup. Or perhaps he had already smashed and was creeping around at night doing things like dragging poor old Bob Herms out of bed and hauling him down to the kitchen. If he had done it, Ross thought grimly, it would mean that he'd cracked wide open because John had always been extremely careful and conscientious with the patients.

Myrtle was in tears. She asked Ross several times if he thought it was an attempted suicide, but he assured her and reassured her that it was merely a mistake.

"Sometimes he gets fussy about taking drugs of any sort, so I didn't tell him what he was getting this afternoon. How the devil was I to know he'd go and swallow another carload himself?"

Catherine came up once to tell them that the police had arrived, and was sent down with instructions to give her version of what had happened. Myrtle and Ross would be down as soon as they could leave John.

Irene had made several attempts to go back to sleep, but all the activity was too distracting, and she decided finally to go downstairs and mix in. She had no idea what it was all about but felt firmly convinced that Elise was in the thick of it, no matter what it was.

She belted herself into a tailored robe of navy-blue silk, combed her hair, applied some lipstick, and went along to John's room, first, to find out what was going on there.

The door was nearly closed, and she put her eye to the crack, but all she could see was the headboard of the bed and a part of Myrtle. She wondered if the platinum-blonde nurse were still in there, and decided that Dr. John must be very ill.

She went on down to the second floor, where Catherine was leaning over the stair rail, trying to see and hear what was going on on the first floor.

"Is it robbery, arson, murder, or just Elise?" Irene asked.

Catherine whirled around with a startled little gasp and then, glad of a fresh audience, told her the whole story in a breathless rush.

Irene shuddered and asked, wide-eyed, "What sort of a place is this? What's going on?"

"You tell me!" Catherine said in a scared whisper.

Irene went on down to the front hall and unexpectedly found it rather crowded. Five hastily dressed members of the Herms family were huddled together at one side, while Elise and two men held the limelight in the center. Beatrice had stuck her gum under the switchboard while she drank a cup of coffee and was now frantically hunting for it with both hands while her eyes goggled at Elise and the two men.

Elise had evidently been holding the floor and was just warming up.

"I assure you, gentlemen, that I have never, in a fairly varied lifetime, had such a fearful experience before."

The two men stirred, as though they had been held in restraint for a long time, and turned to face each other.

"What do you think we ought to do, Joe?"

"Frankly, Ed, I don't know."

Elise helped them out. "I think the doctor wanted you to guard the place, don't you know, so that no more terrible things can happen. And, of course, find the maniac."

"What maniac?" Ed asked, startled.

Elise sighed for his density. "My dear gendarme, there must be a maniac around to have done such a thing."

"My name's Ed Posner," he said politely. "Yeah, I guess that's right. Joe, get a couple of the boys and put them in here, and you and I'll go off and find this here maniac."

"No, no," Elise protested. "You mustn't go oh anywhere. The creature is probably hiding right here in the building somewhere."

"But, naturally, lady," Ed said reproachfully, "we're gonna give a gander around here, first."

Elise nodded. "Yes. Well, that's splendid. Perhaps I can help you."

Joe and Ed turned pale in unison. "No, no," Ed muttered. "That won't be necessary, lady."

"My name is Mrs. De Petro, as I believe I have already told you."

Ed said, "Pleased to meet you," rather absently, and, with Joe close behind him, turned away and disappeared out the front door.

Irene descended the last few stairs and approached her mother.

"Elise, for heaven's sake let's go up and pack and get out of here."

"My dear, quite impossible. I am the key witness, and I expect to be of the most vital help to the police."

Irene murmured, "The police could stumble along by themselves," but she knew it was hopeless.

Myrtle and Ross came down at that point, and Myrtle took in the scene with one comprehensive, sweeping glance. The Herms family stood gaping at Irene and Elise, who looked slim and elegant in their night attire—it was not good publicity for the hospital. Especially when it got around—as it was bound to—that this same modish pair were sleeping in the doctor's bedroom. Elise looked no more like a chaperon than Irene—in fact, she looked young and lovely in her shell-pink satin with the delicate touches of filmy lace at wrists and neck. Myrtle caught her lower lip between her teeth and took a moment to wonder how she did it.

But things had to be attended to, and she squared her shoulders and plunged in. In the space of a few minutes she had disposed of the Herms relatives, and Elise and Irene, and had hinted to Beatrice to mind her own business and keep her mouth shut.

Elise and Irene went only as far as the dining room, because Elise insisted that the police would be back and would need her help, and Irene figured that she might as well see the excitement out to its end.

They found Ross there, standing by the window, smoking and staring out into the darkness.

Elise said, "Ah, Doctor," and he turned as Irene asked, "How is Dr. John?"

"He's all right now. Sleeping quietly."

He had been all right, finally. He had talked to Myrtle and Ross and had seemed fairly normal. But Ross's troubled thoughts hovered around him. He felt nearly sure, now, that John had not taken the old man out of bed. He was not insane—but certainly some heavy burden lay on his mind. He had tried to make him tell about it, whatever it was, and Myrtle had begged him with tears in her eyes to confide in them. But John had become cross and irritable, declared peevishly that there was nothing whatever on his mind, and insisted that he was simply feeling a bit seedy. He had been working hard, and the heat was trying.

They had had to be content with that and to let him go back to sleep with his own particular little hell still locked inside of him.

Irene seated herself at the table, shook back her hair, and asked casually, "Who was the blonde nurse who went into Dr. John's room while you were downstairs?"

"What blonde nurse?" Ross asked abstractedly.

Elise turned an alert eye on her. "A platinum blonde? Very nice arrangement of curls?"

Irene nodded.

"There was no nurse up there," Ross said. "You must be mistaken."

"No," said Irene. "No mistake. It was after you had gone downstairs. I heard a noise outside, and I went and looked, and this blonde nurse was just disappearing into Dr. John's room."

Ross shook his head. "There isn't a blonde nurse in the place."

"That's what Myrtle tells me," Elise declared, "but you are both wrong, because I saw her too—going into the kitchen. I noticed her hair particularly."

Ross stared at them and wondered rather helplessly what was going on in his hospital. It could hardly be that they were both mistaken about this blonde nurse, and if they were right, who was she—where was she—and why was she hiding? She must be creeping stealthily around and doing things like hitting him on the head, dragging that old man downstairs, and—possibly—terrorizing John. He shot his cigarette out onto the terrace and suddenly straightened, with a sharp intake of his breath.

It was that girl, that mental case, who was supposedly in Chicago with Clark. Only, she was not in Chicago—she was hiding in or around the hospital.

## TWENTY

ROSS felt, suddenly, that he understood the whole situation. For some reason Clark had never taken that girl to Chicago—he had left her in

John's charge. Only, why would sober, conscientious old John agree to such a thing? Of course he was very fond of Clark—always had been—and Clark could be very convincing when he wanted someone to do him a favor. But why had Clark left the girl, instead of taking her to Chicago? Oh well, that was easy. They were looking for her in Chicago—so she was safer here. Clark's brand of cleverness. He must be very much in love with the girl, and yet that wasn't like him, either. His method was to flit from girl to girl.

Ross shook his head in a troubled fashion and realized that Elise was asking for a cigarette, for the third time. He supplied her, and after she had puffed for a minute or two she said restlessly, "I think I'll just step into the front again—I want a word with Beatrice."

She departed, and Ross said to Irene, "*She's* having fun, anyway."

Irene stifled a yawn and nodded. "I'm leaving tomorrow, and I'll take her with me."

"Why? You're comfortably settled here now, and I don't suppose you'll be able to get a room at the hotel."

Irene grinned at him. "I think you've been punished enough."

"I have not been punished at all. You really should stay until you can get even with me."

Irene shrugged and, after a moment's silence, asked, "Is it actually true that you have no blonde nurse here?"

He shook his heads with a worried line between his brows. "No blondes at all. But I have a theory about that nurse."

"What?"

"I think it's that girl who drove up here with you. Clark probably established her here, with a nurse's uniform, and then went off to Chicago to scatter red herrings."

"Hmm." Irene thought it over for a moment, while the light of interest dawned in her eyes. "That's quite an idea. Except that her hair wasn't blonde—it was about the same color as mine."

"It would be simple enough for her to have it changed, wouldn't it? It's a typical reaction of people who have been held in restraint for some time. And of course it would help to confuse those who were looking for her, too. Anyway, you know what she looks like—and I want you to help me find her."

"Well, I—I don't know what I could do," Irene said doubtfully. "I thought Joe and Ed were handling it."

Ross laughed impolitely. "I went to school with Joe and Ed—and whenever we played hide-and-seek, they never found anybody who was hiding—no matter how hard they sought."

"Still, they are the police."

"Yes—but that girl should be found without delay. And to tell you the truth, I'm worried about John. There's something on his mind, and he's in bad shape. I have an idea that he knows about the girl—he's fond of Clark, and he may have agreed to keep an eye on her—but he knows it's wrong to keep her hidden, and it's wrecking him. I'd like to find the girl and return her to the hospital without his having any hand in it. He'd be out from under, then, and I think he'd clear up. I don't want Joe or Ed to find her because she might implicate John."

"But I don't quite see how I could help you," Irene said uncertainly.

"Well, you know what she looks like. Even with her hair changed, I should think you could recognize the face."

"I suppose so," Irene agreed. "Although I didn't actually see much of her—not so much more than you did yourself."

"You must have seen more of her than I did," Ross protested. "Anyway, you know the sister, and that might help. Family resemblance—that sort of thing."

Irene thought it over for a while but was unable to make up her mind as to whether she'd recognize the girl or not. "What I want you to do," Ross continued, "is to come with me and search for her. At least we can be pretty sure of one thing—that she's not hiding in the building, because there'd be nowhere for her to sleep. There isn't a corner in the place where she could sleep for any length of time without someone stumbling over her. So she's outside. Now, I saw a light in the summerhouse, the other night, and I believe that's where she is." He glanced up at the clock on the mantel. "Dawn will be breaking in about three quarters of an hour, and I want you to come out there with me. You can identify her and help me with her—because I want as few people to know about it as possible."

"We could at least have Myrtle with us," Irene suggested. "She always knows what to do about everything, and she'd be a big help."

Ross frowned and said quickly, "No. I'd prefer to keep Myrtle out of it. She'd be upset on John's account—and anyway, when Myrtle fixes things, anything's apt to happen."

Irene laughed. "All right. But how are we to get the girl to the car—probably struggling and fighting—without anyone knowing about it?"

"There's a path on the far side of the summerhouse that leads to the garage," he explained. "I can handle her while you drive straight to the hospital. You know the way. You see, I really do need your help."

Irene felt a bit flattered, in spite of herself, and her mouth curved in a half-smile. "Well—all right. We'd better go upstairs and dress."

He nodded and took her arm, and they went companionably up the back stairs. When they reached the door of the bedroom, Irene paused and found herself blushing.

"You know this really is a bit beyond the edge. Coming up to the same room to dress."

Ross put his hands on her shoulders and urged her into the room. "Come on—you brought this situation, with much bravado, upon yourself. You have already ruined my reputation—the thing's all over town. Even if you made an honest man of me and married me, there'd still be people to point the finger of scorn at me. So I'm hanged if I care about your reputation any longer."

"Any longer!" Irene repeated. "When did you ever?"

"Who gets the bathroom first?" Ross asked.

Irene answered by walking into it.

John, standing just inside his own door, was waiting for theirs to close—but to his annoyance, they left it half open. He felt dizzy and slightly sick, but he was able to walk, and he had determined upon one more effort to confront Horace. He would go down, now, to the summerhouse—and if he failed this time, he'd have to go away. There was no other way out, for the thing was killing him.

It had not been right to fool Ross and Myrtle as he had done a while ago, either—pretending for so long that he did not hear them and could not answer them. But he had not wanted to talk to anyone, and they wouldn't leave him alone. One of the nurses had been in his room before Ross came, but he had kept his eyes closed and she had gone out again.

He wondered vaguely why so many people were up and about—Dave Cattledge, perhaps. Anyway, it didn't matter.

He slipped past Ross's room and went quietly down the stairs. He avoided Catherine safely, went on down to the kitchen, through the dining room, and out the side door.

John was fortunately ignorant of Joe and Ed and their cohorts, and as it happened, he did not run into any of them. Neither Joe nor Ed knew that there was a side door, so they had left only two men—one at the front and one at the back. Joe and Ed themselves were out on the front driveway, having an argument.

John emerged, therefore, and made his way out across the lawn, unmolested. He was thinking grimly that this was his last attempt—if he failed now, he would have to give up.

He reached the overgrown little path and was conscious of a vague impression that it was considerably more beaten down than it had been.

He stumbled on to the summerhouse, his breath laboring in his throat, and when he reached the entrance he closed his eyes tightly and said in a high, quavering voice, "Horace!"

Only the sounds of the summer night answered him, and after a moment he opened his eyes and peered in. Horace was still there, and this time he could see him more distinctly. The darkness was thinning into dawn, and Horace's figure, on the wicker lounge, was clearly outlined. John forced his eyes up—and stopped breathing.

There was no face. The entire head was missing.

## TWENTY-ONE

JOHN stood at the entrance to the summerhouse, hanging onto the wooden trellis with a clammy hand, knowing that he should go in and investigate and unable to move forward by so much as one step. He turned away after a moment and began to run, stumbling through the path and slowing to a walk only when he was once more on the smooth surface of the lawn.

He'd tell Ross and Myrtle—send them out and let them take care of it. He was all in, anyway—completely exhausted. He was shaking, and his teeth were chattering, but he knew that he was better. The fear and tension had gone, now that he knew Horace was dead. Headless. How had it happened? Who could have done such a thing? But John didn't really care. He admitted it to himself and then hoped that Horace, wherever he was, couldn't read the disloyal thought.

He was trembling in regular shuddering spasms by the time he reached the side door. He had realized that he should certainly have looked in Horace's clothing for the will—he was so convinced that it must be there. He'd tell Ross to do it—he'd have to tell Ross, anyway, about the body lying there, headless, in the summerhouse.

He went into the back hall and was seized by a sudden paroxysm of sneezing. He could not stop it, and presently Myrtle appeared from the front hall to find out what was going on.

"Oh, John!" she cried. "What on *earth* are you doing out of bed? What is it? What's the matter? This is awful."

John mopped at his face with a shaking hand and whispered, "Hush, Myrtle—I'm all right—it's all right now."

He put his arms around her and kissed her, but she said fretfully, "It isn't all right. You look like death, and you ought to be in bed—especially after what has happened here tonight."

John shook his head in an effort to clear it and muttered, "Where's

Ross?" He was suddenly sleepy, so sleepy that it was almost impossible to keep his eyes open.

"He's around somewhere. But you're going to bed," Myrtle said firmly.

"I must see him immediately—it's very important. Help me upstairs, will you? I'm—I seem to be a little unsteady— all that stuff I've had."

Myrtle put a strong hand under his arm and steered him toward the kitchen. She wanted to get him up the back stairs and on to his room without anyone seeing them, if it could be managed.

John was wondering vaguely if he would ever make it to the top of the stairs. The tremendous relief of knowing that Horace was really dead had set up a reaction, and he wanted only to sink into a sleep that would last for many hours.

Ross heard them, as they got to the third floor, and walked out of his room.

"Good God, John!" he exploded, and added in honest bewilderment, "How the devil do you do it?"

"Suppose you leave the small talk until later," Myrtle snapped, "and help me get him back to bed. He's about washed up."

As they were putting him to bed, John tried to tell them all about Horace. In the end, he supposed that he had given them the whole story, but actually he had merely thought the greater part of it. They did gather, from his few muttered words, that he believed Horace's body to be in the summerhouse and that Ross must look in the pockets of the shroud for something—but just what was not made clear.

They both thought that he was raving. When they left him, Myrtle locked the door of his room and put the key in her pocket. She blinked at Ross through a mist of tears and said quietly, "I'll keep the key. I'm going to take care of him."

Ross nodded. "Don't be too upset about it. There's something going on here, and I believe John knows about it. He's been worrying his fool head off, but he'll be all right. I think I know what it is now—and I'm going to fix it."

"Are you going out to look in the summerhouse?" Myrtle asked, and felt a bit foolish.

"Oh yes—I'll go at once. I want to get hold of Irene first, though."

"For God's sake, what next?" Myrtle groaned. "Why do you have to drag her along? I know you're sweet on her, but you shouldn't mix business and pleasure."

"This is purely business," Ross said coldly. "Any pleasure will be incidental. She's necessary to what I plan to do."

Myrtle flung up her hands in an exasperated gesture. "All right—take her along, and justify it by a lot of fancy words. But maybe John wasn't all crazy—and if Horace's body *is* in the summerhouse, that girl will scream. You'd do much better to take Joe or Ed."

"Now, listen, Myrtle," Ross said firmly, "on this excursion I don't want either Joe or Ed—I want Irene. And I have a very good reason for wanting her. As a matter of fact, Joe and Ed would be more likely to scream than Irene."

Myrtle narrowed her eyes at him and nodded her head once or twice. "O.K., brother, I can see the handwriting on the wall—and I wish to state, here and now, that I will not stand for any interference from that chit in the running of this hospital."

She swished off before Ross could choose from several retorts that occurred to him. Irene emerged from their bedroom, fully dressed, at that moment, so he relieved his frustration by taking it out on her.

"What have you been doing all this time? How do you expect to catch that girl when you take all night to put on a few clothes ? She may be miles away by this time."

"I can't chase maidens across the countryside attired only in a form-fitting uplift and a pair of hand-embroidered and monogrammed panties belonging to Elise, and which I put on by mistake," Irene said imperturbably. "Come on, can't you? We're wasting time."

They went on down and in the front hall ran into Joe, who looked peeved and tired. He said, "Listen, Ross, we combed this place good from top to bottom, and there ain't anybody or anything—only what belongs here."

"What do you mean by 'anything'?" Ross asked. "Have you been looking for ghosts?"

Joe blushed, but said defiantly, "I been looking for nothing in particular, because that's the only way you was able to describe what you wanted me to find."

"Well, keep on looking for it," Ross said, heading for the dining room. "It was here earlier, playing tricks—whatever it looks like. Only, don't disturb my patients."

Irene was laughing quietly. In the dining room, she asked in amusement, "How can he make any sort of a search without disturbing the patients?"

"Ahh, I only want to keep his mind occupied while I'm busy on the outside," Ross said.

He took the key to his father's tomb from its hook and slipped it into his pocket. Better investigate thoroughly, while he was about it. Probably John had just been babbling, but he had to make sure. He disliked the idea of entering the mausoleum, but John's mutterings made it necessary to check on it.

As they made their way across the lawn, Irene began to feel decidedly nervous—rather to her own surprise. She decided that it must be the gray early-morning light, because she was not afraid of Doris Miller, even if she was insane.

Ross went ahead through the straggling little path, and she followed, trying to preserve her stockings from the undergrowth.

The summerhouse was deserted and empty. Ross attempted to turn on the electric bulb and found that it did not work, but it was quite light enough to see that the place was unoccupied.

Irene found herself drawing a breath of relief as she said unnecessarily, "No one here."

"No. Come on, we'll try the other place," Ross said, and started off again.

He had never been inside the tomb, but he knew the coffin had not been sealed, and he decided, grimly, that he'd have to open it and see that everything was in order.

The small, neat little building looked gray and blank in the dawn, and Irene stopped, some distance from the door, and protested rather breathlessly: "You—you're not going in there?"

Ross fitted the key into the lock and glanced back at her. "Sorry. I'm afraid it's necessary."

"But she wouldn't be there. How could she?"

The lock turned easily and smoothly, and Ross said, "There's no need for you to come in. I'll bring her out if she's here."

Irene set her teeth and followed him in. She peered fearfully over his shoulder and saw at a glance that the musty little room, with its stained-glass window, was bare, save for the coffin set up in the center. She took a step backward and was horrified to see Ross advance toward the coffin and lay a hand on the lid. He fumbled with it for a moment and then raised it, and stood for so long looking down inside that she crept forward. She clutched at his arm, gave his face a quick, frightened glance, and then looked down into the satin-lined box.

It was empty.

## TWENTY-TWO

ROSS dropped the lid of the coffin and glanced around the bare little room, while Irene stood, scarcely breathing, looking up into his face.

"It's not musty enough in here," he muttered.

She glanced over her shoulder and said with her teeth chattering, "The door is open—we left the door open."

"I know, but it's more than that. Someone has been in and out."

Irene felt suddenly that she couldn't stand the place for another instant, and she turned abruptly and walked out. The summer dawn glowed softly against her face, and she took several long, deep breaths with her eyes closed. After a moment she heard Ross behind her, locking the door.

"John saw the body of my father somewhere," he said, dropping the key into his pocket. "I'm convinced of it. I'll have to talk to him and find out what he knows. In the meantime, suppose we walk around behind the summerhouse and down to the garage. It's possible that the girl may be lurking around there."

They moved off together, and Irene said uncertainly, "It's so completely puzzling. I mean, I can understand why Doris is hiding around here—but the—the body— Why would anyone move it? It's ghastly."

"Well, I think I can answer that one. The mausoleum would be a good place for the girl to hide—no one would dream of looking for her there. But she'd have to get the body out, naturally. I suppose she put it somewhere and John found it—although I don't know why it sent him into such a tailspin. He should have come straight to me."

"But there's nothing there," Irene protested. "In the tomb, I mean. If Doris were sleeping there, she'd have to have *things.*"

"She may hide her things elsewhere in the daytime." He rubbed his forehead with a closed fist and added, "We'll have to keep after it until we clear it up. And if you would like a peep into the crystal ball, I'll prophesy that the doctors and nurses of our hospital will have more rest and leisure in the next few weeks than we've had for a long time."

"What are you talking about now?" Irene asked helplessly. "You skip from subject to subject like a mountain goat."

"I may turn out to be the goat," Ross conceded, "but I am not skipping. I'm still on the same subject. With things of this sort happening around the place, the patients will be removed by their loving relatives as soon as they are fit. I'll go broke, and your mother will no longer eye me as a possible candidate for her daughter's hand."

Irene blushed and wished violently—not for the first time—that she had never put in the phone call that had brought Elise flying out here.

She said, "Don't flatter yourself—Elise wouldn't sell me so cheap. If she's eying you, she must have other plans in mind for you."

"That's right," Ross said mildly. "Kick a man when he's down."

They passed by the summerhouse, which was still deserted, and around to the other side. The path was much more obstructed here, and Ross went ahead to clear the way for Irene, but her stockings were soon mutilated anyway.

She asked in some irritation, "Why couldn't we have gone around the front way?"

"I told you—I'm looking for that girl."

But they did not find Doris. They came at last to the garage, which turned out to be a huge old barn, rather badly in need of repair. They went in through a hole in the back.

"You know," Irene said, trying to get her breath, "you've only to get a slat of wood and nail it on, to repair this particular hole."

"Certainly," said Ross coldly. "And where would I get the time? And where would the combined gardener and handy man get the time? He complains constantly, as it is. Furthermore, if we did have the time, where would we get the slat of wood? The lumber company in the village is very obliging about filling orders, and they definitely promise delivery by 1950."

Irene, busily examining her stockings, begged him to shut up.

There were three cars and an ambulance in the gloomy cavern of the barn. The ambulance and the two cars belonging to Ross and Clark were dusty and travel-stained, but John's conservative black sedan was neat, clean, and carefully polished.

"Damn that fellow Mac," Ross muttered. "I've told him a thousand times to do the ambulance first—and then the others, if he could manage it. And he does John's car, and only John's car."

"Maybe John did it himself," Irene suggested, squinting up at the huge old oak beams that were hand-hewn and pegged into place.

"Oh no—John's a doctor. I have to wash my car, of course—but Mac and John were at school together, and John's the one who counts. I wish to God Mac had gone to school with the ambulance."

"Everyone around here seems to have gone to school with everyone else."

"There's only one school," Ross explained, "so that if you're roughly in the same age group as someone else, you naturally went to school together."

They gave a cursory search, but the barn was obviously deserted, and there was no loft. The raftered roof slanted above them, with daylight showing here and there through the cracks. Irene suggested that a temporary repair—enough to keep the rain out—might be effected with chewing gum, but Ross ignored it.

"Come on. We've missed the girl, but I don't want to spend any more time on it. I'll have to start Joe and Ed looking for my father's body. I'm going to put a stop to that sort of thing, and whoever did it will be punished. Evidently John saw the body—and not much more than an hour ago—but I can't question him now, and I don't want to wait. The body can hardly be very far away—there hasn't been time."

He set off across the lawn, and Irene had to trot to keep up with him. They went in by the back door and entered the kitchen together, and caught Joe and Ed red-handed, regaling themselves with cake and milk.

"Nothing if not thorough," Ross observed, staring at them. "You even looked through the refrigerator."

Ed swallowed some cake that was in his way and looked up with a touch of defiance. "Well, for Pete's sake, Ross, what do you expect? You get us up out of bed, and no breakfast, just because a patient walks himself downstairs. We ain't machines—we're human."

"That's highly debatable," Ross snarled. "I've told you that patient couldn't walk himself downstairs or anywhere else."

"O.K.," Joe interposed. "So another patient—slightly loony, maybe—brings him downstairs. So what are we huntin' for? Why don't you keep them dopes locked in their rooms where they belong?"

Ross sat down and absently helped himself to a piece of cake. He considered the possibility of another patient having dragged old Bob Herms downstairs, and presently came to the conclusion that it was impossible.

Irene pulled out a cigarette and sat down at the table. Joe and Ed looked at her warily, and she flashed each of them a brilliant smile.

Ross stirred and said, "All right—leave the house alone —but I want you to start a thorough search outside. I have reason to believe that that girl who escaped from the asylum is hanging around out there. You know about her, of course?"

Joe and Ed admitted that they did. They had a description of her and had been keeping an eye open, but they understood she was in Chicago.

"Well, she isn't. She's around here somewhere, and you'd better start looking for her." Ross hesitated for a moment and then told them, in a flat, emotionless voice, about the disappearance of his father's body. They seemed rather pleased at having something concrete to look for and went off, after first getting the key to the tomb.

"Now," Ross said, turning to Irene, "we'll do a little sleuthing ourselves. I want you to come with me to the local beauty parlor and tell them you'd like to have your hair blonded—the same sort of job that your friend had done yesterday morning. It must have been yesterday—and I want to be sure that that blonde is Doris Miller. If they admit to having blonded someone yesterday morning, then I think we can be reasonably sure."

"But I don't want blonde hair," Irene said childishly.

"You don't have to have blonde hair. They're busy, and you'll have to get an appointment for a later date."

"How do you know?" Irene asked suspiciously. "Are you one of their customers?"

"Don't be an idiot. I went to school with Marie."

"Oh. Of course."

"Come on—let's go now."

"What's the matter with you?" Irene asked, glancing at her watch. "It's barely six o'clock."

"Oh damn. All right—we'll have some breakfast first."

They clattered around the kitchen together, putting on coffee, which eventually boiled over, and frying bacon, which promptly burned, but in the end they sat down to a meal of sorts and had just started to eat when Myrtle walked in, dressed and starched whitely for the day.

As her eye fell on them and the mess they'd made, she stopped dead and moaned, "Oh, my God! Couldn't you have waited? If Rowena walks in on this, she'll turn around and walk straight out again."

"Sit down and have some breakfast, Myrtle," Ross said amiably. "There's plenty for all."

Myrtle got an extra cup and plate and sat down with them, still shaking her head. After her first cup of coffee she brightened a bit and said, "John's much better—I had a look at him. Sleeping like a baby."

Ross nodded, reached for another helping of charred bacon, and then told her about the rifled coffin.

Myrtle rose up out of her chair, her face suddenly white and her eyes enormous.

"I knew it—I knew something was queer. The coffin was not to be nailed down—the door could be opened from the inside. Ross, Horace is no more dead than you are."

## TWENTY-THREE

IRENE gave a little gasp, and Ross frowned and said, "Don't be silly. He was embalmed."

Myrtle sat down again, and some of the color came back into her face. "Maybe he was embalmed—and maybe he wasn't. He and Knott were friends, after all."

"They probably went to school together," Irene murmured.

Myrtle nodded. "They did."

"The thing's fantastic," Ross said irritably, "and you know it."

"No, I don't know it," Myrtle declared with spirit. "You go around and ask Knott, and see if he doesn't act confused and start to shuffle."

"It won't be necessary," Ross said shortly. "Joe and Ed will find the body—you'll see."

Irene found that her appetite had deserted her, and she was unable to finish the remainder of her meal. She lit a cigarette instead and watched with mild wonder while the other two ate heartily. She supposed, vaguely, that it was their profession. A body was just a body.

"Where is Elise?" she asked presently.

"Sleeping," said Myrtle, with her mouth full.

"Maybe that's not a bad idea."

"I wish I could," Myrtle sighed.

Ross pushed back his chair and said to Irene, "You're not doing any sleeping just yet. There's a little business to attend to first—in case you had forgotten." He lit a cigarette and began to pace the kitchen.

Myrtle turned a bleak eye on him and suggested grimly, "While you're doing nothing, you might as well start washing the dishes."

"What!"

"I'm all out of stories—can't think of another one—and Rowena will quit if she walks in on this mess. You start doing those dishes, Ross Munster, or I'll quit myself."

Irene put out her cigarette, stood up, and began to collect the dishes on the table. "You're both nervous and upset after the night you've had," she said calmly. "There aren't enough dishes to make a major issue out of it. I'll take care of it myself." She carried a pile to the sink and began to wash them under the running faucet, without benefit of soap, while Myrtle and Ross watched in silence. "If Myrtle is all ready to quit over a bit of disputed dishwashing," she added, squinting at an egg-smeared fork, "she must have another job all ready lined up."

Ross picked up a dish towel and began to dry the things, and Myrtle started to clear off the rest of the table.

"I have," she said, dropping a clutter of cutlery into the sink. "Dozens of them, as a matter of fact—I could have my pick. Perhaps the situation will change soon, and I'll have to hold my tongue again, but right now I claim the right to threaten to resign several times a week. Like Rowena. The only trouble being that she may really do it."

Irene laughed, and Ross said, "Hurry, can't you? I'm all caught up with you."

They reduced the kitchen to spotless order, and Irene surveyed it with pride. "Rowena won't threaten to leave for at least a week, after this. She doesn't even have to get breakfast for us this morning."

"Yes, she does," Myrtle said hastily. "We're keeping this meal under our hats. I'll tell her we'll have a late breakfast—nine-thirty. She won't mind that because—"

But Ross had Irene by the arm and urged her out of the kitchen, so that she never discovered why Rowena would not mind a nine-thirty breakfast.

"Marie opens at nine," Ross said, "so you be ready to come to the village with me then. I'll have to work fast, but I think I can manage it at that time. I'll take you to Marie's, and I'll drop in on Knott, just to shut Myrtle up."

"All right," Irene agreed. "I'll go upstairs for a while."

He gave her a suspicious side glance and said, "No going to sleep."

"Of course not. But I have to change these stockings that you ruined by dragging me through that path."

They went through to the front hall and found it deserted and no one at the switchboard.

Irene glanced up at Ross and murmured, "Easy now, remember your blood pressure."

At the same moment Beatrice stepped back from the front door, where she had been peering out, and, as soon as she saw them, assumed a defensive expression.

"Dr. Munster, that Jean is late every morning, and me sitting overtime, here, while she makes up that thing on the front of her head she calls a face. After this I'm goin' on the stroke of seven, and the switchboard can ring its fool head off till she comes."

"You'll do no such thing!" Ross yelled. "If I find that switchboard sitting by itself again, there'll be trouble."

Beatrice, slightly intimidated, drew her defiance about her and grumbled, "Well, why should I do her work for her? She won't do mine for me."

"All right," Ross conceded, "we'll institute a new system. For every minute either of you is late, the other one gets a percentage of the offender's salary."

"Come again?" said Beatrice, puzzled but courteous.

"He's going to dock Jean for being late, and give you what he docks her," Irene explained.

Beatrice, entirely mollified, said that would do very well.

Ross gave Irene a cold stare, and she said, "Pardon me. But just the same, you should put things more clearly." She started toward the stairs and added, "I'll be down at ten to nine—precisely."

She went on up and found Elise sleeping prettily and soundly in the double bed. She looked relaxed and comfortable, and Irene sighed and went out to the balcony. She found a deck chair there, with a footrest, and she stretched out in it with her arms folded behind her head. Her watch said just seven, and she wondered idly whether Jean had arrived. It was the last thought she had before she drifted into a comfortable sleep.

She awoke sometime later and yawned and stretched comfortably before taking a casual glance at her watch. She was astounded to find that it was nine o'clock, and she was wide awake in an instant. She went into the bedroom, where Elise was still sleeping it off, and after a hasty wash and brush-up, which necessarily included removal of her ruined stockings, she hurried downstairs.

Ross was waiting in the front hall, and he looked up and said sarcastically, "Ten minutes to nine, precisely."

"Well, I had to make up the front of my head, like Jean. I can see why she's always late, now."

Jean looked over the switchboard and declared indignantly, "I am not always late."

"We have it on good authority " Irene began, but Ross caught her by the arm and ran her out the front door.

"Come on—do you think I have all day? Where's your car?"

"Why don't we use yours?"

"Time," he said shortly. "We haven't any."

She climbed in behind the wheel of her car, and he settled himself beside her. He gave her directions for getting into the village and to Marie's shop and then said thoughtfully, "If I'm right, Marie blonded Doris's hair yesterday, and I want you to get all the information you can out of her. Hairdressers dig up a lot of gossip, and probably Marie knows more about Doris, by now, than any of us. You'll have to get it out of her."

"Oh, sure," said Irene. "I'll just ask for Doris's address."

"Don't waste time trying to be funny—you know what I mean. First, of course, you'll have to find out definitely whether she did a blonding job yesterday."

They drew up in front of Marie's shop, and Irene said, "I'll be out again in a minute or two—because hairdressers haven't time to stand and chat; they do their gossiping while they work—but I'll get what I can."

As she entered the shop, Marie emerged from a booth with an expectant smile which changed to polite inquiry when she saw Irene.

"I'd like an appointment," Irene said. "I ran across a girl yesterday who had the loveliest platinum hair, and she said she had it done here yesterday morning."

Marie nodded, her eyes lighting up. "That *was* a good job, wasn't it?"

"Indeed it was. And I should like to have mine just the same."

"So you shall," Marie agreed cheerfully. She squinted critically at Irene's hair and nodded. "Yours should do up quite as well as hers."

"She told me her hair was about the color of mine before it was done?" Irene said tentatively.

"Just about. Now listen, dear, you're in luck. I'll do your hair right now. My customer is late, and I'll just put you in her place."

Irene turned pale and swallowed air, but before she was able to articulate, Marie went on. "There was something sort of queer about that girl, you know. She asked me if any of the patients at the Munster hospital were about to die."

## TWENTY-FOUR

MARIE urged Irene into one of the booths, seated her in the chair, and then turned to draw the curtain with one vigorous motion of her wrist. She draped her in a coverall apron and then tucked a towel about her neck with firm, efficient fingers.

Irene scarcely noticed these preparations. Her mind was busy forming a remark that would bring forth further revelations and yet would sound casual enough. She said at last, "What an odd thing to say—that girl, I mean."

Marie nodded. "I just gaped at her, and she looked me right in the eye and said, 'Well, is there?' I told her I'd heard Dave Cattledge wasn't expected to live, and do you know what she said to that?"

"No! What?" Irene breathed.

But someone entered the shop at that moment, and Marie said, "Pardon me," and went out. It immediately developed that the new arrival was the woman who was late for her appointment, and Irene sensed that Marie was enjoying herself.

"I'm so sorry, Mrs. Downs," she was saying with false courtesy, "but you have missed several appointments with me entirely, so naturally, when this customer came in, I took her."

"But, Marie, my dear," the lady wailed, "I don't miss any appointments now—you know I don't—they're much too hard to get. You *knew* I'd be here—even if I am a little late."

"I'm so sorry, dear, but you were nearly half an hour late when she walked in, so—"

"I'm only twenty minutes late *now.* Marie, you'll just have to sandwich me in."

"I'll make another appointment for you as soon as possible," Marie said, and added musingly, "Now, let's see— how about three weeks from today, same time?"

There was an anguished cry from the customer, who presently departed in dudgeon, slamming the door behind her.

Marie returned to the booth with a cheerful smile stretched across her face.

"Sorry to keep you waiting, dear—but I couldn't pass up a chance to tell her off. Always late for her appointments, sometimes not bothering to keep them at all—and I had to take it. But I don't now. I can't get any help here, and I'm rushed off my feet."

"Don't bleach my hair," Irene said nervously. "Just a shampoo and set."

Marie, with all ten fingers digging into Irene's scalp and a faraway look in her eyes, murmured, "There are one or two other customers who could stand a little booting around, and it'll be a pleasure to give it to them."

Irene asked, "Did that girl, yesterday, ever explain why she was interested in which patients were dying at the hospital?"

"No, she didn't. I was astounded, of course, and after I told her about Dave, I asked her why she wanted to know, but she said she was just curious."

Irene thought it over for a while. "I wonder where she's staying," she said presently, still trying to sound casual. "I met her out on the lake, yesterday afternoon. I admired her hair, and we talked a little—and she said she'd had it done here. But I don't even know her name."

"Jane Wills," Marie said promptly. "She's staying at the hotel."

"Oh." Irene was so lost in intrigue, by this time, that she had no thought for Marie's hands, which were dealing so efficiently with her hair. "That's odd—I'm sure I haven't seen her around the hotel. Have you seen her since she was here?"

"My dear, I haven't. She just walked in, you know, and I was able to give her a canceled appointment. But I work hard all day, and at night I'm so tired I just mostly go to bed."

"Is she married?"

"No, but she's engaged—or anyway, she said so. She didn't have a ring, but that doesn't mean anything—the men are so stingy these days. I know lots of girls who were promised a ring later on and foolishly got married without one—and naturally no man is going to bother buying a diamond ring *after* he's married—at least not for his wife. They haven't the money to spare, after they get through drinking, gambling, and taking other girls out."

"Isn't it the truth?" Irene agreed mournfully.

Marie exhibited her left hand, which was adorned with a diamond solitaire above the wedding ring, and laughed heartily. "I stuck out for it. He wanted me to wait—said he'd get me a ring that would knock my hat right off on our first anniversary but that right now he needed a new suit to get married in. I told him, nothing doing—no ring, no wedding, and I didn't care if he got married in his bathing suit. So I got the ring—and a good one, too, because I went along to choose it—but, believe me, that's the last thing he ever gave me.

The door of the shop opened with a bang, and next instant Ross's stentorian voice yelled, "Marie!"

"Well, forever!" Marie said in mild astonishment, hastily drying her hands. "If it isn't Ross Munster."

She went out to the front of the shop and called laughingly, "What in the world do you want? A shampoo and finger wave?"

There was a short silence, and Irene felt that she could almost hear Ross thinking, then he said hesitantly, "I—er—I was passing—just thought I'd drop in and see you. Are you busy?"

"Sure I'm busy."

Ross walked toward the cubicles and sent a hasty glance into each one until he found Irene.

"Hey!" Marie yelled. "You're not supposed to look in there—I have a customer. Get outa there."

"Hello, Miss Hastings," Ross said loudly. "What are you doing here? Marie fixing you up?" At the same time he exhibited his watch and raised his eyebrows in an inquiring manner.

"In about an hour," Irene whispered.

Ross nodded and muttered, "I'll come back."

Marie had come up behind him, still protesting. "I never heard of such a thing—spying on a lady when she's sitting under an apron with her hair all over the place. You take yourself out, Ross Munster."

"I always did want to see what went on behind the front of a beauty parlor," he said mildly.

"Well, now you've seen, and probably lost me a customer, so beat it."

Ross departed, wondering impatiently why Irene should have wasted time over a shampoo, or whatever it was, when she could just as well have made a future appointment, pumped Marie a little, and come right out again. But women were forever messing around with their hair. In Irene's case it was a pity, because her hair was nice the way it was—and now, probably, she'd come walking out with swirls and curls all over her head, like her mother.

When he arrived back at the hospital he found that John was up and going about his daily work. He looked much better, but as soon as he saw Ross he said fretfully, "Myrtle is sleeping. Do you think I should wake her? It's going on for ten—I've never known her to do such a thing."

"Leave her alone," Ross said easily. "We'll struggle along somehow. She didn't get much rest last night. I didn't get much myself, as a matter of fact." He yawned and rumpled his hair. "Sit down for a minute, will you, John—I want to talk to you."

John sat down with an eager light in his eye. Now, he thought, Ross would tell him about Horace and the will—he hadn't wanted to mention it himself, hadn't wanted to sound greedy. But if Ross had found the will and was about to tell him so—

"John," Ross said soberly, "where did you see the body of my father last night?"

"In the summerhouse," John said quickly, and with an uneasy feeling that something was wrong.

Ross frowned. "He wasn't in the summerhouse—I looked. And he—isn't in the coffin. Do you know anything more about it?"

John's face began to look pinched, and Ross drew a quick, impatient little sigh. The old boy had seemed so much better this morning, he thought, and now he looked as though he might start his prowling and fainting all over again.

"John," he said sharply, "I know you've had something on your mind for some time—for God's sake tell me what it is, so that you and I can get together and clear the thing up. This way, we're both groping in the dark. I know that something's going on around here, but I don't know what it is. However, it's pretty serious when a patient is taken from his bed and dragged downstairs—and subsequently dies."

John had heard that Mr. Herms had died during the night, but nothing more. Yet, when Ross gave him the whole story, he was conscious only of a dull sort of apathy. Yesterday he had been frightened—now, somehow, he did not care so much. Perhaps Horace *was* still alive, and his head had been in shadow, there in the summerhouse—no, it wasn't a shadow—but anyway, it didn't matter. He got to his feet, murmuring that he was busy and would have to go.

"But wait a minute," Ross protested. "You haven't told me anything."

John shook his head stubbornly and moved away. "I don't know anything. I saw him lying in the summerhouse, as I told you—and if he was not there later, someone must have dragged him away."

Ross swore softly and went on about his own work. Two patients had left, carried off by politely noncommittal relatives, and he realized that rumor was already going the rounds. His father had built up the hospital, and he hated to think of it being destroyed. He determined to fight hard to save it—and in the meantime he shrugged away any worry about it. If it went in spite of all he could do, he'd have a much-needed vacation and start over again.

When he left to go back to Marie's, he was a little late, but when he parked outside the shop, there was no sign of Irene. He lit a cigarette, slumped down in the seat, and prepared to wait.

The village was somnolent under a blanket of heat, and Ross drowsed with half-closed eyes until a solitary promenader approached with lagging footsteps. Ross glanced up and then opened his eyes wide.

It was Clark, looking both shabby and depressed.

## TWENTY-FIVE

ROSS leaned out of the car and called peremptorily, "Clark!"

Clark jerked his head up in a startled fashion, and then his face relaxed into a half-smile. "Oh—hello, Ross. I was just going to wander up your way and see if the tent is still unoccupied."

He was completely disarming, as always, and after a silent moment of exasperation, Ross asked flatly, "Where's your bag?"

"I left it at the station—didn't want to lug it all the way out."

"You'd better get in," Ross said, opening the door of the car.

Clark climbed into the back seat and, leaning against the cushion, began to mop at his damp face.

Ross turned around and looked him in the eye. "Now, what about that girl—where is she?"

"She skipped. I suppose she was just using me to get away. She disappeared as soon as we got to Chicago—must have had a friend there. Anyway, I was subsequently surrounded by coppers, all demanding that I produce her. In the end, I managed to convince them that I was only an innocent bystander, and they let me go—so I came back here. I'm sorry about it, Ross—all the trouble I must have caused you—but I really loved that girl. Still do, as a matter of fact—but I'll have to get over it. I couldn't believe there was anything really the matter with her when they put her away—I thought someone was railroading her, and that's why I helped her to escape."

"All right," Ross said abruptly, "forget it. There's plenty to do out at the hospital, and I'll be needing your help."

Clark nodded and declared earnestly, "I want to help— I'll do anything I can. Fact is, I was thinking of earning my living with you and taking a medical course at the same time. Might as well be handing out pills to dopes with a bellyache as anything else."

"What sort of a doctor do you expect to be, when you go into it with an attitude like that?" Ross said coldly. "You should have a real interest in it and—"

"Well, blast my poor old eyes!" Clark interrupted in a refreshed tone and sitting up straighter. "Look at that fancy dish coming out of Marie's!"

Ross turned and beheld a girl with a cloud of silvery, sunlit hair and a face that was marred by a dark scowl. She crossed the sidewalk to the car, stuck her head through the open window, and spat at him, "I hope you're satisfied now, with your crazy ideas. Look what's happened to me! It'll take a year to grow out, and it cost me a fortune."

Ross got out of the car, shaken with helpless laughter. When he could speak, he said soothingly, "It looks lovely—really. I don't see why you want to let it grow out at all— you should keep it like that."

"You're just trying to get out of paying for it," Irene said wildly. "I didn't know she was doing it—we were talking—and then it was all done. I told her not to—right in the beginning "

"Stop worrying," Ross said, still laughing. "It's gorgeous. But if you want it changed back again, I'll pay for that and this session as well."

Irene got into the front seat of the car and dropped her head against the back. She felt a bit better now, but the shock had been terrific—and all she had been able to think of was that she looked exactly like Elise's daughter.

Ross indicated Clark, in the back seat, but Irene merely sent him one fierce glance and turned away again. When Ross had got the car going, however, she leaned close to him and whispered, "What's he doing here? Why has he come back?" Ross shrugged, and she added, "You'd better drive around to the hotel and see if Jane Wills is registered there. That's the name she had her hair blonded under."

Ross nodded and swung the car around, and after a moment Irene murmured, "I wonder you let him come back. What's his story?"

"She ditched him in Chicago, and now he's going back to the tent to build a new life for himself."

"Did you tell him that she's hanging around the hospital?"

"I've no intention of telling him anything," Ross said shortly.

Irene took a small mirror from her purse and gazed at her hair from various angles, while she told him everything that she had learned from Marie.

He digested it in silence, and when they arrived at the hotel he went in, and was not surprised when it developed that no Jane Wills was registered there. He returned to the car, to find Irene twisted around in her seat, talking to Clark.

''Yes—but where did you first meet Doris?"

"I've told you—at a canteen, when I was in the army. She was one of the hostesses."

"All right—but the canteen must have been in a city or town or village or on a plain or something."

"No doubt," Clark agreed imperturbably, "but I have been in so many cities, towns, and villages, and on so many plains, that I have no idea where this particular one was located."

They drove to the station and picked up Clark's bag, and Ross, glancing at his watch, swore grimly.

"I should have been back half an hour ago. John's not much good just now—something on his mind—and whatever it is, it has him running around in circles." He glanced into the little mirror above his head, for a cautious look at Clark's face, reflected from the back seat. But Clark merely looked hot and uninterested and, after stifling a yawn, said idly, "The old boy has to carry a worry around with him, or he'd be lonely. Never had a real problem in his life, and yet he's fretted himself gray-haired." He laughed and mopped at his damp face again, and Irene compressed her lips. She reflected that if John did a little less worrying and Clark a little more, they'd both be better off.

Ross was wondering whether he ought to tell Clark that his brother's tomb had been violated, and decided at last, for no particular reason, to let him find it out for himself. But Clark should be able to help them find the Miller girl—he'd be better able to recognize her than any of them, no matter what color her hair was. She ought to be found without delay, or God knows what would happen. Evidently a dead body had some sort of morbid fascination for her—probably she had thought poor old Bob Herms was dead when she dragged him out of his bed. And she had the body of his father hidden somewhere.

A line appeared between his eyebrows, and he remembered that he had not checked up on his father's embalming. Well, he wouldn't bother; Myrtle's theory was ridiculous. He put his foot down on the gas and swung into the driveway with gravel spitting out from the wheels.

"I wish I had a hat to cover me," Irene moaned as she descended from the car.

"But—er—why did you have it done?" Clark asked, grinning amiably.

"It was an accident," Irene said shortly.

Ross hurried into the front hall and immediately asked Jean where Joe and Ed could be located.

She shook her head. "I don't know, Dr. Munster—but they want you upstairs, right away. Mr. Cattledge, I think."

Ross mounted, two steps at a time, and ran into Myrtle in the upstairs hall.

"So here you are at last!" she exclaimed, and added, in answer to his inquiring look, "Old Dave's all right—still with us. His relatives have pulled out their handkerchiefs so often, and had to put them away again, that they're mad at everybody—including Dave. He must have the constitution of a bull."

Ross said, "Good!" rather absently, and asked, "Where are Joe and Ed?"

"I don't know—catching up on their sleep, probably. But listen, Ross—John says your father's body was out in the summerhouse and that it—it had no head."

"Oh God!" Ross muttered. "Do you mean he's repeating all that lurid stuff he was gabbling about when we were trying to get him quiet last night? About the body having no head, and that we were to look in the pockets of the clothing for something."

Myrtle sighed. "He was talking about it quite sensibly this morning—I mean, he seemed perfectly normal. Said he had remembered, quite suddenly, that Horace had told him there would be something of interest to him in one of the pockets of his clothing. And John declares he saw the body in the summerhouse—and that it had no head." She sighed again. "I think he's mistaken about that, though—perhaps the head was in shadow. Anyway, I believe that Horace is still alive."

"Oh, talk sense," Ross said crossly. "You know perfectly well that the old man was always a big noise. He couldn't possibly have lived in that tomb all this time so quietly that none of us knew it."

Myrtle shrugged and said presently, in a different tone of voice, "Ross—three more patients have left. It looks bad."

They were interrupted by Clark, who came up the stairs and advanced on Ross with an almost timid expression. Myrtle exclaimed in surprise at sight of him, and he gave her an engaging grin before turning back to Ross.

"Look—could you lend me five? I think Doris is around here somewhere—and I think I know where to look for her. I'll get her and take her back to the hospital for you."

# TWENTY-SIX

In spite of her shrewd knowledge of him, Myrtle had a soft spot for Clark—a reflection of John's feeling for him. She did not allow it to betray her into lending him any money—and John would not have parted with a nickel for the Angel Gabriel, so that it was always Ross, like his father before him, who kept the wolf from Clark's various doors.

While Myrtle fluttered a little, with suggestions of food for the wanderer, Ross asked sourly, "What do you want money for now?"

"To buy gasoline."

Ross frowned. "I thought your car was out of commission?"

"It is—but surely one of the ladies would lend me a car. I'm certain they wouldn't mind, but of course I'd like to have some gasoline in it when I'm through. Always the gentleman, you know."

"Come and have something to eat," Myrtle interposed.

"Let him wait," Ross said impatiently, and asked Clark, "Where are you going to look for the girl?"

Clark's face closed up, and he said distantly, "I'd rather not say."

"No—of course you'd rather not say, because you have no idea where the girl is, and you want the five so that you can go and ask Irene out for a date."

Clark denied to high heaven, while Myrtle laughed heartily.

"Pretty tough," she said, wiping her eyes. "Borrowing five dollars from a fellow to take the fellow's girl out."

Clark shot a glance at Ross and asked in mild surprise, "You interested in that girl?"

"Damn it! No!" Ross yelled. "Myrtle and that woman are always stuffing her down my throat, and I'm getting sick and tired of it. But I'm not lending you any money for anything—and that's final."

Clark said, "O.K.," and turned away, and Ross called after him, "If you have any idea where that girl is, it's your duty to tell us. The hospital has lost several patients already, and if it goes on, we may be ruined."

Clark stopped and turned around, his eyes evasive and an embarrassed expression on his face.

"Look, Ross," he said uneasily, "if you'd just let me go—You can't go, anyway—and I'll get her for you— I'm nearly sure of it."

Ross set his jaw. "She's around here somewhere—no matter what Ed and Joe may think—and you'd better get out to your tent and try and contact her there. She's been inside the hospital, and she flits around the grounds as well."

Clark shrugged and started slowly toward the stairs. "I don't see how she could be around here right now," he called back. "What with Joe and Ed beating through the bush, and everyone else looking for her."

He went on down the stairs, and Ross turned away, feeling far from satisfied. He had a nagging idea that Clark knew exactly where the girl was but would not tell for reasons of his own. Anyway, there was no use worrying about it. He shook it away from him and followed Myrtle into one of the rooms.

Irene had gone up to the communal bedroom, where she found Elise lingering over a prolonged toilette. Elise glanced up and immediately screamed, "Darling! How simply too wonderful! Really marvelous! But why didn't you tell me you were going to have it done, and I'd have come along and supervised?"

"I couldn't tell anyone," Irene said, beginning to divest herself of her dress, "because nobody told me. I was as surprised as you are." She flung the dress over the back of a chair, kicked off her shoes, and crawled into the unmade bed. She turned over, shut her eyes, and muttered, "Wake me up for lunch."

Elise, who had been all ready for a lengthy chat, clicked her tongue in annoyance and turned back to the mirror. She was encased in the severe, perfect lines of a simple white dress and wore a heavy brooch of silver and amethysts on the left shoulder and a huge amethyst and silver ring on her slender, beautifully groomed hand. She patted her hair, cocked her head to left and right, and at last tore herself away from the mirror and tripped lightly downstairs.

She met up with Myrtle, on the second floor, and Myrtle told her about Clark's return.

"But my dear Miss Warner, are you telling me that he is walking about a free man? Why isn't he in jail?"

"Why should he be?" Myrtle demanded, antagonized.

"He helped at the escape of a lunatic, didn't he? Isn't that a criminal offense?"

Myrtle didn't know whether it was or not, so she changed the subject.

"I have a little time this morning—we've lost some patients—so come on to my room, and we'll sit down and have a cigarette."

Elise, who had nothing whatever to do, hesitated as a matter of course and then brightened. "Why, yes—I believe I can manage. Delightful."

They went to Myrtle's room, which was at the end of the second-floor corridor, and Elise sent a critical eye around the small, pleasant little apartment. She began almost at once to tell Myrtle how the furniture should be rearranged and what was wrong with the drapes and bedspread. Myrtle replied stiffly that their tastes were no doubt different, but Elise brushed it away impatiently. There was a right way, and there were many wrong ways, of furnishing a room. Some latitude might be allowed in the matter of pattern, color, and material, but that was all. Myrtle's room was wrong, and Elise could show her, very simply, how it could be made right.

She fingered one of the drapes at the window, frowning thoughtfully and pursing her lips, and Myrtle said sharply, "Leave the curtains be. I like them, and since I'm the one who has to sleep with them, that's all that matters."

Elise flicked the length of chintz away from her and delicately dusted her hands. People were so wrong-headed, she thought tolerantly—but what could you do? If they wished to pass their lives among antipathetic colors and haphazard, badly arranged furniture, in the face of superior and freely given knowledge, there was nothing to be done about it. She gazed idly out of the window, which overlooked the curving drive in front, and, picking out her own car, wondered whether she could get someone to wash and polish it for her. Her eyes suddenly became fixed and more attentive, as it seemed to her that the car was moving—and the next instant it shot down the driveway and disappeared onto the main road.

Elise let out a yell. "My car! Someone has stolen my car! I just saw it go!"

"Who was in it?" Myrtle asked, and was immediately requested not to be a fool.

"How could I possibly tell from up here, looking only at the back of it?"

"You probably left your keys in it," Myrtle said severely, "so it serves you right. Anyway, I expect it was only Irene."

"It was not Irene—she's upstairs, sleeping. As for my keys, I always leave them in the car, because otherwise I'd lose them."

"Oh, sure," Myrtle said heartily. "Much better to lose the whole car."

Elise closed her eyes and pressed her fingers against the lids, then she opened them very wide and looked at Myrtle.

"You think you are being sarcastic—but as a matter of fact, it is better to lose my car, which is insured, rather than my keys, which are not."

Myrtle shrugged. "O.K., pal, just as you say. But come on—I have a few things to do before lunch, and you might as well come with me. Be good for your figure."

Elise's eyes gleamed from narrowed lids, and Myrtle added hastily,

"Keep it slim, the way it is."

Elise left the room and went on downstairs to the front hall, where she inquired of Jean if anyone had just gone out.

"Well, yes, ma'am," Jean said vaguely. "Several people have sort of been going and coming."

"But who in particular?" Elise asked.

"Oh, no one in particular, Mrs. De Petro," Jean replied, with an obliging desire to be helpful.

Elise frowned in annoyance and went out the front door with briskly tapping heels. She walked along the driveway to where her car had been parked but, after a certain amount of peering, was unable to find a clue of any sort. She remembered, then, that the police were about the place somewhere, and decided to put the case in their hands. She walked around to the back of the house and saw two men standing by the barn, but as she approached them they moved off in the direction of the summerhouse.

Elise followed slowly, picking her way carefully through the matted undergrowth, and she had almost reached the summerhouse when she felt her stockings go. She cursed freely but quietly and bent to examine them. One was ruined, but she thought the other might be saved, and she had started to swear again when her eye fell upon an envelope lying half hidden in the rioting weeds. She picked it up and looked it over curiously.

She could feel that there was something inside, but the envelope was sealed with red wax. On the front, in a neat, flowing hand, was inscribed, "Instructions for finding the last will and testament of Horace Munster, M.D."

## TWENTY-SEVEN

ELISE examined the envelope, turning it over curiously in her hands. It was somewhat weather-beaten, but apparently it had not been lying out in the open for any great length of time. She started to rip the flap and then hesitated, glancing at the two men, who were only a short distance away from her. She decided to wait until she was alone, and reflected irritably that policemen were never there when you wanted them but were very apt to be interfering at your elbow if you did not.

She slipped the envelope down the neck of her dress and then picked her way daintily through the summerhouse and out across the lawn. She threw a nervous glance at the mausoleum and had a mental picture of Horace, piously reposing inside with his hands folded, which made her shiver. Had she known that the place contained only his empty coffin, she would have abandoned all intrigue and left for the city on the spot.

She knew that the hospital belonged to Ross, and she wondered, with a little quiver of excitement, if this will left it to someone else. Or perhaps there was a pile of money hidden somewhere for Ross, and Irene would be a rich man's wife—which would be very satisfactory. Irene, she thought, might as well marry this Ross—in fact, she'd better. The other two that hung around her had no money at all—and they'd be back soon, too. Better hurry the thing along.

Elise stubbed her toe on a stone at this point, and so forgot Irene and Ross for the time being. She limped through the kitchen, where she gave Rowena a gracious bow and a smile. She received a rather awed acknowledgment and went her way with a complacent reflection that no one knew better how to do these things than herself. You simply, for the moment, thought of yourself as being a queen, and the people around you sensed it and automatically extended homage.

She went up the back stairs to save time and found Irene still sleeping peacefully in the double bed. She did not disturb her, but seated herself quietly in a chair and, without further delay, ripped open the envelope.

A single typewritten sheet said:

DEAR JOHN,

*I have hidden that will in my room for safekeeping. You should be able to find it, if you exercise a little ingenuity. Sincerely,*

HORACE

Elise wrinkled her nose in disappointment. Nothing exciting about that. Probably the will to which this Horace referred had been found long ago. Or perhaps it hadn't, since the letter was sealed. Elise pursed her lips and examined the envelope again. Had someone thrown it away deliberately? No, of course not—much safer to destroy it, if someone had wanted to get rid of it. She shrugged her shoulders and flipped at the letter with a polished fingernail until it occurred to her that she ought really to deliver it to John, since it was addressed to him. She got up and walked across the hall to John's room, where she rapped smartly on the door.

John was knotting his tie. He felt much better and had decided to do his work conscientiously and forget all about Horace. It was absurd for them to say that Horace was missing. He started to laugh and hastily swallowed it as Elise's knock sounded on the door. He gave his tie a final pat, squared his shoulders, and called, "Come in."

Elise opened the door and stuck her head prettily around the edge, while she held the letter out to him.

"Doctor, I'm so sorry—so stupid of me—I seem to have opened this by mistake."

John took the envelope and felt the blood suddenly burning in his face. He extracted the letter with shaking hands and read it twice—once so fast that his confused senses could not take it in, and again, very slowly and carefully.

So that was it. The will was right there in Ross's room, and Horace, with his monstrous sense of humor, knew that John would have the utmost difficulty in making any sort of a search there. Probably he had amused himself by imagining John waiting his opportunity, as the years went by, to slip into Ross's room when Ross was not there. Only he was wrong, this time, as it happened—because John intended to show Ross that letter, and the search would be made openly. Ross would never destroy the will if he found it when he was alone—the boy was honest to the core. He felt anger surging in him that Horace could have supposed he was such a fool.

Elise had been watching him curiously, and she asked now, "Is this a new will?"

John became aware of her with sudden embarrassment and stammered, "I—er—I believe so."

Elise's interest revived. "But how exciting! We must look for it at once. Which room does he mean?"

John became purposely a little vague and nodded in the general direction of Ross's room. "But it is lunch time, and we must not be late. May I escort you down?"

Elise protested that lunch did not matter, the will should be found, but John shook his head gravely. "I'm convinced that it will take some time. He gives us no hint as to where it is, and we shall simply have to start a systematic, methodical search."

He urged her toward the stairs with a hand on her arm, but she remembered Irene and detoured into Ross's room to get her. John felt that he was bound to wait, after offering to escort Elise, so he paced the hall, looking at his watch every five seconds and quietly fuming, while Irene leisurely dressed herself. In due course Elise galloped out into the hall again and gave a little shriek when she saw him. "Are you still here? Why, you dear, patient soul—how sweet of you. Now we can all go down together."

John stiffened. What sort of masculine manners was the woman accustomed to? He had said he would escort her—

His eye fell on Irene, and he froze to the spot. "That woman! These women!" he thought wildly. He had always taken such care that no breath of scandal or even vulgarity should touch the hospital, and now this creature was running around with bleached hair—and sleeping in Ross's bedroom. He would have dismissed any nurse who flaunted hair like that, but what could he do with this brazen girl? It was out of his hands.

Irene smiled at him. "Just don't look at it, Dr. Girsted. It was all a mistake, and I'm going to have it restored to the original color as soon as possible. In the meantime, we might as well have lunch."

"But, darling," Elise protested, "why not leave it? I think it's chic. You could at least try it for a few weeks to see how you like it."

Irene made no reply, and John shuddered.

There was no one in the dining room when they got there, which was a relief to John, who hated to be caught coming in late. He was holding Elise's chair for her, when Myrtle and Ross walked in with a pair of distinctly gloomy expressions.

"We can all put our feet up and take it easy," Ross announced. "We've so few patients left that we might as well reduce the staff."

John went pale. "No, no, Ross—don't do that. It will die down—I'm sure we can weather it."

Myrtle laughed. "For heaven's sake, don't start worrying, John. Ross is exaggerating—we're not going to fire anyone. Anyway, we all need a rest."

John began to fumble in his pocket, with agitated fingers, for Horace's letter. If only the will could be found, he'd be head of the place, and then he'd take charge and bring the hospital through this trouble. And first and foremost he'd put those two women out.

Clark lounged into the room, and John forgot the letter and sprang to his feet. "Clark! My dear boy! I didn't know you were back."

Elise demanded shrilly, "Did you go off in my car? Without my permission?"

Clark said, "Just for a short ride. I didn't hurt it." He saw that there was no place set for him and went leisurely through to the kitchen.

Myrtle called after him, "She's forgotten my napkin—bring me one, will you?" and let him go, because she knew that he had an uncanny talent for getting on well with the help. He reappeared shortly with her napkin, an assortment of cutlery, and a sandwich for himself, and sat down at the table, looking sleepy.

"Clark," Ross said at once, "what did you mean by that silly message you left in Irene's car? About a headless nurse."

Clark began to arrange his cutlery with meticulous care, but he made no reply. He looked uncomfortable and decidedly less sleepy.

"Well," Ross asked sharply, "were you trying to scare someone, or were you merely drunk?"

"I was not drunk," Clark said with sudden heat, "and I saw it quite clearly. She—she was on the lawn, up near that damned morgue of Horace's, and she was just standing there. And I tell you, she had no head."

"Perfectly plausible," Ross said grimly. "No doubt she opened the door to Father's tomb and went in."

There was a heavy silence, while Clark stared across the table with the color draining out of his face, and at last he muttered hoarsely, "How did you know?"

## TWENTY-EIGHT

CLARK pushed back his chair and flung out of the room, and after a moment Ross stood up and followed him. In the back hall he caught him by the arm and said, "For God's sake, Clark, snap out of it—we've had enough trouble with John without you bringing up all this childish nonsense."

Clark wrenched his arm free and muttered furiously, "Leave me alone. I know what I saw."

He went off without a backward glance, and Ross frowned after him for a while and then went slowly back to the dining room. Everyone looked at him expectantly, which antagonized him, so that he resumed his luncheon in silence.

"Well!" Elise exclaimed on an expelled breath. "I hope he hasn't gone off in my car again—in that mood."

"Why did you let him have it?" Ross asked crossly.

"She can't help herself," Myrtle explained. "She has to leave the keys in the car so that she won't lose them."

John, eating slowly and chewing well, was conscious of the conversation about him only as a vague annoyance. His mind was nibbling at Horace again. Did Ross and Clark know that Horace had lost his head? And where was Horace now? Ross had not told him. Better not mention it in front of the women—he could ask Ross later.

"Ross," Myrtle said suddenly, "have you seen Joe and Ed?"

Ross shook his head sourly.

"Then you don't know whether they found Horace or not?"

"Horace," Elise said thoughtfully. "Now, who is Horace? I seem to have forgotten."

John choked and laid down his fork, and Ross glanced up at him. "John, could you take over this afternoon? It's not so heavy now, and I simply must get out and clear up this trouble. That insane girl is running around loose somewhere, and my father's body has disappeared. I want to see what I can do."

Myrtle observed in a low, firm voice, "Horace is living."

John's face was almost green. "Oh no, Myrtle—no, no. He—he has no head. I saw him."

Elise rose up out of her chair and gave a highly cultured little scream.

"I shall have to leave. I cannot stand it."

"Any time you like, Mrs. De Petro," Ross said amiably. "You could start your packing after lunch. I haven't said anything, but as a matter of fact, we're a little crowded up in that bedroom."

Elise dropped back into her chair, looking thoroughly offended. "Very well. But you understand, of course, that I shall take Irene with me."

"Don't worry, Ross," Myrtle said heartily, "the girl has a mind of her own. She won't go."

Ross looked straight into Myrtle's face and said levelly, "Shut up!"

Irene finished her lunch, at this point, and folded her napkin, because she was not sure whether they were the same napkins for several meals or a clean one each time.

"Come on," she said to Ross, "I'll drive you wherever you want to go. You'll have to work fast if you're going to clear this mess up in an afternoon—and there are several unexplored territories that we might cover."

"Irene has one very valuable quality," Elise murmured admiringly. "She remains calm and unaffected in the face of gibes and sneers."

Ross nodded at Irene and said, "Thanks. I can use some help."

Elise and Myrtle tittered, and John, who didn't know what they were all talking about, said gravely, "May I have a word with you in private, Ross?"

Ross put down his napkin in a resigned fashion and stood up, and he and John went into the back hall. John produced Horace's letter, as found by Elise, and waited in silence.

"But what will is he talking about ?" Ross asked presently, in a puzzled voice. "You remember he always said he was not going to make a will. Said the stuff would come to me as a matter of course and why bother."

"Yes," John said quietly.

Ross raised his head and looked at him. "Come on, John—what is it? I can see that you know something about it. Did he ever say anything to you about making a will?"

John's reserve broke and he poured out the whole story. Horace had promised him the place and then, as Ross grew up, repented of the promise, but kept to the letter of it by making a will that he hoped would never be found.

Ross was considerably affected. He knew that John would never lie or even exaggerate about a thing of that sort, and after a moment he said, "You should have told me— there's no need to find the will. I wish you had told me earlier. The place evidently ought to belong to you, and I'll arrange it as soon as possible. Let's go back and finish eating."

Ross returned to the dining room, and John stood and watched him go with his head in a whirl. He was willing to relinquish the hospital, just as easily as that, after all the years of secret worry.

But Ross was rather floored himself, although he had tried not to show it. The thing had to be done, of course—his entire heritage. He was uncomfortably aware that this was just like one of his father's tricks—to go on deviling people even after he was dead.

John must have the hospital, Ross decided, and he would get out—perhaps try the city. He'd never been anywhere else, except for his army experience, and the city intrigued him. He was slightly deflated to discover that handing over the hospital to John was not entirely noble unselfishness; it meant also burning his bridges so that he could do as he liked.

He returned to the luncheon table where Myrtle and Elise were having a hot argument about woman's place not being in the home. They both appeared to be on the same side, but for different reasons, and each was striving to air her opinions.

Ross said, "God Almighty!" and slid into his seat.

"What are you going to do first?" Irene shouted at him through the din.

"Find Joe and Ed," he yelled back.

Irene shook her head. "Waste of time. If they had anything to report, they'd have come bounding in with it. Let them go on turning over stones in peace."

Ross shrugged. "What do you suggest, then?"

"Phone the state hospital and find out what you can about that girl. Tell them you have reason to think she may be around here somewhere, and get all the information you can about her—because it's much easier to find someone when you know which way she's likely to turn."

"All right," Ross said, "but Clark should know all that."

"Certainly he knows all that, but he isn't telling."

Myrtle turned to them and asked worriedly, "What's the *matter* with Clark?" She appeared to be quite unconscious that she had interrupted one of Elise's most elaborate reasons for the necessity of bringing woman out of the kitchen.

Ross rumpled his hair fretfully and said he didn't know what was biting Uncle Clark and didn't care. "But you get together with John and take care of things this afternoon—because I'm going to find that girl."

Myrtle belched politely into her napkin and said cheerfully, "O.K.—where is John?"

"He was out in the back hall when I last saw him. Perhaps he's still there."

They found him there when they left the dining room in a body, and although he was still a bit dazed, he assured Ross that he would see to everything during the afternoon.

Ross nodded and took Irene's arm, and the two of them went off to his private office. He phoned the state hospital, who obligingly offered to send Dr. Babcock down again, since he was thoroughly familiar with the case. They put Dr. Babcock on, and Ross talked to him for some time; but although Irene listened carefully—at least to Ross's end of the conversation—she was unable to make head or tail of it.

When he hung up at last, she asked impatiently, "What was that all about?"

Ross looked at her vaguely and then broke into a grin. "Stripped of the medical technicalities—which impressed you, I hope—it all boils down to this. Doris is a nut, and when she was picked up at the hospital where she was a student nurse, it was largely because she had taken to spending most of her time down in the morgue, playing around happily with the stiffs. There's no doubt that it was she who dragged old Bob Herms downstairs."

There was a knock on the door, and John fussed into the room.

"Ross, I want to find that will. I can't allow you to do anything without the will—it would not be right. I simply cannot rest until it is found."

Ross stood up and said resignedly, "All right—come on —we'll go up and find it now." He glanced at Irene. "You wait here. I'll be back in about fifteen minutes, and then we'll go out."

Irene stretched out on the couch and promptly went to sleep—which was just as well, because Ross did not return for over two hours. He spent the time alternately cursing and searching, because Horace had hidden the will very effectively—in fact, it was finally located behind the wallpaper.

John had gone down to see one of the patients, but he came back in time to read the will—and found that Horace had double-crossed him again.

The hospital was left to Ross, provided that within two months it was still successful. But if Ross had run it down to a certain number of patients, it reverted to Clark—with the provision that John was to take charge without interference from Clark. Clark's interest would be purely financial.

## TWENTY-NINE

ROSS looked at the names of the two witnesses to the will and vaguely recalled them as a former patient and her brother who had since moved to Canada. Horace would have selected them, of course, because he knew that they were leaving the country and therefore would not be apt to upset his plans.

John, looking stricken and old, was silent, and Ross glanced at him uncomfortably.

"Listen, John," he said presently. "I think the old man had gone a bit whacky when he made this will—it's absurd. We'll just keep the place going until the two months' period is up, and then I'll sell it to you for a nominal fee."

John raised his hand in a gesture of protest, and Ross added quickly, "It's no great sacrifice on my part—I'm tired of the place, anyway, and I want to try the city. I've remembered several things my father said, now, that indicated his intention of leaving the hospital to you. So you take over, this afternoon, while I try and clear away the cause for the loss of our patients."

He gripped John's arm for a moment and then went off, leaving John still speechless and clutching the will in a shaking hand.

Clark had seen that will at some time, Ross reflected, and their recent troubles were the result of his efforts to reduce the census of the hospital to the required minimum. He must have gone off and left that wretched girl with instructions which she had not the wit or will to carry out.

Probably she had been told to act the part of the headless nurse in some manner—as an extension to Clark's written message that he had seen the headless nurse. And instead of that she appeared from time to time with her head gleaming and adorned with platinum blonde hair.

Ross remembered John's repeated assertions that Horace's body was headless, and wondered, frowning, if the girl could have done a thing like that. Anyway, she'd have to be found—and his father's body, as well.

He must find Clark, Ross decided, and try again to drag out of him what he knew. He went downstairs and out through the front lobby, ignoring Jean, who raised her voice and called to him. He had a vague idea that Clark must have gone into hiding and was therefore mildly astonished to find him in plain view, smoking a cigar that appeared to have size without too much quality and seated on the running board of Elise's car.

Ross went up to him and said bluntly, "We found that will."

Clark gave him a quick sidelong look, puffed on the cigar, and said nothing.

"Of course you knew about it?"

Clark shrugged and flicked ash onto the grass.

"So you turned that girl loose around here and hoped that she'd scare the patients away."

Clark looked up through narrowed eyes. "I love that girl. I don't believe she's insane, and I intend to marry her as soon as it's possible."

"Where is she?" Ross asked sharply.

"I don't know—and I wouldn't tell you if I did." He began to puff on the cigar furiously, and Ross backed away from the smoke, which carried a blend of fertilizer and old rope. He made a rude comment, and Clark said sulkily, "They're all I can afford."

Elise came up presently and informed Ross that she had been looking for him. "I want to drive into the village, and this man refuses to get off my running board."

Clark spoke through his clenched teeth. "I wish you'd both go away—do you hear? I'm trying to think where Doris could be, and if you'd leave me alone, I believe I could figure it out. You can come with me to get her, if you like—I'll give her up—I suppose it's the best way— but you'll have to leave me alone while I think about it."

"You see?" Elise cried indignantly. "He just won't budge. And anyway, I object to his smoking that filthy weed there. My car has been carefully scented with sachet on the inside, and then he comes and smokes all over it with a cigar that smells as though it had been washed up out of a sewer."

Clark's face had darkened, and the veins began to stand out on his forehead. His mouth twitched oddly, and Ross, after a glance at him, took Elise by the arm and led her away.

"Leave him alone—as requested," he said when they were out of earshot. "He has an attack of the vapors, and he was getting ready to scream—which would have been unbecoming to a man and an uncle of mine. Just let him stew alone until he works his way out of it—or asphyxiates himself with that cigar."

"But that's absurd," Elise protested, "giving way to him like that. After all, it's my car. Suppose I got the sulks and went and sat on your operating table and wouldn't get off when you wanted to use it. You wouldn't just tell them to wheel the patient downstairs again and wait until I got over it, now would you?"

"Sure," said Ross absently. "I'd carve you, instead of the patient."

Elise went into peals of laughter, but Ross was still thinking of Clark. He was under a strain, and a bad one, and perhaps the thing to do was to go back and needle him until he broke out into screaming hysterics. Probably it would all come out then—where the girl was hiding, and what she had done with Horace's body, which she quite obviously had been hauling around. The body should be back in its tomb and the girl back in the asylum—and, even more important, Clark should be straightened out. He ought to have some work of his own in which he was interested, Ross thought with a sigh—something to keep his mind occupied, so that he wouldn't be resorting to underhand tricks in an effort to make an easy living out of someone else's property. He half turned to go back to Elise's car and then stopped. No—better, perhaps, to find the girl and put her away, and that should be the end of it.

Elise had wandered off into one of the flower beds and was picking a bouquet. This was strictly forbidden by Mac, the sometime gardener, to all except a favored few, but Ross decided that Elise could handle any row which was likely to blow up. He had started for the house, when a car turned in at the driveway and presently disgorged Joe, Ed, and a man whom they introduced to Ross as Lieutenant Domer, from the city. The lieutenant was slick, and Joe and Ed looked somewhat provincial beside him and were not a little nervous.

Ross led them inside with more haste than ceremony, since he did not want them to see Clark. He took them straight to his office, and immediately felt himself blushing all over. Irene was still sleeping on the couch, her silvery hair spread over the pillow and her slim brown legs exposed to some inches above the knees, to which point her navy linen dress had retired during her restless nap. Lieutenant Domer whistled, and Irene woke up. She blinked, yawned, and said lazily, "Oh. I thought you were coming back in fifteen minutes."

Joe and Ed grinned, and Ross blushed again. He said formally, "This is Lieutenant Domer from the city, Irene. I presume he's come down to help Joe and Ed."

"No," said Domer. "I came down to get Miss Miller and return her to the hospital."

Irene adjusted her skirt and said courteously, "I don't believe she's around here just now."

Lieutenant Domer cleared his throat and said, "If you don't mind, Miss Irene, I'd like to talk this matter over privately with these three gentlemen."

Irene got to her feet and shrugged her gleaming hair away from her face. "Of course. But it seems to me that if you'd talk less and act more, you might get somewhere."

She departed, looking offended, and wandered through the front hall. Jean was engaged in conversation on the telephone, and there was no one else about, so Irene went on outside. Clark was still sitting on the running board of Elise's car, but he looked so forbidding that she turned away from him and went over to where Elise was politely quarreling with Mac, who had just caught her picking his flowers.

Clark watched them from his seat on the running board. He was a little afraid of Elise, fearful that she might come back at any minute and demand her car. It was an odd car, at that, with a small collapsible table in front of the back seat and the trunk all cluttered up with camp beds and pots and pans. A car belonging to an outdoors sort of person—a camper and a picnicker—and the De Petro woman looked far more like a sheltered hothouse blossom.

The cigar began to burn his fingers, and he threw it away. He immediately pulled another one from his pocket, stared at it in distaste for a moment, and then lit it. There was a bad taste in his mouth, and his tongue felt burned—but it was a good thing he'd had the cigars, though. He'd won them on a bet and had put them in his pocket with the idea of trading them for cigarettes.

"Oh God!" he muttered, and stared at the sky that stretched bright and blue above him. If the darkness would only come—but it would be hours yet, hours and hours. And Ross had found that will. How the devil had he done it? Not that it mattered, although it would have been nice to have owned the place, with John managing it and the money rolling in without work or trouble. Ross could always have gone to the city and made money—doctors always seemed to be able to make money. But that was no use now; he was a fool not to have seen it before. No doubt about that. He was going to make a run for it, anyway. No—couldn't do that. He'd face her. After all, surely he could defend himself.

The cigar was making him feel a bit sick. He held it a little away from him and let the smoke rise in a column into the warm, still air.

Presently his head dropped and a tired, beaten look came into his face. It wouldn't matter what he did—he was convinced now—she was going to kill him.

## THIRTY

SOMETIME later Ross flung out of his office in a temper and slammed the door behind him. Lieutenant Domer had been smooth, superior, sarcastic, and generally annoying, and Ross's dignity had suffered in front of Joe and Ed, who had always looked up to him.

John walked through the hall, and Ross glanced at him and then stopped him with a hand on his arm. "You'd better let me take over for a while, John—you look all in. Go on up to bed and have a rest."

"Have you found Horace?" John asked.

Ross scowled and shook his head. "No need for anyone to worry any longer. They've sent a superman down from the city who guarantees to find anything up to and including the lost chord. Forget it. Go on upstairs and take a rest."

John began a nervous outline of the condition of each patient, but Ross stopped him abruptly. "I'll read it on their charts or ask Myrtle," he said impatiently. "Or wait until they write their reminiscences."

"All right." John's frown showed disapproval, but he turned away and went on upstairs. Ross noted, with a certain amount of concern, that he used the elevator. The patients were always taken up in it, of course, but the rest of them never bothered with it because it took too much time.

The will must have hit him pretty hard, Ross thought. It was a mean trick for Horace to have played on him—honest, sober old John. You wouldn't dream of doubting his word. Ross shrugged and muttered, "No doubt about it—if I ever have any children, they'll have to be taught not to point with pride to the portrait of Grandfather Horace."

There was a faint gasp, and he turned to find Jean regarding him with round, shocked eyes. He winked at her. "You needn't noise it around," he said, and added, "Get Miss Warner for me, will you?"

Jean was unable to locate Myrtle on the house phone, but Ross eventually found her in the back wing of the second floor.

"I'm alerting you," he said, grinning at her. "I've put John back to bed. He looks as though he'd been sent out and returned in the wet wash by mistake."

"He worries me half out of my mind," Myrtle said fretfully. "Eating his soul out and ruining his health—and for what?"

"Nothing," said Ross. "You keep an eye out here, like a good girl. I want to work on this trouble we've had and clear it up."

Myrtle gave him a cold stare. "Oh, sure—and you'll have to take that dizzy blonde with you, because she knows what the other one looks like. Why don't the two of you go and search in the movies, and you can hold Irene's hand to make sure that she doesn't get away."

They had come down to the front hall, and Ross realized that Jean was listening avidly. He gave Myrtle a meaning look, but she brushed it away impatiently.

"Jean knows I'm only kidding," she said loudly. "Sure I'll take over while you go out sleuthing. But I'm fast getting to be a nurse in name only. You ought to pay me a doctor's wages.,'

"The place will be all yours before long," Ross said obscurely. "Be reasonable, will you? I can't work when my father's body has disappeared and there's a blonde lunatic running around loose."

Domer had approached on his smooth detective's feet and now said nastily, "Where do you propose to start your search, Doctor?"

"You turn over your stones, and I'll turn over mine," Ross said furiously.

Myrtle looked the lieutenant over and asked, "Who's this ?"

Ross introduced them and then slipped away when Domer started to question Myrtle.

Where *do* I propose to start my search? Ross thought, and damned Domer thoroughly. There was nowhere else to search—they'd looked everywhere. Doris evidently had a secure hideout for the daytime, but she might return to the hospital after dark. If she did, they'd have her.

He went outside and saw that Clark was still sitting on the running board of Elise's car. Joe and Ed were visible in the distance, on a little hillock, and seemed to be measuring something, and Elise and Irene were sitting on the lawn. The sun was getting lower, and the slanting rays touched Irene's hair into shimmering silver.

Ross decided to join the ladies. He knew of Myrtle's dark foreboding that they would be the ruin of him, and it seemed sensible to enjoy some of the pleasures along the primrose path.

Elise hailed him with cheerful chatter, and he sat down on the lawn between them. Elise leaned toward him, lowered her voice, and said she'd heard that a detective had come out from the city.

Ross nodded. "He says he's here to pick up Doris Miller."

Irene plucked a blade of grass and chewed on it thoughtfully.

"It's so silly," she said presently. "Because Clark knows where Doris is—he must. Can't you get it out of Clark?"

"I'd rather leave him alone just now."

"Well, but if he's ill," Elise said reasonably, "he ought to be in bed, instead of on the running board of my car."

Ross, absently digging a small hole with a flat stone, shook his head. "Don't bother him—we'll keep an eye on him. How long was he gone with your car this morning?"

Elise frowned and said, "I don't know."

"Well, he went somewhere, and then he came in to lunch, but only for a few minutes before he lost his temper and went off again—presumably to his perch on the running board."

"He fixed up a sandwich first," Irene said, "and took it with him."

Ross looked up at her. "Perhaps he has something in the car—and he's guarding it."

"Doris!" Irene exclaimed. "'He must have taken the sandwich to her. I'll bet she's on the floor in front of the back seat."

Elise pursed her lips. "But how uncomfortable. Why didn't he just take her somewhere else?"

"He had to bring the car back," Ross explained, "or you'd have had the police after him. Now he's waiting until it's dark, so that he can get her out and hide her somewhere."

"Then why on earth don't we just go over and get her right now?" Elise suggested practically. "What are we waiting for?"

Ross said, "Right," and got to his feet.

But Clark had been watching them, and although he could not hear what they were saying, he rightly interpreted the purpose in their sudden movement. He was into the car and flying down the driveway while they were still some yards away.

"We must follow him," Elise shrilled excitedly, but Ross shook his head.

"He drives like a demon—we wouldn't have any chance of catching him. We'll have to wait until he comes back."

"I don't know why you didn't search the car before," Irene said accusingly.

"I had no idea he was guarding anything—I thought he was just sitting there. It was the sandwich that made me think of it."

He took out his cigarette case and handed it around.

They all puffed together, and when the smoke had cleared away they found that Myrtle was among them.

She looked a bit grim. "Just run in and take care of the patients, Ross—I'll go on with the search. I've been watching you from the window. First you lounge on the lawn with your lady friends, after which you take a stroll, and then you all have a cigarette. Nice searching. Have you proposed to the girl yet—or are you waiting for the mother to leave you alone for a few minutes?"

"What good would it do me to be alone," Ross yelled, "with nurses snooping from every window?"

"He really was searching," Irene said mildly. "He made a little hole on the lawn with a stone and looked in it."

Ross turned to her. "I don't know whether Myrtle is jealous or what's eating her, but will you become my betrothed until you go, so that she can settle down? Or, if you'd rather not, perhaps Elise will oblige."

Elise gave a silvery trill of laughter. "No, no, Irene can do it—much more appropriate—age and all that, you know. Besides, she's engaged to two men already, so that one more can do no harm. There is such safety in numbers."

Ross asked Irene quickly, "You are engaged to two men? Even before you became such a howling blonde?"

Irene started to say something, but Myrtle drowned her out.

"Don't pay any attention, Ross. You can always get rid of the competition by telling them she's been sleeping in your bedroom."

"Myrtle Warner, that is not funny," Elise thundered.

Ross put an arm around Irene's shoulders. "You can hardly complain, Myrtle, if I take an evening stroll with my fiancee?"

"Go right ahead," Myrtle said, flinging up her arms. "Dave Catledge is dying again, and John is in bed, but good old Myrt can attend to everything."

Ross dropped his arm from Irene's shoulders, muttered a curse, and then said briefly to Myrtle, "Come on."

Elise watched them go with a speculative look in her eye. "You know, my dear, you can have that young man, if you play your cards properly."

"I play cards for ashtrays or money," Irene said. "If any man wants me, he can ask, and I'll say yes or no."

"That's all very well for talk," Elise replied imperturbably, "but you have to be practical too."

"The new woman does not resort to tricks of any kind."

"Poor thing," Elise murmured serenely. "If she knew any, she'd resort to them quick enough."

Lieutenant Domer approached holding something out before him. "Could either of you ladies tell me what this is?"

Elise and Irene turned and saw what seemed to be a rather outsize black stocking with the foot cut off.

## THIRTY-ONE

ELISE examined the mutilated stocking very carefully, but her mind was not really concerned with it. She was thinking that Domer was actually a detective from the city and she must impress him with the analytical brilliance of her mind.

"Let me see." She dangled the stocking in one hand and tapped against her lip with her forefinger. "As far as I can make out, it is a stocking—or rather, it was a stocking, but it has been made into an anklet. Or, no—what do you call those things? I've seen men wearing them, doing folk dances with a feather in their hats. They sell them in the stores, but they are not anklets—they cover the calves, you know. What am I thinking of, Irene?"

"Calvelets?"

"Don't be absurd." Elise turned to Domer. "I don't know what they call them, but anyway, this is one. It has been made from an ordinary stocking by the simple process of cutting off the foot. But of course it has no significance—here."

"Why?" Domer asked.

"Well, because in a hospital they use all sorts of bits and pieces like this to keep various parts of the patients warm."

"It's summertime—and hot," Domer pointed out.

"My dear man, that makes no difference at all. Some patients—particularly the very old and the very young—are apt to be cold in any temperature."

Domer cleared his throat. "But don't they use—er— white wool on the patients?"

"Not these days," Elise said firmly. "Woolen anything is hard to obtain, and nobody is going to fuss about the color."

"This is a woolen stocking?" Domer asked.

Irene reached across and felt it. "No. Rayon and cotton —or something like that. Where did you find it?"

"Over in the woods, not far from the lawn. There's a path that runs in from the road—a lane really—and a sort of picnic ground, with a fireplace and a trash container."

"Did you get this stocking out of the trash ?" Elise asked.

"No," Domer said slowly. "I picked it off the ground." He hesitated for a moment and then added, "I don't think it had been lying there long—doesn't seem to be weathered —and I wondered what it could be."

"Well, I shouldn't waste any more time over it," Elise said with decision. She lowered her voice and in a confidential tone told him all about Clark, and how he had gone off with her car again, and of her certainty that the girl was in the car too.

Domer let out a wounded howl and roared, "Why in hell didn't you tell me before?"

"I'm telling you now," Elise said coldly, "and I'll thank you to mind your language."

Domer caught her by the arm. "Come on—we'll follow them in my car. You can identify your car for me if we catch up with it."

They went off together, Elise happily excited to be on a manhunt with a real detective.

Irene watched Domer's car out of sight and then walked slowly toward the hospital, while she admitted to herself that she was vastly uneasy. Perhaps, she thought, it was just the hospital atmosphere—people who were ill and dying, like that poor old Dave Cattledge. It was no place for a healthy girl to be living—why was she staying on, anyway? That Myrtle woman probably thought it was because of Ross. Irene colored and made a sudden decision. She would leave today—now—no matter whether Elise stayed on or not. She could try for a room at the hotel and, failing that, she'd drive straight back to her apartment.

She went upstairs to start packing without delay and discovered that the bedroom was in wild disorder. Parts of the wallpaper had been pulled off, and the furniture was standing away from the walls, with gaping drawers. The mattress on the double bed lay exposed, with a long rip down the middle. Irene surveyed it all, shook her head, and decided that the sooner she was out of this madhouse, the better. Elise might object to being left in 301, with Ross occupying 301A—but Elise could always look after herself.

She began to pack her things, and had almost finished when Ross came quietly into the room behind her. He knew at once what she was doing and stood for a while, looking at her and trying to get used to the realization that Myrtle was right. He did not want the girl to go—and if he followed that to its logical conclusion, Elise would be his mother-in-law. Elise. Well, he thought, so what did it matter? Elise was enjoying herself and her life, which put her well out in front of the great majority of people.

Irene caught sight of him, turned, and said, "Hello."

"What do you think you're doing?"

She patted a folded dress into her suitcase and said shortly, "I'm leaving. I think it's high time."

"Are you packing your mother's stuff too?"

"Elise thinks she's an important witness or something—doubt if she'll be going."

Ross leaned against the wall and took out a cigarette. "I suppose you're going back to those two fellows to whom you're engaged."

"No—not exactly. They haven't come home yet."

"I see. What do you intend to do? Take the first one that comes out?"

"Certainly not," said Irene with dignity. "That would be hardly fair."

"No, I can see that. How are you going to decide between them?"

Irene turned away from the suitcase, pushed her hair back from her hot face, and sat down. She asked for a cigarette and, when he supplied her in silence, took a few puffs and looked away from him, out of the window.

That was the old trouble—trying to decide between George and Bill. Well, she wasn't going to do it—not now. She'd just let things ride and see what happened.

"You'd better stay on here," Ross said, with his eyes on her face. "Perhaps they'll find out that you and I share the same bedroom, and then they'll throw you over, and you won't have to decide a question like that. Because you must know that when you pick one, it will be a matter of only a few years—or perhaps months—before you realize that you should have chosen the other one."

"If I stay here," Irene said, "and they throw me over, I'll be forced to take you, and maybe it will be a matter of weeks before I realize that I should have chosen one of the others."

Ross grinned at her. "Oh well, you can't go through life without picking up a few regrets."

He went over to the suitcase, took out two handfuls of clothes, and dropped them into one of the open drawers. "I'll help you to unpack."

Irene let out a sharp cry and began to try and rearrange the jumbled mess in the drawer, but he caught her arm and pulled her away.

"Come on—we've time for a stroll before dinner."

He urged her down the stairs, talking loudly all the way, so that her protests were drowned out.

They went out onto the front veranda, and Ross paused and looked down the driveway with a worried frown. "He isn't back yet," he said grimly.

"Perfectly all right," Irene assured him. "Lieutenant Domer and Elise are in pursuit together."

Ross shrugged. He still held her arm, and he led her down the steps and across the lawn to the woods.

"Slow up, will you?" she begged after a while. "I'm panting and perspiring. When George and Bill stroll—they stroll. And talk about my eyes, and the stars, and so on."

"Hurry has become chronic with me," he explained. "And as for George and Bill, I guarantee that neither one of them ever told you that your eyes are slightly myopic—which at least has the novelty of truth."

"I'd have spit in one of theirs, if they had. Where's this picnic ground where Comer found the sock?"

"Did he show it to you too? That's where we're going now—to see if we can find anything else lying around there."

"Oh, I see. We're taking a romantic stroll, with a little business attached to it."

"It takes time to woo a girl," Ross said easily, "and I never have much time. It's necessary for me to combine business with pleasure, if I want any pleasure."

They found Elise's car parked in the small clearing that Domer had called a picnic ground. They looked inside immediately, but it appeared to be empty, and there was no sign of Clark. They poked into the surrounding shrubbery a little but found nothing, and Ross presently suggested that they take the car and drive out to a place he knew of, for dinner. "I can phone Myrtle and tell her I found something and had to follow it up," he said carelessly.

Irene considered for a moment and then nodded, her eyes sparkling. Ross kissed her, when they were both in the car, but she drew away and said severely that she had not yet lost Bill or George and he would have to wait.

They drove off down the lane leading to the main highway, and Clark watched them, from where he lay concealed in the undergrowth, with frozen horror.

## THIRTY-TWO

CLARK was feeling decidedly unwell. He supposed it was the cigars he'd smoked—he hated cigars. He had run the car into the picnic clearing and then stretched out on the grass, a short distance away, in the hope that his troubled stomach would calm down. He could see the car from where he lay, and anyone who might approach it, but he had made the mistake of falling asleep. It had been a restless, feverish sleep, shot through with lurid dreams.

He had awakened in time to see Irene and Ross drive off, but he had been too late to stop them—and what could he do now? No use trying to follow them, when he had no idea where they were going. Perhaps, though, they were just moving the car to the front of the hospital again. He scrambled to his feet and stumbled through the woods and across the lawn, but when he arrived at the driveway there was no sign of Elise's car. He'd have to try and follow them, he thought desperately—he couldn't just let it go.

He sat down on the grass with his arms clasped around his legs and his forehead resting on his knees. Where could they have gone? On an errand, perhaps—or maybe out to dinner. It must be almost dinner time. He turned his head from side to side, rubbing his forehead across his knees. He ought to go in to dinner and try to eat something, might make him feel better. Perhaps Irene and Ross would be back soon—he'd wait a little, anyway.

A car turned in at the driveway, and Clark sprang to his feet, with his heart thudding. The driver parked it carelessly, slammed the door, and went around to the other side to assist his companion to alight. They were Domer and Elise.

Clark watched them morosely. When Domer turned and his eye fell on Clark, he swore quietly for at least a minute. He'd been chasing the fellow all over the countryside, to no avail, only to find him waiting on the steps when he got back. Domer felt that he'd been made to look silly, and there was nothing he hated more. He opened his mouth to start relieving his feelings, but Elise was well ahead of him. "What have done with my car now?" she demanded. "We've been looking high and low for you. I shall definitely start an action of some sort if you don't leave my things alone."

Domer wished that she had left out the part about their having looked high and low. He felt more of a fool than ever.

Clark said indifferently, "Irene and Ross are out in your car."

Elise and Domer spoke together, got tangled up, and were drowned out by Myrtle, who had appeared on the veranda.

"Why don't you people postpone this social gathering until after dinner? It's been ready and waiting for some time."

"Good," said Elise. "I am starving. Come, Lieutenant." She took Domer's arm and started for the steps.

"Well, I'll probably see you all after dinner," Domer murmured, and tried to disentangle himself.

Elise held onto him firmly. "Nonsense! You're tired out, as I am, chasing that irresponsible creature all over the countryside, when actually he was sitting here on the front lawn. So stupid and irritating. You must come in and have some food and some good, strong coffee. We shall not take no for an answer—shall we, Myrtle?"

Domer still hung back, blushing and perspiring, and Myrtle, looking him over coolly, felt inclined to say, "No cops at the table," but she reflected that she had never been one to let a person down, so she said instead, "We certainly can't take no for an answer. Come on, Mr. Domer."

She took his other arm and called over her shoulder to Clark to come on and not wait for Irene and Ross, as they had phoned to say they would not be back for dinner.

Whereupon she and Elise ran the embarrassed Domer into the dining room and sat him down. Clark followed—more to find out where Irene and Ross had gone than because he was hungry.

Elise smoothed her plumage and explained to the trapped Domer that she was simply starved for conversation with an intelligent man.

It had always been Domer's rule never to look at a woman while he was working, but he did, at this point, look squarely at Elise—and he was impressed. He cleared his throat but never got any further, because Elise leaped in ahead of him and did all the talking until Myrtle stopped her.

Myrtle said firmly, "Mr. Domer, you must have had some thrilling experiences. Won't you tell us about some of them?"

Domer glowed into sudden life and looked at Myrtle almost affectionately. He at once launched forth, while Elise looked bored and played fretfully with her jewelry, and Clark talked into Myrtle's ear in an undertone. Myrtle answered in a mumble, without moving her lips, because Domer was looking straight at her during the recital of his experiences, and she did not want to seem discourteous. It got to be more and more of a strain as Clark became more insistent. "But where *are* they, Myrt? I must know, I tell you."

"What's so important about it?" Myrtle mumbled peevishly. "Anyway, I don't know. They're out to dinner."

Domer had got to a tense point in his story, and his voice rose accordingly—only to sink to a whisper, in the next few seconds, because he was now hidden in a closet and did not want to give his whereabouts away.

"I know perfectly well that Ross would never go out without telling you where you could get in touch with him," Clark muttered. "For God's sake, Myrtle, tell me—"

"Quiet!" she said out of the corner of her mouth, and added, "I'm not going to have you disturbing him and plaguing him to death. He's having a good time for once."

Domer was still reminiscing, but the fervor was gone. In the first place, he had realized that he did not have Myrtle's full attention, and secondly, his mind had clicked back onto the job again and he was sizing up Clark. He had decided that business was out while they were still at dinner with the ladies, but the instant it was over, he intended to collar Clark and squeeze him dry. He thought it looked a bit as though Myrtle were in collusion, and filed it away in his mind for future investigation.

Food was set before him, and he dropped the flow of personal biography and set to. Elise took over the conversational angle at once, since she had always been able to eat and talk at the same time.

Irene and Ross had gone to a roadhouse, where they were established in a dimly lighted booth. Ross had ordered drinks, and because he had had nothing to eat for some time and was overfatigued, the drinks had disordered him a trifle. He proposed to Irene without further ado.

She knew that he was a bit drunk and told him to shut up, but he merely became loudly insistent, so that eventually, in a bit of a panic, she informed him that he was accepted.

He behaved much better after that, and they began to enjoy themselves over the dinner. The hot food steadied him somewhat, but toward the end he made one last drunken remark.

"There's only one drawback to marrying you, darling— I mean, having a flighty sketch like Elise for a mother-in-law."

Irene froze on the spot. Drunk or not drunk, she thought, that was right out beyond the pale. When she could speak at all, she said in a cold, flat voice, "I feel a bit hesitant, myself, about marrying a man whose father seems to have been a lunatic."

It was the last word spoken between them until they were getting into the car.

Ross, feeling cold sober by that time, said stiffly, "I'm afraid I was a bit tight in there—I should have known better. I hope you won't take anything I said too seriously."

"Certainly not," Irene replied in a fury. "I could see you weren't used to anything stronger than lemonade. No," she added as he opened the front door, "I'll sit in the back."

Ross bowed coldly and opened the back, and she mounted with dignity, tripped over something on the floor, and fell into the back seat.

Ross gave her a supercilious look of concern. "I trust you didn't hurt yourself?"

She pulled the door shut in his face and fell to cursing Elise, silently but thoroughly. Always leaving things lying around on the floor of her car—why couldn't she clean it out once in six months, anyway? And it smelled, too smelled abominably, whatever it was. She'd probably done some marketing for perishables, several weeks ago, and then forgotten all about it. Just like Elise's scatter-brained behavior.

Ross started the car, and as the fresh air blew in, the odor was less objectionable. Irene stirred, and her bag fell to the floor from her lap. She leaned over and groped for it and, when she couldn't find it, tried to turn on the overhead light, but it didn't work. Perspiring and cross, she swore at Elise afresh. Elise's lights wouldn't be working, of course. But even so, that was no reason to sneer at her as a mother-in-law. Elise would make a better mother-in-law than a lot of grim specimens she knew about. The whole thing was particularly annoying because she was certain that Ross had been nearly sober when he made the remark.

She curled her feet under her and swung sideways, settling back more comfortably. Her eyes had become accustomed to the darkness, and it seemed to her, suddenly, that something white glimmered at the end of the seat. A towel, or a sheet? Elise's careless untidiness again? But there had been nothing white on the seat when they had looked into the car earlier.

She had found her bag, and she began to grope in it now, feeling feverishly for matches. The first one that she struck promptly blew out in the wind, but the second one, shielded by her cupped hand, glowed just long enough to show her that there was a man sitting on the seat beside her. A man in a dress suit, with a dead, crumbling face.

## THIRTY-THREE

IRENE dropped the dead match and, with no very coherent thought beyond a terrified desire to remove herself, began to scramble frantically over into the front seat. One of her feet kicked Ross's head a smart blow and knocked all the frozen dignity out of it.

"What's the matter with you?" he asked crossly. "Can't you make up your mind where you want to sit?"

She caught at his arm and whispered, "Stop! Stop the car at once!"

Ross glanced at her face but could not see much in the faint glow from the dashboard light. He stopped the car and looked at her again, more fully.

"What's the matter?" he asked sharply.

Irene, breathing in short gasps, did not attempt to speak but pointed behind her.

Ross twisted around but could see only a glimmer of white. He got out of the car, walked to the back, and, opening the door, lit a match.

He was not sure of anything at first, and it was only after he had used up several matches that he realized that his father's body lay awkwardly back against the seat. The face was hardly recognizable. It was decomposing, and the features were peculiarly flattened.

He closed the door and turned away, feeling sickened and angry. Irene was emerging from the front seat, and he ordered her back peremptorily. She obeyed in silence and sat clutching her bag and barely breathing while he drove to the hospital at breakneck speed and on the left-hand side of the road for at least half the trip. When he parked at last in the driveway, she heaved a long, quivering sigh of relief and got out at once. Ross got out on the other side and stood leaning against the mudguard. He called after her, "Get me some sort of a cop, will you? There must be one around somewhere."

Irene found Domer in the front waiting room, where he had been attempting to grill Clark—with very negative results. He was in a fury, which he tried to conceal, as a good detective should. He was convinced that the fellow knew where that girl was hiding, and he felt that it was his duty to batter him down until he told. But Clark had proved to be irritatingly impervious to battering, and it began to look like a tedious affair that would stretch far into the night.

When Irene walked in and told him that he was wanted, he said tersely, "I can't come now—I'm busy."

"I think you'd better—" Irene began, and then glanced at Clark, who was staring at her in horrified fascination. "We found it," she said, nodding at him.

Clark stood up and jammed his hands into his pockets, and Domer looked from one to the other of them. "What is this? What's happened?"

"There's a—a dead man in the car out there," Irene said faintly.

Clark started out, and Domer followed on his heels. Ross was still leaning against the mudguard, but he straightened up as they approached, and indicated the tonneau of the car. Domer took a flashlight from his pocket and peered inside.

There was an interval made noisy only by the crickets and katydids, and then Domer turned around.

"Where did you get this body? When did you put it here?"

"I don't know anything about it," Ross said flatly. "We looked in the car before we left, and it appeared to be empty. Miss Hastings discovered it there when we were on our way home after dinner."

This sounded a bit confused to Domer, who was trying to think up a series of concise, probing questions and keep an eye on Clark, in the darkness, so that he wouldn't get away.

"This body has been in the car all day, hasn't it?" he demanded.

Clark backed up a step, cleared his throat, and murmured, "Well—er—"

That was the way he had been going on all the evening—vague, indefinite, and obviously stalling. Domer turned to Ross and unexpectedly met a fury to match his own.

The body, Ross said, was that of his father, which had been taken from the tomb, by ghouls, some time ago. He understood, of course, that in difficult and complex cases the police procedure was to goggle, stammer, and then go out and buy a large sponge and throw it up—but when it was a simple matter, like finding a missing body and restoring it to its tomb, it would seem that the police should attempt to handle it.

Domer's control began to slip, and his voice rose several notes higher. It was the business of the local police, he stated, to find all lost children, dogs, cats, bodies, and other miscellany. Lieutenant Domer was concerned only with the apprehension of a girl—one Doris Miller—who had been certified as insane and committed to a state institution, and who had escaped and was now at large. At the very least he had expected cooperation from the residents of the vicinity—he had supposed that self-interest would have prompted it—but instead nobody bothered to tell him anything, and, in fact, they were all complicating his work to the best of their various abilities.

He turned on Clark and said furiously, "You knew that body was in the car all day, and you deliberately sat on the running board to prevent anyone from finding it."

Clark pulled himself together with an effort and spoke with a certain amount of assurance. "Nothing of the kind. That body must have been put there later. I was sticking by the car in case I heard from Doris. My car is out of order, and—well—you know how I feel about Doris. If she'd appealed to me, I'd like to have gone to her."

Domer's eyes glazed over and he thought longingly of his bed at home. He had never, in all his career, wanted so badly to have done with a case, and yet he was frustrated at every turn. He began to think that the girl was not here, after all, and that Clark did not know where she was. Of course Clark was obviously a born liar, but still Domer shrugged and decided to go and telephone. Perhaps the girl had been picked up in town, and his troubles would be over. The sister had been released yesterday, with two tails, in the hope that Doris would contact her, but the last he'd heard, there'd been nothing doing. Ann Miller had gone straight home to bed and hadn't telephoned anyone. Today she had gone to business and had been carefully watched, but she had not contacted anyone. Domer sighed. Perhaps, by now, the sisters had got together and Doris had been picked up, and he could go home and have a highball.

He made his call and was disappointed to hear that Ann Miller had gone to the movies with a girlfriend, while her tails sat directly behind her. What next, then? No use trying to talk to Joe and Ed—they probably had union ideas and were fast asleep in bed.

He glanced at his watch, saw that it was nearly eleven, and went out to the front again. He realized that he had wronged Joe and Ed, for they were out there, talking to Clark. Elise's car was still where Ross had parked it, and Domer, after a moment's hesitation, took his flashlight and went over to examine it. The body had been removed, and he swung the light over the back seat and across the floor. Gadgets of all sorts, and a loose strap. He shook his head. The incredible woman had a folding table there, a magazine rack with magazines bulging out of it, and two packs of cards. He glanced up to the roof and saw a network of heavy straps—no doubt for the storing of additional baggage—blankets, perhaps, and things of that sort.

Domer squinted up at the straps for some time and then nodded his head. That's where the body had been all day— strapped up against the roof. That was why the doctor and his girlfriend had thought the car was empty when they started out. And then the movement of the car had dislodged it and it had fallen into the back seat. There was no doubt that that Clark fellow had known it was there all day—in fact, it seemed probable that he had put it there himself.

Domer put his flashlight away, walked over, and plucked Clark out of Joe's and Ed's hands.

Joe and Ed didn't mind. They had put Horace Munster back in his tomb, locked him in, and were going home to bed with a feeling of the day's work well done. Since the arrival of Lieutenant Domer they had put Doris Miller comfortably out of their minds.

Clark regarded Domer with a stubborn, weary eye. He could see that Domer had decided to grill him again, and with an idea that he might just as well be as comfortable as possible while it was being done, he suggested amiably, "Come to my room, and we can talk there."

"What do you mean, 'talk'?" Domer said sourly. "You're not telling me anything."

"I have nothing to tell."

"Where is your room?"

Clark started to indicate the tent and suddenly changed his mind. He didn't want to sleep there—not tonight—it would be too easy. He'd better sleep inside. Some of the patients had left, and there was sure to be a room for him. It would be much safer, with nurses walking the floors all night. He turned swiftly and walked inside, and Domer followed him.

In the front hall, Beatrice referred him to Myrtle and told him to look for her in the dining room. Myrtle, seated at the table with a penciled list before her, assigned him to a room and absentmindedly gave one to Domer as well.

Domer swallowed an automatic protest and decided to use the room. He was tired, and anyway, he had come to the conclusion that the best way to find Doris Miller was to stay as close to Clark as possible.

They went up to the second floor, where their rooms were next door but one. Domer asked Catherine if he could move the patient who had the room that separated them, but her expression of astonishment and indignation decided him to drop it. He went into his room, removed his shoes, and stretched out on the bed, where he presently fell into an uneasy sleep.

Clark had not brought any of his things from the tent, so he rang for Catherine and asked for a hospital shirt from the linen room. She supplied him, and he undressed and went to bed. He tried to sleep, but it was useless, and he had known it would be useless. He was hoping that she wouldn't come—and knew all the time that she would. It was no use hoping or wishing—she'd come. He shivered slightly as another thought struck him. She would almost certainly appear headless.

## THIRTY-FOUR

ROSS went upstairs, feeling tired and shaken. He had gone with Joe and Ed while they replaced the body in its tomb, and fortunately there had been no onlookers. When the door was once more securely locked, Joe had handed Ross the key, and he still had it in his pocket. It was not to hang in the dining room any longer, but must be hidden safely away from casual curiosity and meddling.

He reached the top floor and, hearing a murmur of voices from John's room, walked over and entered, after a perfunctory knock. He found Myrtle and John talking in low voices, and as they turned inquiring faces to him, he told them, briefly, that his father's body had been found and restored to the mausoleum. Rather to his surprise, they seemed considerably relieved. They both asked him, more than once, if he were sure that it was really Horace, and he gathered that they had been genuinely afraid that Horace was still alive.

Myrtle became cheerful at once, and the pale gloom that had draped John so persistently seemed to fall away.

"I thought I had seen his body lying in the summerhouse without a head," he explained, mopping at his face. "But later, when he couldn't be found, I was afraid there was some mistake and that he was still alive—still—still deviling people. I'm glad there is no longer any doubt about it—it's a great weight off my mind. But what about the head?"

"It's there. It's decomposing, and the features are oddly flattened."

John nodded. "It's been out in the open for some days. Of course it was embalmed, and in the tomb it would have lasted fairly well "

Myrtle shuddered and then pulled herself together and broke in firmly. "Horace is dead and in his tomb. It's settled and finished, and I don't want to hear any more about it." She drew a long breath and patted her starched bosom. "The problem, now, is to get another patient in here tonight. You two probably haven't given it any thought, but according to that will, tomorrow is the deadline, when there have to be a certain number of patients if Ross is to keep the place."

Ross ran a bothered hand through his hair and muttered, "Tomorrow?"

"Yes. John told me all about the will. It was a scandalous thing, Ross, and your father had no right to do it."

John was silent, but he thought, too, that it was scandalous. In the end, Horace had deliberately broken his word.

He had supposed, probably, that John would never find the will and would spend the rest of his life looking for it.

"Now look," Myrtle was saying. "Clark played right into my hand—he came in and asked me for a room, and he looked so ill that I admitted him as a patient. Domer was with him, and I gave him a room too—but he didn't really look sick, actually, so I couldn't make a patient out of him. I wish he'd come down with something. I wonder—"

Ross laughed suddenly and freely and felt the tension go out of him.

"Then there's Elise," Myrtle went on. "I admitted her too—she's in 203—she says you can diagnose heat exhaustion—says she certainly is exhausted after the time she's had trying to chase after Clark, and that she's been like to die of the heat for two days. She's sitting up with two pillows, in a lace bedjacket, with a book, candy, cigarettes, and a row of medicine bottles on the bedside table. The bottles look silly, and I tried to take them away, but she wouldn't let me. I think they're actually flavoring extracts."

Ross laughed again, and even John gave her a pale smile.

"Irene didn't cooperate," she continued. "I stopped her when she came in and told her she looked terrible, but she merely gave me a nasty look and said, 'So do you.'"

"Where is she now?" Ross asked.

"She's in your room—getting to bed, I guess."

John colored, glanced at Ross, and said quickly, "But she can't sleep there tonight, with the mother in another room."

Myrtle shrugged. "What's the difference? They're going to be married anyway."

"We are not," Ross said coldly.

Myrtle looked up at him and raised her eyebrows. "Oh? Lovers' quarrel?"

"We'll convert her into the missing patient," Ross said with a faint grin. "Come on, Myrtle."

John stayed where he was, because he disapproved of the whole thing as being dishonest, but as long as his own conscience was clear he couldn't help hoping that they'd be successful in converting Irene to the status of patient.

She was propped up in bed, reading, when Myrtle and Ross entered, and she gave them a distinctly cold stare.

Myrtle said, "You see what I mean, Doctor?" and Ross nodded and advanced to the bedside.

Irene dropped her book and looked up at him, and at that critical point his Hippocratic oath began to trouble him. It was easy for Myrtle to talk, he thought resentfully; she had no scruples and her ethics were elastic, and anyway, no one had ever administered the Hippocratic oath to her. He seriously doubted that her nurse's oath and her present actions were compatible, but that was her affair.

He backed away from the bed and, avoiding Myrtle's eye, muttered, "I can't do it."

Myrtle indicated the door with a jerk of her head and said in a low, angry voice, "Get out of here."

Ross departed, closed the door behind him, and immediately put his ear against it, but was not able to hear much.

Myrtle sat down on the side of the bed, but after one look at Irene's face she gave up any idea of subterfuge. She simply presented the problem and asked if Irene would help by developing an illness, so that they could admit her as a patient.

"It isn't honest," Irene said, after thinking it over for a moment. "He's supposed to have a certain number of patients, and he doesn't."

"Oh, put the hymnbook away," Myrtle said dryly. "Do you think it would be very honest to let Clark take over? Can't you see what he's been doing around here? He knew about that will; he deliberately hauled that crazy girl out here to play headless nurse, and then he left that absurd note in your car. He knows very well how things get around in a hospital, and he counted on the patients up and leaving at the first rumor of a ghost on the premises. He's never done a lick of work here, and it's most unfair that he should get the place, when Ross has slaved over it, just because Horace was a malicious, nasty old man."

Irene closed her book, threw it to the end of the bed, and said, "You'll have me in tears. So you want me to connive—"

"No, no," Myrtle interrupted hastily. "It's just that you look pale."

"That's fury."

Myrtle sighed and murmured, "These men! Tear the heart right out of you."

"Oh, rubbish!" Irene stretched, yawned, and suddenly laughed. "All right—I'll go in for observation. Only it's to be distinctly understood that the observing is to be done by eye. I don't want anyone lowering little buckets into my stomach for samples of last night's dinner."

"That's swell, honey." Myrtle jumped up, looking cheerful and busy. "Let's get your things together, and I'll take you down to your room."

Clark, lying sleepless in his high, narrow bed, heard them come down. They didn't worry him, because two sets of footsteps was not what he feared. He was waiting for one—and anyway, it would come from downstairs. He thought he knew Catherine's steps by now—busy, quick, almost staccato. He heard Myrtle's voice as they passed his door, and later he heard her again, apparently leaving. It sounded as though she had brought someone down from upstairs—but who could it be? He wondered about it for some time.

Catherine stuck her head in at his door and cheerfully offered him a sedative for the third time. He refused angrily and added that all he wanted was to be left alone. Catherine shrugged and removed herself.

He lay back again with his arms folded behind his head and stared at the ceiling. He wasn't going to take any of their damned pills—he wanted to stay awake—all night—he had to. When she came, he wouldn't let her kill him—he'd have it out with her.

He did doze, after a while, and awoke to find that it was three o'clock. Well, he thought, she was due about now—any time. He began listening for footsteps. He heard Catherine go along to the front, and then it was silent again. The silence was bad—any sound at all would have helped, even the footsteps he was dreading. He couldn't stand waiting for them this way.

They came at last—slow, quiet, stealthy in the surrounding silence. She was a little late.

He wondered whether she'd run into Catherine, and knew that she hadn't when his door opened, slowly and without sound. His heart was thumping heavily, and he wished wildly that Catherine would come; but his hand never moved to press the button by his pillow that would switch on the red signal light above his door.

He forced himself to turn and look at her—and shuddered. She looked horrible—a nurse without a head. He tried to say something and saw that she had raised her arm and that a small revolver gleamed with deadly menace in her hand.

There was no sound, but he saw a wisp of smoke and relaxed into a darkness that was shot through with golden stars which presently burned out into nothing.

## THIRTY-FIVE

DOMER was restless. His pillow was hot and felt crumpled and uncomfortable under his head, and his clothes were damp and heavy on his body. But his mind troubled him more than the physical discomfort. He should not be trying to sleep until he had finished the job—a simple little thing like picking up a nut and putting her back inside. But the girl was not in the building or on the grounds—that seemed pretty certain. She'd gone off somewhere, and he should be able to trace her. She'd dyed her hair a fancy blonde color like the Hastings girl—or maybe the Hastings girl had dyed *her* hair like the nut.

Domer sat up and gave his head a vigorous shake. No use lying around all night with thoughts drifting in and out of his skull—better get up and start thinking logically. He rolled off the bed, put on his shoes, and lit a cigarette.

That black stocking with the foot cut off—they were selling them at the local five-and-dime. They'd sold several pairs lately, but of course nobody remembered who'd bought them. Who would wear stockings like that, anyhow? Certainly no woman that Domer had ever known—not even during the war. They'd rather have gone barelegged—up to and including his grandmother, who was eighty-nine and still wore her skirts too short because she was vain about her legs. Anyway, it was probable that he was wasting his time over the stocking—more than likely it had nothing to do with anything.

There was a sudden sound of footsteps and voices out in the corridor—quiet and restrained, but giving an unmistakable sense of emergency. He opened his door and peered out, and saw Ross, Myrtle, and Catherine go into a room across the hall. He heard Catherine say, "I'm sure he's going this time, Doctor."

Domer backed up and closed his door again. Some poor devil passing in his checks. He lit another cigarette and began slowly to pace the room.

Irene was restless too. She kept dozing and then waking, with remarks half formed in her mind which would shatter Ross and his dignity if only she could get them properly thought out.

She heard Ross's voice after a while, and then Myrtle's, but apparently they went into one of the rooms, and then everything was quiet again. She switched on the light and looked at her watch—twenty past three. She heard another voice—a woman's—weak and old and complaining.

"Nurse! Oh, Nurse! Come quickly! Nurse! Nurse! Nurse!"

Irene got up and put on a robe and slippers. She regretted having left her door open, so that she could hear these things, but it was impossible to ignore the querulous, frightened old voice, and evidently Catherine, Myrtle, and Ross were busy over some emergency.

She went out into the hall and followed the cries of "Nurse" to a room two doors down. She found an old lady with snow-white hair, lively dark eyes, and tiny, blue-veined little hands, who looked her up and down and observed resentfully, "You're not a nurse."

"No—but if you want something, I can get it for you."

The old lady clutched at the sheet with her little hands, and her mouth quivered. She was frightened, but game.

"I think they're busy with someone who is very ill," Irene explained. "Won't you let me get whatever you want?"

"I don't want anything."

Irene smiled and brushed a wisp of white hair away from the dry, old forehead. "Shall I get the nurse for you, as soon as she's free?"

"The nurse was here—she was here—but she had no head. She was walking around without a head. You stay with me, child—I'm afraid to be alone."

Irene's face set, with the smile still on it, but she could feel her scalp tingling and her heart began to pound. The poor old soul must have seen something—she wouldn't pick a headless nurse out of the air. Irene shivered and thought, no—she's heard the nurses talking, that's all, and she's scared.

"Nonsense!" said the old lady loudly. "Absurd! I must have been dreaming." And suddenly, in the manner of the very old, she was asleep.

Irene heaved a quick sigh of relief and crept softly out of the room. She glanced down the corridor and saw Domer peering out of his room, and made for him with all speed. She badly wanted company, and he looked solidly dependable. She told him about her experience with the old lady, and he said, "For God's sake! A nurse without a head, yet. What did they feed the old lady for supper, to give her dreams like that?"

"Well, maybe she was dreaming," Irene said doubtfully, "but it's not the first time a headless nurse has been reported around here."

"What do you mean?" Domer asked quickly.

She told him what she knew about it, and when she had finished he nodded happily.

"One nutty patient starts the thing, and then this Clark fellow reopens the idea in order to empty the hospital and grab off the inheritance. And he gets this poor girl from the squirrel commissariat to help him."

"The—" Irene shook her head, feeling a bit confused. "But she couldn't walk around with her head under her arm."

"Her head," said Domer in a satisfied voice, "stayed right on her neck. Remember the black stocking?" He started briskly up the hall.

"Hey, wait!" Irene called, running after him. "What about the black stocking?"

"You just slip it over your head," Domer explained. "If it's fairly dark your head wouldn't be seen at all—but you could see through the mesh well enough to get around."

Irene was surprised at the feeling of relief that flooded over her. "Oh. Yes. I see. Where are you going now?"

"The old lady saw that girl only a short time ago, and maybe she's still around here. Anyway, the first place to look is in the boyfriend's room."

Domer pushed into Clark's room without knocking, but Irene remained out in the hall, because it was a hot night and she decided that she might as well save a double embarrassment in case Clark had cast off all his coverings.

Domer came out again almost immediately, and she saw at once that something had happened. "She must have been good and damn mad at him," he said briefly.

Myrtle and Ross emerged from one of the rooms, talking quietly together. Myrtle looked up, caught sight of Irene, and broke away.

"My dear, you must not be walking around like this—you must stay in bed until you're better, or we shall have complications."

Domer directed a sudden grin at Irene and asked, "You sick?"

She grinned back at him. "I'm in for observation. They haven't seen anything yet, but I intend to give them something to observe when I get the first week's bill."

Ross and Myrtle gave her a pair of cold looks, and Myrtle said curtly, "You'd better go back to bed at once."

"Certainly not. The doctor told me to get up and exercise if I couldn't sleep at night."

Domer cleared his throat and became official. "You'll have to contact the local police at once, Doctor. Clark Munster has been shot and killed."

In the ensuing commotion he slipped away, still intent on his own particular job of tracking down Doris Miller. He went outside and was annoyed, but not daunted, to find that it was raining. He turned up his coat collar, headed into it, and made a quick, comprehensive search of the grounds, but found nothing. He ended up at the small clearing, beyond the lawn, where he had found the stocking, but there didn't seem to be anything except dripping shrubbery and wet grass. He made one last sweep around with his flashlight and then held it steady, cursing softly to himself.

Tire tracks—unmistakable. There were patches of mud where the pattern of the tread was quite distinct, and he filed it carefully away in his mind. So she had come by car—and gone, too. God knows where, by this time. He straightened slowly, pocketed the flashlight, and started back toward the hospital.

He felt acutely dissatisfied. He had not been quick enough—and perhaps he should have prevented that Clark fellow's death too, in some way. But how could he know that Clark's life was in danger? Well, he should have known. He was a detective, wasn't he? And a good one. That will— But the will didn't mean that the fellow was in danger of being shot. He was losing out on that in any case, what with that Myrtle roping in pseudo-patients all over the landscape. He liked Myrtle—nice, understanding woman.

He wondered, with sudden uneasiness, whether he'd been registered as a patient himself. He couldn't be a party to that sort of thing, no matter how much he might sympathize.

He heard a faint cry and stopped in his tracks, his head raised alertly. He strained his ears through the continuous drip and patter of the rain and heard it again—an anguished cry for help. He thrust his hand into his pocket for the flash, but he was still fumbling to draw it out when there came a shrill, terrified scream. He looked up at the building and saw a white figure slide over the wet tiles of the roof and come crashing to the ground almost at his feet.

## THIRTY-SIX

DOMER advanced and played his flashlight over the crumpled figure. Platinum-blonde hair, blood-drenched, and from a pocket of the white uniform a length of black stocking hung limply. The foot had not been cut off this one, but the leg was stretched and shapeless. Domer knelt down, frowning, and gave his head a little shake. She was dead.

Ed came running around the corner of the building, his face a white blur in the darkness and his voice trembling with excitement. "What is it? What's happened here?"

Domer stood up and played the flash again, so that Ed could see. "It's Doris Miller. Fell from the top of the building, up there. Slid down over the roof."

He turned away abruptly, leaving Ed to his duty, and went inside and up to the third floor. Several people loomed in his path with excited questions, but he brushed past them all, his mind concentrated on the section of roof from which Doris had fallen. His sense of direction was unusually good, and it led him straight to Ross's bedroom. The room was empty, and he stood for a moment looking around, until his eye fell on the door that gave on the small balcony. He was quite unconscious of the fact that a small crowd of people had pushed in behind him, as he went over and stepped out onto the balcony.

There was a section of sharply slanting roof directly beside the projection of the balcony, and he decided that was where she had gone. It was not an easy climb, and he wondered how she had managed it—unless she came around from a window somewhere. His foot hit against something, and he glanced down and saw a small ladder lying on the floor. He picked it up and set it against the roof. It fitted snugly and led straight to a small chimney.

Domer pulled a long breath and nodded. That was how she had done it, and she'd kicked the ladder away so that it fell back onto the balcony after she had climbed up. She had shot Clark and then come up here to hide, but the roof was so steep she must have been mad indeed to think she could have done anything but fall off it, once she had kicked the ladder away.

He went back into the room and came face to face with Elise, Myrtle, Irene, and several other people who were strangers to him.

John was standing beside Myrtle, trembling a little and trying not to show it. Things were getting too much for him again. Clark dead—murdered—right here in the hospital. And now this—a nurse—fallen from the roof and killed. That's what they were saying; one of Ed's men had run in looking for Joe, and he had told them.

Domer went to the telephone to send in his report, and although Myrtle would have liked to stay and listen, she had John on her mind and felt that he came first. She took him by the arm and drew him away. "Come on downstairs with me, John—I'm going to get you a strong, hot cup of coffee."

Domer presently put down the phone and stood for a moment frowning in thought. Irene and Elise watched him in silence, until he looked up and asked suddenly, "Do you know the telephone number of Doris Miller's sister?"

Irene nodded. "I do. But are you sure that that's—Doris—out there?"

"No doubt about it. Will you phone the sister? She'll want to come out."

Irene agreed and picked up the telephone with reluctant fingers. She wished that she had stayed downstairs now—this was a rotten job to have been roped in for. The phone hummed monotonously against her ear, and then her stomach turned over as Ann's sleepy voice spoke to her.

It was her way to be direct, and even blunt, and she was so now—in her nervousness even more than usual—and Ann's response was a sharp scream. Irene removed the instrument from her ear for a moment, and when she put it back, Ann had subsided into hysterical sobbing. She promised to come out with as little delay as possible, and Irene hung up and wiped her brow. "That was awful," she muttered. "Don't anybody ask me to do a thing like that again."

Elise was flinging questions at Domer, who was thinking of something else and hadn't yet answered one of them. So Elise, in her excitement, answered them herself and, when Domer turned to leave the room, hooked herself firmly onto his arm and went with him.

Irene trailed along behind, but parted from them on the second floor and went on down the back stairs to the kitchen. She knew that sleep was out of the question and decided on a cup of coffee with Myrtle and John.

The kitchen was brilliantly lighted, and the only occupant was Ross, who stood staring gloomily at a furiously percolating coffeepot.

Irene hesitated, and he glanced up and said, "Hello."

"Fine, thanks," she responded, being a bit confused, and added a few embarrassed words of condolence.

Ross shook his head. "It's a shock, of course—but Clark and I have never been at all close since we grew up."

There was a short silence, and Irene asked abruptly, "Isn't that coffee done yet?"

"Coffee ? Oh—yes. Myrtle told me to let it perk four minutes by the clock. That was ages ago. Here—I'd better take it off."

He lifted the coffeepot, dropped it down again with a rude exclamation, and then got a pot holder and picked it up again and put it on the table. Irene gave voice to a milder exclamation, picked it up, and slid a magazine under it.

"It's maple—do you want to burn a nasty ring on it?"

"Sit down," Ross said, "and let's have our coffee before the others get here."

They sat down together, and Ross began to talk about Elise—what an entertaining and colorful personality she had, and how interesting it must have been for Irene to have lived in the same house with her. Irene listened for a while and then pulled herself together and observed that Ross's father must have been a clever and skillful doctor to have built up such a fine hospital.

They hardly noticed when Myrtle and John came in. Myrtle put John into a chair and then compressed her lips into a thin line when she saw that there was nothing to eat on the table, nor any cups, saucers, spoons, sugar, or cream.

Only a pot of overpercolated coffee. Just waiting for a workhorse like herself to come in and see to everything. She began to throw things onto the table, but John was the only one who noticed the clattering and banging. He frowned in a vaguely pained sort of way but said nothing.

Myrtle was just about to sit down when Elise and Domer came in, still linked arm in arm. She sighed loudly and got out two more cups, and Elise exclaimed, "Coffee! How delightful! "

Ross got to his feet and said courteously, "You'll have some, won't you? I made it myself."

Myrtle gave him a withering glance and, as they all sat down, turned to Domer and asked, "Have you found out yet who shot poor Clark?"

"It's nothing to do with me," he said with a shrug. "I came to find Miss Miller, and I have found her."

"Well—but—but who's going to get that—the killer?" Myrtle gasped. "You can't just walk off and leave us here with a murderer."

"Local police," Domer murmured indifferently.

"Myrtle," Elise said, "don't you see? It was that girl—that lunatic. Mr. Domer and I had the particulars from Joe and Ed. She shot that poor young man—I know that I was angry with him, but I think now that he was more misguided than malicious—and then she hid on the roof. She wore a black stocking over her head—just to terrify people, you see—and it gave the impression that she had no head at all. Not that her actual head was much good to her, poor creature—her brain was all snarled up in knots, like worsted."

John, soothed and revived by the strong coffee, thought uncomfortably that Horace must have had that stocking on his head when he had seen him in the summerhouse. The girl must have done it. He should have gone into the summerhouse then and investigated, and perhaps it would all have come out and Clark might have been saved.

"Mr. Domer and I have traced her movements exactly," Elise was saying. "She went up to the doctor's room and out onto that balcony he has, and climbed up that little ladder to the roof, and then she kicked the ladder back onto the floor so people wouldn't notice it and get ideas. So she hid there until it started to rain, and of course it must have been very uncomfortable, hanging onto that little chimney, and I guess she got restless, so she decided to risk a move—and she lost her balance and fell."

Domer sipped his coffee in silence and stared at the wall just above John's head, which made John distinctly uncomfortable, though Domer was unaware of it.

Joe and Ed came in and, ignoring everyone else, made straight for Domer.

"We can't find the weapon," Joe said plaintively. "We looked everywhere—been through everything. Nothing doing."

Domer raised one eyebrow and said, "Tch, tch."

Joe rattled the change in his pockets and waited hopefully, but Domer resumed operations on his coffee.

Ed said, "Listen—we found a will of Clark's, dated about six months ago—right, Joe?—and it leaves everything which he dies possessed of to this here Doris Miller."

"He wasn't possessed of anything," Ross said flatly. "Not a dime."

"He might have had the hospital, though," Myrtle said in a low voice. "From midnight—it might have been his today." She directed a meaning look at Irene and Elise, who ignored her.

"Who would inherit from Doris ?" Domer asked thoughtfully.

"There's only Ann," Irene told him.

"Well, perhaps Ann did it," Elise suggested. "Tried to make it appear as though Doris had done it, you know, and then fixed things, somehow, so that Doris would fall from the roof and kill herself, and everything would be nicely settled—for Ann, I mean."

"Lady," said Joe peevishly, "that's a lot of—er— You're mistaken. We checked on that—we just finished checking it—and that Ann dame hasn't been out at night or telephoned or anything since they turned her loose."

Elise bit her lip in annoyance and glanced at Domer to find him gazing at her in unmistakable admiration.

She's dead right, he was thinking buoyantly. Ann Miller had killed them both.

## THIRTY-SEVEN

DOMER was staring through John again, with his thoughts turned inward, but John became so uncomfortable that he presently took his coffee cup and went over to stand by the stove. Although he had had nothing to do with the terrible things that had been happening, he felt as though guilt were written large across his face.

Myrtle finished her coffee and then began an efficient rounding up of Irene and Elise, who were driven back to bed forthwith. They were invalids, Myrtle said firmly, and should be on their respective backs with hot-water bottles to their feet. John knew that she had the good of the hospital in her mind, but he thought she was overdoing it a bit.

Domer stood up and stretched. Have to get going, he thought, and wondered how that girl had covered herself so well—he'd have to find how she'd done it. Clark would have to be killed first, of course, so that the batty sister would inherit, and then the sister had to be put out of the way. All this prefaced by carefully laid plans to scare enough patients out of the hospital to insure its coming to Clark in the first place.

Ann had worn that stocking over her head when she killed Clark, and one of Doris's uniforms left over from her nursing days, so that she would be thought to be Doris if seen, and then slipped into the old lady's room—probably scared out of the hall by someone's footsteps. Later she'd picked up Doris and probably had tried to induce Doris to put the stocking on her head—but Doris either had refused or had removed it subsequently and stuffed it into her pocket. Ann had taken her up to Ross's room then and out onto the little balcony. This could not have been planned ahead; Doris probably would not stay where she was supposed to stay, and Ann, trying to keep her hidden, got up to Ross's room and took her chances as she found them. She probably told Doris it was a good hiding place for her and she would be back for her, and then went off, after removing the ladder, knowing that Doris would get restless after a while and try to get off herself, which made it highly probable that she would slip and fall—and even if she was saved—well, there would be other chances.

He came out of his abstraction to find Ed at his elbow.

"Should I list that girl as an accident or a suicide, should you say?" Ed asked diffidently.

Domer brushed past him. "Don't list it at all until you know what it is," he said carelessly, and made for the front door while Ed sent a helpless look after him.

The rain had stopped, and it was cooler outside now, with the fresh feeling of dawn in the air. Domer breathed deeply as he got into his car and headed toward the city.

Ann had come out by car, he thought, and had brought Doris with her. She must have been keeping Doris in her own apartment. Somehow, after her release, she had eluded whoever was tailing her and had picked Doris up in a car—he'd have to find out how she'd managed it. During the time that Ann was being held, Doris had been loose around the hospital, scaring the patients, according to Ann's carefully laid plan. Only she'd gone off the track a bit, Domer reflected. Instead of lurking around as a headless nurse with a stocking over her head, she'd had a fancy blonding job done on her hair and had been more inclined to show it off than to cover it up. She had even come in in the daytime through the side door, evidently armed with something heavy, as she had used it on Ross when he had come out of the dining room. But apparently she had fallen into her old habits and had tried to make off with Bob Herms, who, if he wasn't a corpse at the time, seemed due to become one at any minute—and that had been as effective as the stocking.

Domer absently passed through a red light and thought back over some of the numerous things that Elise had confided to him. The old doctor's body—how had the poor, mad creature managed to get it out of the tomb, since the key had been hanging in the dining room all the time? There'd been another key made, of course—Clark and Ann planned to have Doris live in the tomb while she was terrorizing the hospital.

Ann must have dominated Clark in the planning, and double-crossed him too. He had shown himself as being far the weaker member of the team. Everyone was supposed to think that he and Doris were together in Chicago, but he was not skillful enough to keep himself hidden, and as soon as they had picked him up it became known that Doris was not with him. So Clark returned, defeated, and probably Ann was furious at the miscarriage of their plans.

Domer doubted that Ann had intended to kill them both so soon—after all, there was no particular hurry. But Clark was going to pieces, and it became necessary to get rid of him at once. She must have seen him, to have known his condition—and how could she have seen him, when she had been so closely guarded? Well, she'd found some way, that was certain.

The dark gray dawn was suddenly shot through with rose and gold, and Domer shifted his tired body and switched off the headlights.

Clark, he thought, had been desperate to get a car, and had finally stolen Elise's, because she had left the keys in it. He had gone in to see Ann then, but Ann had worked all day and lunched at her usual cafeteria. Perhaps that was it—her usual cafeteria. Clark knew that she always lunched there, and so went in and sat somewhere near her, and they whispered together without it being obvious to anyone around them. She had told him where the old doctor's body was, and he had picked it up and strapped it to the roof of Elise's car. Elise had explained that she strapped the tent up that way when she went camping, and there was a canvas hammock for odd things like pots and pans. The body had been strapped up there, with the hammock to conceal it, and no one had seen it until the straps had broken and it had fallen down. Evidently Ann had not been able to control Doris's insane craving to play with dead bodies, and this one had had to be hidden somewhere until Clark could pick it up.

Domer turned off at a diner, where he had some breakfast and telephoned in four information. He was told that Ann had hired a taxi to take her out to the hospital and had left some time ago. He hung up, grinning faintly as he pictured Ann's reaction when she discovered that Myrtle had raised the census to the required number by hospitalizing Elise and Irene.

He supposed that Clark had seen his brother seal that will into the wall and had later taken it out, read it, and pasted it in again. He couldn't have known of the letter to John, indicating the whereabouts of the will. Perhaps the old man had put it into his funeral clothes, before he died, and it had fallen out when Doris was carrying the body around. If either Ann or Clark had known about it, they would certainly have removed it.

Domer returned to his car and drove straight to the apartment house where Ann lived. It was a rather old building, but decent, with a single narrow entrance at the front. He pushed open the outer door and entered a small tiled lobby that smelled of soapsuds. There was a row of brass mailboxes, and he saw that Ann's apartment was on the third floor. The inner door was locked—one of those buzzer arrangements, he decided—so he went out again and walked toward the back of the building. There was an entrance into the basement, with the door standing partly open, and inside, a self-service elevator which obligingly dropped down in front of him when he pressed the button. He went on up to the third floor without having seen anyone.

Ann's apartment was at the front of the building, and it took Domer one minute and thirteen seconds to open the door with a nail file. It was a one-room-and-kitchenette arrangement—a crowded, untidy little place, with a couch covered with rumpled bedclothes. But she'd had to leave in a hurry, of course.

The kitchenette had an unusual number of modern, timesaving gadgets, and Domer inspected them rather idly, until he was struck with an idea. He went into the living room and over to a big lamp that stood near the window, and almost immediately his mouth relaxed into a satisfied smile. It was another gadget, really—one of those arrangements whereby you could turn the lamp on and, at a certain time, it would turn off of itself. Well, that was one hurdle. She could be out at the hospital, while her tails were supposing, comfortably, that she had just turned out her light and was getting into bed.

Domer left the apartment and headed for the roof. She had got out twice without being seen, and he ought to be able to find out how. The roof was squared and flat, and the adjoining building, on one side, was too far away for her to have got over—he could think of no gadget that would have served her there. He walked to the other side and was a little taken aback to discover that the space was even wider, until he looked along toward the back and saw a projection that nearly touched the roof on which he stood. He stepped over, made his way across tarred gravel, and entered the building through a heavy metal door.

She would not have gone out the front way, he decided— it was too close to her own front entrance, and she might be seen. He went to the basement and out a back door to a rear yard. There was a high wooden fence separating this yard from the one behind Ann's building, and Domer chuckled. This apartment house had a good deal more elegance than Ann's, and the fence appeared to have been put there to keep the neighbors apart and make sure that the genteel white sheep, here, did not mix with the goats from Ann's place.

He followed a path that presently forked—one fork leading to the front of the building and the other to a large garage at the rear. He made for the garage with a spring in his step. This was it, all right—she'd borrowed a car from somewhere.

He went into the cool, shadowed space of the garage and approached a man, attired in overalls and rubber hip boots, who was busily washing a car. He asked, without preamble, for information concerning a Miss Ann Miller, and was met with an indifferent shrug and the response that the garageman had never heard of her.

A customer, on his way out, stopped for gas, and when the attendant had dropped his hose and gone to serve him, Domer took the opportunity for a quick look at the cars parked against the walls. He was feeling somewhat sobered, since he did not see how Ann could have taken a car when the attendant did not know her—but he looked anyway.

Two of the cars showed signs of having been out in the recent rain—a large green sedan and a black coupe. With the tire pattern that he had seen in the mud of the picnic grounds well in his mind, he inspected the tires of these two cars. The green sedan was out, but when he looked at the black coupe he was conscious of a little inner thrill. The pattern was the same.

He straightened up and, glancing at his watch, saw that it was a few minutes after seven. The garageman was approaching him with a certain amount of belligerence, and he decided to show his badge. It cleared the air, but the subsequent questioning was a disappointment. The attendant was on duty all night, went off at eight in the morning, and declared that nobody could take a car out without his knowing it.

Domer was discouraged, but he made a search of the black coupe. He found nothing, and had not really expected to find anything. Ann had certainly had a revolver with a silencer, but it was not likely that she had left it lying around anywhere. Those things were too easily traced.

He turned back to the attendant, who had lost his truculence and was regarding him with open-mouthed interest, and asked suddenly, "Don't you eat during the night? Do you bring a lunch with you and eat it here?"

"I go across to the diner at one o'clock and at five. But it don't take more than a few minutes—cuppa coffee and a snack."

Domer smiled on a long breath. That settled it, then. Ann had watched, and knew just when to take the car out and when to bring it back again. The keys were left in all the cars, so that they could be moved for washing and service—it was quite simple.

He indicated the black coupe and asked abruptly, "Who owns this car?"

"Mrs. Elliot. She's in California—won't be back till next month."

Domer nodded. Probably a friend of Ann's—easy to check on it.

He glanced at the car with a faint frown. Ann would assume that there was nothing to connect her with it, and where could she find a better hiding place for the gun? She could always come back and get it, after the furor had died down, and dispose of it at her leisure.

It's in the car, all right, he thought, and began another and more thorough search.

## THIRTY-EIGHT

ANN paid off her taxi and stood for a moment surveying the hospital. She gave it a comprehensive going over with her eyes and then mounted the steps and went in, her face falling into lines of grief.

Ed was at the door and Myrtle in the hall, and at her request they escorted her to where Myrtle had laid Doris out as prettily as possible.

Ann wept. She mopped ineffectively with a sodden handkerchief while Myrtle told her the whole story, and broke in at intervals with a dull, unvarying eulogy. "She was a lovely girl."

When Myrtle came, with some embarrassment, to the part about Doris having shot Clark and hidden on the roof, Ann was appropriately shocked.

"I don't believe it. Doris wouldn't have hurt Clark or a living soul. She was a lovely girl."

Her tears continued to flow. It was easy to cry now, and there was relief in it—relief after all the strain of Clark breaking up, like the poor weak thing he was, and Doris being so hard to control. Getting her hair bleached, like that, and then refusing to wear the stocking because she did not want to hide it. However, it had worked out all right. Doris had dragged the old man downstairs, and that had scared enough patients into going home.

There had been plenty to worry her, though. She'd had to get out and pick Doris up, because she was afraid that if the police got to her first, she'd spill everything. And that had been dreadful—it made her shudder to think of it. She'd been on her way back, when Doris had suddenly asked her to drive more carefully, because she had a friend in the back seat. She'd glanced over her shoulder—and there it was. That hideous decomposing body from the mausoleum. It had taken every ounce of self-control she possessed not to abandon the wheel and go into screaming hysterics. Later she realized that Doris must have put the body in the car while she herself was off looking for Doris's suitcase. She had located it, eventually, in the summerhouse—with no aid from Doris, who had turned sulky and refused to help. She had not wanted to go back to the apartment, and Ann had had a good deal of trouble in persuading her.

There had been no way to dispose of that ghastly body, either. The car had to be slipped into the garage at five, and there was not time to return to the hospital. She tried to stop and throw it out onto the road, but Doris started screaming and fighting, and she had to drive on. In the end, she had driven into the garage—when the attendant was having coffee at five o'clock—and had simply left the body in the car. But it had worried her nearly to distraction, and she had been intensely relieved when Clark appeared at the cafeteria where she had always lunched. She had warned him to pretend not to know her, since she knew she was being watched, but they had managed a fairly comprehensive conversation nevertheless.

Clark told her that the will had been found, and she expressed her satisfaction—it was time for that. In return, she told him about the body of his brother, which was still in the borrowed car. She described the car and the attendant's habits, and was vastly relieved, later on, when she discovered that Clark had somehow managed to remove the dreadful thing.

Myrtle was still soothing her, though rather absently by this time, and she presently put her limp, wet handkerchief away and asked weakly, "Is my friend Irene still here?"

Myrtle hesitated. Irene, dewy-eyed and blooming, looked far too healthy to be exhibited; but on the other hand, she could hardly keep them apart.

"Irene hasn't been well, you know—she's sleeping now, and the doctor doesn't want her disturbed."

Ann continued to hang her head, but her eyes slitted and the line of her jaw became rigid. So that was the game! They d found the will and they'd taken steps without delay. She wondered how they'd found it. Clark had seen his brother pasting it inside the wallpaper and had later taken it out, read it, and replaced it. But he had told no one, except Doris. Always Doris. He had never looked at Ann. He'd dropped into her cafeteria sometimes and talked to her—about Doris. It didn't make any difference that Doris was insane—of course he always believed her stories of having been framed. He believed her so thoroughly that it had been a tremendous shock to him when he learned that she had carried the old man downstairs and violated his brother's tomb. He had supposed that it was because Doris had been a nurse that she consented so eagerly to hide quietly in the mausoleum and come out occasionally with the stocking on her head, pretending to be a headless nurse, so that all the patients would be scared away. Poor Clark—charming enough, in his way, but no brains or courage.

Ann took a long breath and turned her drenched eyes imploringly to Myrtle's face.

"Oh, please—please let me see Irene. She's one of the few real friends I have—and I need a friend now. I won't bother her or be a nuisance, but I'd just like to sit with her for a little while, until I feel better."

Myrtle sighed, muttered, "All right, come on," and led the way to Irene's room.

As they approached the door they heard a murmur of voices—low, intimate, and harmonious. Myrtle slowed up and said, "Will you wait a minute? The—er—doctor is with her now." But when she pushed grimly into the room, Ann was right behind her.

Ross was sitting on Irene's bed, and they were both smoking. Ann took them in at a glance and felt anger surge up within her. She began to cry again. Myrtle stepped over to Ross and put her face within a few inches of his. "*Will* you get out of here?" she hissed through her teeth. "I don't suppose it would matter to you if the patients were all dead and dying and the building on fire."

He stood up, disposed of his cigarette, and exchanged a glance with Irene in which there was intimacy and humorous understanding. "Not much," he said to Myrtle indifferently. "It's really John's concern now—not mine."

His eye fell on Ann, and after Myrtle had hastily introduced them he offered a word or two of condolence. Irene started to get out of bed, but Myrtle pushed her back with a firm hand on her shoulder and said out of the corner of her mouth, "For God's sake, stay there—just for today, at least."

Ann, with her face once more buried in what was left of her handkerchief, heard, and perfectly understood the implication.

Myrtle urged Ross out of the room and in the hall outside asked curiously, "What do you mean by saying it's John's concern?"

"Just what I say. I intend to hand the place over to him and then I'm going to try the city. This village is no place for a girl with platinum-blonde hair."

"Are you out of your mind?" Myrtle asked helplessly.

"No—just being honest, upright, and noble to make up for some of the old man's didos—and who should know better than you that he cut a good many before he died?"

"He did promise the place to John," Myrtle said soberly, "but you know perfectly well that he never meant it—and John should have known too."

Ross shrugged. "A promise is a promise. If John had not been depending on it, he could have gone out on his own and probably done a good deal better. My mind is made up, so there's no use in arguing. Come on and we'll look in on all these dead and dying patients you were talking about."

At the head of the stairs they ran into Elise, who was elegantly dressed and bejeweled for the day, and their argument was lost in the ensuing struggle, during which Elise was disrobed and returned to her bed, with Myrtle more or less sitting on her chest.

Ross left them to fight it out and went down to the first floor, where he presently ran into John. John had overheard enough of the talk between Ross and Myrtle to make it a little difficult to keep his face in lines of befitting gravity. Clark was recently dead, and he was grieved and ought to show it—and yet, at intervals, he found himself beaming happily.

"We'll have to work hard to get the place on its feet again," Ross said, "but we'll manage it—and then you and Myrtle can take over, John."

Irene was feeling decidedly uncomfortable. Ann had collapsed into the armchair beside her bed and was weeping drearily, impervious to the few murmured and rather stilted words of condolence that Irene offered from time to time. In the end, she fell silent and merely extended a dry handkerchief.

Ann mopped busily for a while and then raised her head and stammered timidly, "Are you—I mean, that doctor—do you like him?"

Irene gave her a surprised glance, yawned, stretched with her arms above her head, and suddenly laughed.

"He's all right."

"No, but—what I mean is—are you going to marry him?"

"I suppose so. I think it's the only way I can get him to pay for having my hair restored."

Ann dropped her head again, and while her hands twisted and worried the handkerchief her mind raced furiously.

They'd pulled this trick on her—it was perfectly obvious that Irene was bursting with health—she'd sue them.

She was conscious, suddenly, of an immense fatigue—a weariness so devastating that the tears dripped over her face because she felt unable to raise her hand to wipe them away. Suppose someone were to come, now, to that door—someone who knew all about it, who had discovered everything she'd done.

The handkerchief fell from her hands and lay in a damp ball on the floor, but she was too tired to pick it up. Only she must not go to pieces the way Clark had done—she'd have to shut out these terrifying thoughts.

The gun, though? She'd put it into a canvas bag in the trunk of the car—a bag that held the skid chains. You could not feel the gun or even see it, readily, if the bag were opened, when it was mixed in with a heavy mass of chains. She'd never go near the car again, and she could taper off her friendship with Barbara Elliot.

Fear surged up in her again, drying her tears and pounding against her temples. Someone was coming along the hall—not a nurse—slow, heavy footsteps—a man. A doctor. It must be a doctor. She closed her eyes and had a sudden clear picture of Doris cutting off the foot of one of those black stockings and pulling it over the face of that dreadful corpse, not wanting to hide his nice hair, but thinking his face was in bad shape and ought to be covered. And, later, pulling it off again just before she put the body into the car.

The footsteps slowed and stopped. She fastened her eyes on the door, her hands clammy, her stomach turning over, her breath coming shallow and fast. Someone knocked.

Irene called, "Come in," and Ann struggled to her feet, her hand feeling for the back of the chair to keep herself from falling.

Domer walked in, and there was no need for words—she knew at once that it was all over.

Domer said mildly, "I found that gun."

THE END

# Rue Morgue Press Titles as of May 2000

**Brief Candles** by Manning Coles. From Topper to Aunt Dimity mystery readers have embraced the cozy ghost story. Four of the best were written by Manning Coles, the creator of the witty Tommy Hambledon spy novels. First published in 1954, *Brief Candles* is likely to produce more laughs than chills as an English couple vacationing in France runs into two gentlemen with decidedly old-world manners. What they don't know is that the two men, James and Charles Latimer, are ancestors of theirs who shuffled off this mortal coil some 80 years earlier when, emboldened by strong drink and with only a pet monkey and an aged waiter as allies, the two made a valiant, foolish and quite fatal attempt to halt a German advance during the Franco-Prussian War of 1870. Now these two ectoplasmic gentlemen and their spectral pet monkey Ulysses have been summoned from their unmarked graves because their visiting relatives are in serious trouble. But before they can solve the younger Latimers' problems, the three benevolent spirits light brief candles of insanity for a tipsy policeman, a recalcitrant banker, a convocation of English ghost-busters, and a card-playing rogue who's wanted for murder. "As felicitously foolish as a collaboration of (P.G.) Wodehouse and Thorne Smith."—Anthony Boucher. "For those who like something out of the ordinary. Lighthearted, very funny.'—*The Sunday Times.* "A gay, most readable story."—*The Daily Telegraph.* The other three ghost books will appear within the next year. **0-915230-24-0** **$14.00**

**The Black-Headed Pins** by Constance & Gwenyth Little. "...a zany, fun-loving puzzler spun by the sisters Little—it's celluloid screwball comedy printed on paper. The charm of this book lies in the lively banter between characters and the breakneck pace of the story. You hardly grasp how the first victim was done in when you have to grapple with outlandish clues like two black-headed pins."—Diane Plumley, *Dastardly Deeds. With* her bank account down to empty, orphaned Leigh Smith has no choice but to take a job as a paid companion and housekeeper to the miserly Mrs. Ballister. However, once she moves into the drafty, creaking old Ballister mansion in the wilds of New Jersey, Smithy has reason to regret her decision. But when Mrs. Ballister decides to invite her nieces and nephews for Christmas, Smithy sees the possibility for some fun. What she doesn't expect is to encounter the Ballister family curse. It seems that when a dragging noise is heard in the attic it foretells the death of a Ballister. And once a Ballister dies, if you don't watch the body until it's buried, it's likely to walk. The stockings are barely hung from the mantle when those dreaded sounds are heard in the attic, and before long, corpses are going for regular midnight strolls. Smithy and a pair of potential beaux turn detective and try to figure out why the murderer leaves black-headed pins at the scene of every crime. First published in 1938. **0-915230-25-9** **$14.00**

**The Black Gloves** by Constance & Gwenyth Little. "I'm relishing every madcap moment."—*Murder Most Cozy.* Welcome to the Vickers estate near East Orange, New Jersey, where the middle class is destroying the neighborhood, erecting their horrid little cottages, playing on the Vickers tennis court, and generally disrupting the comfortable life of Hammond Vickers no end. It's bad enough that he had to shell out good money to get his daughter Lissa a Reno divorce only to have her brute of an ex-husband show up on his doorstep. But why does there also have to be a corpse in the cellar? And lights going on and off in the attic? First published in 1939. **0-915230-20-8** **$14.00**

**The Black Honeymoon** by Constance & Gwenyth Little. Can you murder someone with feathers? If you don't believe feathers are lethal, then you probably haven't read a Little mystery. No, Uncle Richard wasn't tickled to death—though we can't make the same guarantee for readers—but the hyper-allergic rich man did manage to sneeze himself into the hereafter in his hospital room. Suspicion falls on his nurse, young Miriel Mason, who recently married the dead man's nephew, an army officer on furlough. To clear herself of murder as well as charges of being a gold-digger, Miriel summons private detective Kelly, an old crony of her father's, who gets himself hired as a servant even though he can't cook, clean or serve. First published in 1944. **0-915230-21-6** **$14.00**

**Great Black Kanba** by Constance & Gwenyth Little. "If you love train mysteries as much as I do, hop on the Trans-Australia Railway in *Great Black Kanba*, a fast and funny 1944 novel by the talented (Littles)."—Jon L. Breen, *Ellery Queen's Mystery Magazine*. "I have decided to add *Kanba* to my favorite mysteries of all time list!...a zany ride I'll definitely take again and again."—Diane Plumley in the Murder Ink newsletter. When a young American woman wakes up on an Australia train with a bump on her head and no memory, she suddenly finds out that she's engaged to two different men and the chief suspect in a murder case. But she's almost more upset to discover that she appears to have absolutely dreadful taste in clothing. It all adds up to some delightful mischief—call it Cornell Woolrich on laughing gas. **0-915230-22-4** **$14.00**

**The Grey Mist Murders** by Constance & Gwenyth Little. Who—or what—is the mysterious figure that emerges from the grey mist to strike down several passengers on the final leg of a round-the-world sea voyage? Is it the same shadowy entity that persists in leaving three matches outside Lady Marsh's cabin every morning? And why does one flimsy negligee seem to pop up at every turn? When Carla Bray first heard things go bump in the night, she hardly expected to find a corpse in the adjoining cabin. Nor did she expect to find herself the chief suspect in the murders. Robert Arnold, a sardonic young man who joined the ship in Tahiti, makes a play for Carla but if he's really interested in helping to clear her of murder, why does he spend so much time courting other women on board? This 1938 effort was the Littles' first book. **0-915230-26-7** **$14.00**

**Murder is a Collector's Item** by Elizabeth Dean. "(It) froths over with the same effervescent humor as the best Hepburn-Grant films."—Sujata Massey. "Completely enjoyable."—*New York Times*. "Fast and funny."—*The New Yorker*. Twenty-six-year-old Emma Marsh isn't much at spelling or geography and perhaps she butchers the odd literary quotation or two, but she's a keen judge of character and more than able to hold her own when it comes to selling antiques or solving murders. When she stumbles upon the body of a rich collector on the floor of the Boston antiques shop where she works, suspicion quickly falls upon her missing boss. Emma knows Jeff Graham is no murderer, but veteran homicide cop Jerry Donovan doesn't share her convictions, and Emma enlists the aid of Hank Fairbanks, her wealthy boyfriend and would-be criminologist, to nab the real killer. Originally published in 1939, *Murder is a Collector's Item* was the first of three books featuring Emma. Smoothly written and sparkling with dry, sophisticated humor, this nearly forgotten milestone combines an intriguing puzzle with an entertaining portrait of a self-possessed young woman on her own in Boston toward the end of the Great Depression. **0-915230-19-4 $14.00**

**Murder is a Serious Business** by Elizabeth Dean. It's 1940 and the Thirsty Thirties are over but you couldn't tell it by the gang at J. Graham Antiques, where clerk Emma Marsh, her would-be criminologist boyfriend Hank, and boss Jeff Graham trade barbs in between shots of scotch when they aren't bothered by the rare customer. Trouble starts when Emma and crew head for a weekend at Amos Currier's country estate to inventory the man's antiques collection. It isn't long before the bodies start falling and once again Emma is forced to turn sleuth in order to prove that her boss isn't a killer. Emma is sure there's a good reason why Jeff didn't mention that he had Amos' 18th century silver muffineer hidden in his desk drawer back at the shop. Filled with the same clever dialog and eccentric characters that made *Murder is a Collector's Item* an absolute delight, this second case offers up an unusual approach to crime solving as well as a sidesplitting look at the peculiar world of antiques. **0-915230-28-3 $14.95**

**Murder, Chop Chop** by James Norman. "The book has the butter-wouldn't-melt-in-his-mouth cool of Rick in *Casablanca*."—*The Rocky Mountain News.* "Amuses the reader no end."—*Mystery News.* "This long out-of-print masterpiece is intricately plotted, full of eccentric characters and very humorous indeed. Highly recommended."—*Mysteries by Mail.* Meet Gimiendo Hernandez Quinto, a gigantic Mexican who once rode with Pancho Villa and who now trains *guerrilleros* for the Nationalist Chinese government when he isn't solving murders. At his side is a beautiful Eurasian known as Mountain of Virtue, a woman as dangerous to men as she is irresistible. Then there's Mildred Woodford, a hard-drinking British journalist; John Tate, a portly American calligrapher who wasn't made for adventure; Lieutenant Chi, a young Hunanese patriot weighted down with the cares of China and the Brooklyn Dodgers; and a host of others, any one of whom may have killed Abe Harrow, an ambulance driver who appears to have died at three different times. There's also a cipher or two to crack, a train with a mind of its own, and Chiang Kai-shek's false teeth, which have gone mysteriously missing. First published in 1942. **0-915230-16-X $13.00**

**Death at The Dog** by Joanna Cannan. "Worthy of being discussed in the same breath with an Agatha Christie or Josephine Tey...anyone who enjoys Golden Age mysteries will surely enjoy this one."—Sally Fellows, *Mystery News.* "Skilled writing and brilliant characterization."—*Times of London.* "An excellent English rural tale."—Jacques Barzun & Wendell Hertig Taylor in *A Catalogue of Crime.* Set in late 1939 during the first anxious months of World War II, *Death at The Dog,* which was first published in 1941, is a wonderful example of the classic English detective novel that first flourished between the two World Wars. Set in a picturesque village filled with thatched-roof-cottages, eccentric villagers and genial pubs, it's as well-plotted as a Christie, with clues abundantly and fairly planted, and as deftly written as the best of the books by either Sayers or Marsh, filled with quotable lines and perceptive observations on the human condition. Cannan had a gift for characterization that's second to none in Golden Age detective fiction, and she created two memorable lead characters. One of them is Inspector Guy Northeast, a lonely young Scotland Yard inspector who makes his second and final appearance here and finds himself hopelessly smitten with the chief suspect in the murder of a village tyrant. The other is the "lady novelist" Crescy Hardwick, an unconventional and ultimately unobtainable woman a number of years Guy's senior, who is able to pierce his armor and see the unhappiness that haunts the detective's private moments. Well aware that all the evidence seems to point to her, she is also able—unlike her less imaginative and more snobbish—fellow villagers—to see how very good Inspector Northeast is at his job. **0-915230-23-2 $14.00**

**They Rang Up the Police** by Joanna Cannan. "Just delightful."—*Sleuth of Baker Street* Pick-of-the-Month. "A brilliantly plotted mystery...splendid character study...don't miss this one, folks. It's a keeper."—Sally Fellows, *Mystery News.* When Delia Cathcart and Major Willoughby disappear from their quiet English village one Saturday morning in July 1937, it looks like a simple case of a frustrated spinster running off for a bit of fun with a straying husband. But as the hours turn into days, Inspector Guy Northeast begins to suspect that she may have been the victim of foul play. On the surface, Delia appeared to be a quite ordinary middle-aged Englishwoman content to spend her evenings with her sisters and her days with her beloved horses. But Delia led a secret life—and Guy turns up more than one person who would like to see Delia dead. Except Delia wasn't the only person with a secret...Never published in the United States, *They Rang Up the Police* appeared in England in 1939. **0-915230-27-5 $14.00**

**Cook Up a Crime** by Charlotte Murray Russell. "Perhaps the mother of today's 'cozy' mystery . . . amateur sleuth Jane has a personality guaranteed to entertain the most demanding reader."—Andy Plonka, *The Mystery Reader.* "Some wonderful old time recipes...highly recommended."—*Mysteries by Mail.* Meet Jane Amanda Edwards, a self-styled "full-fashioned" spinster who complains she hasn't looked at herself in a full-length mirror since Helen Hokinson started drawing for *The New Yorker.* But you can always count on Jane to look into other people's affairs, especially when there's a juicy murder case to investigate. In this 1951 title Jane goes searching for recipes (included between chapters) for a cookbook project and finds a body instead. And once again her lily-of-the-field brother Arthur goes looking for love, finds strong drink, and is eventually discovered clutching the murder weapon. **0-915230-18-6 $13.00**

**The Man from Tibet** by Clyde B. Clason. Locked inside the Tibetan Room of his Chicago luxury apartment, the rich antiquarian was overheard repeating a forbidden occult chant under the watchful eyes of Buddhist gods. When the doors were opened it appeared that he had succumbed to a heart attack. But the elderly Roman historian and sometime amateur sleuth Theocritus Lucius Westborough is convinced that Adam Merriweather's death was anything but natural and that the weapon was an eighth century Tibetan manuscript. It's murder, who could have done it, and how? Suspects abound. There's's Tsongpun Bonbo, the gentle Tibetan lama from whom the manuscript was originally stolen; Chang, Merriweather's scholarly Tibetan secretary who had fled a Himalayan monastery; Merriweather's son Vincent, who disliked his father and stood to inherit a fortune; Dr. Jed Merriweather, the dead man's brother, who came to Chicago to beg for funds to continue his archaeological digs in Asia; Dr. Walters, the dead man's physician, who guarded a secret; and Janice Shelton, his young ward, who found herself being pushed by Merriweather into marrying his son. How the murder was accomplished has earned praise from such impossible crime connoisseurs as Robert C.S. Adey, who cited Clason's "highly original and practical locked-room murder method." **0-915230-17-8 $14.00**

**The Mirror** by Marlys Millhiser. "Completely enjoyable."—*Library Journal* . "A great deal of fun."—*Publishers Weekly*. How could you not be intrigued, as one reviewer pointed out, by a novel in which "you find the main character marrying her own grandfather and giving birth to her own mother?" Such is the situation in Marlys Millhiser's classic novel (a Mystery Guild selection originally published by Putnam in 1978) of two women who end up living each other's lives after they look into an antique Chinese mirror. Twenty-year-old Shay Garrett is not aware that she's pregnant and is having second thoughts about marrying Marek Weir when she's suddenly transported back 78 years in time into the body of Brandy McCabe, her own grandmother, who is unwillingly about to be married off to miner Corbin Strock. Shay's in shock but she still recognizes that the picture of her grandfather that hangs in the family home doesn't resemble her husband-to-be. But marry Corbin she does and off she goes to the high mining town of Nederland, where this thoroughly modern young woman has to learn to cope with such things as wood cooking stoves and—to her—old-fashioned attitudes about sex. In the meantime, Brandy McCabe is finding it even harder to cope with life in the Boulder, Co., of 1978. **0-915230-15-1 $14.95**

**Death on Milestone Buttress** by Glyn Carr. Ambercrombie ("Filthy") Lewker was looking forward to a fortnight of climbing in Wales after a grueling season touring England with his Shakepearean company. Young Hilary Bourne thought the fresh air would be a pleasant change from her dreary job at the bank, as well as a chance to renew her acquaintance with a certain young scientist. Neither one expected this bucolic outing to turn deadly but when one of their party is killed in an apparent accident during what should have been an easy climb on the Milestone Buttress, Filthy and Hilary turn detective. Nearly every member of the climbing party had reason to hate the victim but each one also had an alibi for the time of the murder. Working as a team, Filthy and Hilary retrace the route of the fatal climb before returning to their lodgings where, in the grand tradition of Nero Wolfe, Filthy confronts the suspects and points his finger at the only person who could have committed the crime. Filled with climbing details sure to appeal to both expert climbers and armchair mountaineers alike, *Death on Milestone Buttress* was published in England in 1951, the first of fifteen detective novels in which Ambercrombie Lewker outwitted murderers on peaks scattered around the globe, from Wales to Switzerland to the Himalayas. **0-915230-29-1 $14.00**

## About The Rue Morgue Press

The Rue Morgue Press vintage mystery line is designed to bring back into print those books that were favorites of readers between the turn of the century and the 1960s. The editors welcome suggestions for reprints. To receive our catalog or make suggestions, write The Rue Morgue Press, P.O. Box 4119, Boulder, Colorado 80306.